Archangel's Gambit

Fangs & Halos Book 4

Charlayne Elizabeth Denney

Heavenly Fangs
17003 Blackhawk Blvd
Friendswood, Tx. 77546

Heavenly Fangs and the halo/fangs symbol are trademarks of Heavenly Fangs Books

Cover Illustration © Charlayne Elizabeth Denney
Layout by Paul & Nnew, BB eBooks
Chapter Charms © Dreamstime.com: Russel Shively, Zts, Kuzzie, Risto Villaten, Dagadu

Dedication

To my sister-of-the-heart, Lynn Rudd Bell, who encouraged my writing, my passion for vampires, and was there for everything since 1979. I'm missing you so much, I start to pick up the phone and say "Hey, do you think this will work?" and remember that you're now hanging out with Mikhail, Sethiel, and the other angels, along with your husband, Buddy, and little Nicole. I miss you so much and more every day. Hope the book makes it to Heaven so you can read it. Tell me in my dreams if Mikhail looks like John Barrowman......

Chapter One

THE BIG, BLACK bulletproof Cadillac Escalade streaked through the stifling humidity of the Florida night. The dark, almost squat, surly man scowled as he stared blankly out the window. The potentially lucrative business trip to Russia and Eastern Europe had not gone as planned. Nelson Mishkoph had hoped that the meetings with his potential clients would result in orders for security services and arms. Damn Marcus Lancaster!

Damn him to Hell.

He had somehow gotten ahead of Nelson and circumvented the attempt to negotiate a contract with the Serbian arms company that Nelson had wanted to add to the portfolio. Not only did Lancaster stop the negotiation, he managed to keep Pricor from even getting into the neighborhood where the door was.

He had a mind to kick the back of the seat in front of him, except that it would ruin the leather and startle his driver.

A roll-over wreck was never a good way to get rid of the anger he was carrying.

He let his head fall back on the headrest. Lancaster's face and smart-assed grin haunted him even when he tried to relax.

That man would have to be taken down by force. The message he had sent through Marcus's gay lover should have provoked a reaction. Nelson had heard nothing. Not even a threatening phone call. This non-response was curious and somewhat disturbing, he should have heard, if nothing else, a threat for having the little fag beaten to a pulp.

Nothing. Not one damned word. The whole beat down and the shooting of the chauffeur and poisoning of the fag in the hospital came to a grand total of $295,000. The paltry sum would never be missed from petty cash; he wouldn't have to take it out of his own pocket, or the Pricor budget.

Money he would delight in taking out of Lancaster's hide once he took his company from him.

Then the curdled visage of his harridan wife, Lauren, loomed to the front of Nelson's thoughts.

He was not joyously anticipating the incessant haranguing he was sure to encounter as soon as he walked in the front door. She was going to be a bitch once he walked in from this trip. He had been in an important meeting with the Serbian Deputy Minister of Industry and Privatization, Dragan Popovic. It had taken him almost a year and almost a million dollars in 'incentive money' to get an audience with the guy to discuss the possible purchase of Radulovic Arms. In the middle of the critical negotiations, Lauren called.

She bitched about a florist messing up a delivery of flowers to her mother. What the fuck? She wanted him to call, from the other side of the fucking world, to straighten out the florist. She had ordered daisies and the florist had delivered roses...her mother hated roses. Yes, the world, no, the universe, revolved around Lauren Rabinowitz. He ground his teeth so hard his jaw ached.

All the way to Serbia, like he could do anything about it, even if he would. Was she...worth it? He would love to divorce the bitch, if it wouldn't cost him all of his money and his company, but he would walk away with nothing...maybe even less than nothing. Her parents not only had bank-rolled his company start-up, but they also, to guarantee his slavish loyalty, had all the paperwork and proof of every questionable and illegal thing he had ever done. Even though his father-in-law was dead, and gratefully it was a long, painful death, his mother-in-law was just as evil. She was helping Lauren suck him dry.

He would love to give that bitch of a wife to Lancaster, make her his problem so the ass would not pay attention to his job for once. Even better, he would love to make Lancaster the killer when she was found dead.

Which, if she kept up the shrew personality, would be happening sooner than later.

When the hell did life get so damned complicated? All he wanted to do was build the world's finest mercenary company, grease a few palms, and find a nice, leggy blond with no brains to hang on his every word.

Instead he gets Lauren Rabinowitz, her mafia parents, and Marcus Fucking Lancaster. Who the hell did he screw in his past life?

The Escalade slowed, the ornate iron gates opening automatically to allow entrance into the ostentatious Aventura estate. He let loose an audible groan, the light was on in her room as well as downstairs in the formal. She was waiting to pounce on him and launch the latest tirade about how miserable her life was and what a petty disappointment he was, just what he wasn't looking forward to.

He made a mental note: next trip back from the airport, take the limo. It had a bar and was equipped with several bottles of Grey Goose vodka. Then he could get nicely toasted, to properly prepare him for what awaited.

The big SUV slid to a stop and the chauffeur opened his door. Mishkoph exited and looked up at the white stucco facade and wished he could be back in Europe. Anywhere but where Lauren was.

The car pulled away and out the gates. The luggage left on the curb by the driver would be carted up by the security staff, after they were checked out. He took a deep breath to brace himself for the invariable onslaught. He entered the house to the blaring caterwauling opera shit that she supposedly loved. Nelson knew it was pure affectation. Pretentious fucking shit. He peeked into the formal, great luck was with him, Lauren was nowhere to be seen.

He hastened to the bar and grabbed a chilled

bottle of Goose. He lovingly glanced at the blessed clear liquid. With this he could drink himself into oblivion. He grabbed a second bottle, just to make sure. Now, if he could just make it to his room, he would be safe in his sanctum until morning. He quietly and quickly bolted up the stairs, two at a time.

This was the dangerous part. He had to get past Lauren's suite undetected. He crept past her door. Out of the corner of his eye he noticed something quite odd. A white linen napkin, folded into the shape of a cone, was sitting on the floor in front of Lauren's door on the polished marble floor. Curiosity overwhelmed his desire for stealth and he put one bottle of Goose on the floor and lifted the cloth, recoiling immediately in horror.

It was a finger, adorned with an obscenely huge diamond wedding ring and impeccably manicured scarlet lacquered fingernail, severed at the main knuckle.

Lauren's finger.

He roared her name and grabbed the doorknob to her room, trying to open the door.

Locked.

He beat on the wood, screaming her name. The door stayed solid. He looked up at the camera that was supposed to be monitoring the hall, searching for the lens.

Gone. A couple of screw holes where the thing should have been.

His shrieks of alarm echoed into silence. Suddenly the solitude he had reveled in only a moment before was now uncomfortably eerie.

Where was everybody? He paid his guards good money to be there and to guard his stuff and the bitc....his wife.

"Joseph! Grant! Someone, get in here now!" He yelled out, trying to summon the guards. "Adelaide!" He called the maid's name.

Nothing...

He hurried to his room, to the safe where he kept his gun collection. He grabbed the first one he could and ran back down the hall, still carrying the open bottle of Goose. He ran from room to room, nothing seemed out of place but the cameras were all... gone. No alarms blaring, nothing.

He ran down the stairs, shouting the entire way, hoping for any response. He reached the French doors that lead to the pool.

Suddenly, it was if someone had dropped an ice cube down his back. A chilly shiver shook his entire body and a cold sweat erupted across his forehead.

He ripped open the left French door, rushing out into the humid night. Rounding the shrubs that protected the pool from prying eyes, he slid to an abrupt stop.

The now blood red pool contained the bloated bodies of his wife, her maid, his mother-in-law, the cook, and three of his best men, the guards of the estate, all floating in the bloody water.

He dropped the Gray Goose, the bottle shattering on the concrete.

Attached to the broken umbrella over one of the poolside tables, was a note. Once he could move again, Nelson walked to the paper and looked at it.

You're Next. M.

In one respect, Marcus Lancaster had done him a great service. However, what irritated Nelson most was now he was going to have to hire a whole new household staff. And he was probably going to have to pay triple or higher to get anyone decent for those positions...Damn it.

He calmly removed his cell phone from his pocket and punched in 9-1-1. As he waited for the answer, he thought...

"Game On..."

Chapter Two

MARCUS HELD JESSE'S hand, the first time since the two week nightmare that was the Hurricane Rita bug-out.

He was grateful for anything he got, Jesse was angry but there was really nothing to be done about it. He either got brought over, or died, and Jesse's death was never going to happen while Marcus Lancaster drew a breath. The ghoul-turned-vampire's feigned fury and depression over having been turned had been very profitable indeed over the holidays, lasting well into the new year. Marcus Lancaster had been so contrite and remorseful that showering Jesse with expensive gifts was his way of assuaging him.

So, Jesse intended to take full advantage as long as it lasted. Their relationship began during the Civil War and this was the first time that Jesse ever felt he was at an advantage. Not an unpleasant experience at all. However, he knew he had just about reached the end of Marcus' patience.

"You're awfully quiet, Marcus. Thinking on what that woman is going to do?" Jesse snarled sarcastically. He felt a certain amount of sadistic self-satisfied pleasure recalling the agonized form of Lilly as he closed the door. Crying blood tears of despair as she cradled the unconscious form of Essex. He was sure he didn't want to discuss relationships right now, but he couldn't resist another little dig. It was betrayal, and Jesse knew from experience that it was something that Marcus did not, would not, forget, or forgive.

But, not before he extracted every delicate morsel of revenge and benefit that he could.

Revenge also for having brought that bitch into their lives. After Hurricane Katrina had devastated New Orleans, Marcus discovered that his obsession, Lilly Marchantel, was alive. After almost a century, he still had not forgotten her. That octaroon whore from Storyville. Her reappearance had made Jesse's life a living hell, now an unliving hell. He had been firmly and comfortably ensconced in Marcus' affections and his bed. But she had made his position precarious.

But that threat was over.

A sly grin crept across his face, now he was not going to be replaced since he knew that Marcus did not forgive betrayal.

Marcus had still not suffered enough for bringing him across. It was a promise broken, Marcus had promised that he would never let Jesse be turned. But he did. He did it, but he was going to eventually have to forgive the sod, he always did.

He heard Marcus talking and shook himself out of his reflection.

"...a fucking angel! In my employ. I could not care less what the hell she did to him. Turn him and I'll make him a soldier, let him die and he's not even my problem. So no." Marcus glanced across at his lover, hoping that he was going to be able to be with him tonight. He really needed to have sex with his lover.

"So you don't care what she does, either way, huh? Then why put her into the situation in the first place?"

"Because it gives me a chance to watch her, see what side of this whole war she is going to be on. She's still not over that angel progeny of hers and I'm sure that it's going to be one of the problems we have to deal with. I am quite sure that the pain in my ass is going to show up at the most inconvenient time." Marcus actually growled, his bright blue eyes momentarily flashing red.

Jesse laughed, running his unoccupied hand through his blond hair, "You have yet to meet the idiot, how could he be a pain in your ass. I would think either that damned cat or the angel we just drained would be more problematic."

"The cat is not long for this world, turning my championship Sheltie into a vampire was way over the line that I will tolerate."

"Without that, you wouldn't have your Sheltie. At least I'm not the only one that was turned without permission." Jesse loosened his hand to drop Marcus's, turning away so that Marcus couldn't see the smirk that tickled the edges of his mouth.

"Don't start. We've been over this before. It's a futile argument. You're turned, a vampire, I've been threatened with Hell over it, the only reason I'm not there is because of the Ghoul Rule, you gave permission to me to take your blood for over one hundred years so I had tacit approval to turn you."

He stopped walking and took Jesse's hands, looking into his eyes. "I could not lose you. I would not lose you. You should have never been attacked, Mishkoph was coming after me. He should have just come at me and left you alone. He's paying for that mistake, it will be long, drawn out, and exceptionally painful. He will regret ever crossing me. He will fear me, I promise you it will be a long, excruciatingly painful process, only multiplied by as many dollars as I will get for taking his piddling empire apart."

Jesse snorted, "You really think you can make that man afraid of you enough to make up for my being turned? He wants your company, your money. And he wanted my death to be the message. He must have thought that you would just roll over and hand him everything once he killed me. He obviously doesn't know you"

Again Marcus's eyes glinted red, "He thinks I am a human, and a weak one at that. It may work for people like Erik de Verro, that CEO from DynBlack, you remember the problems that cropped up for them in 1997 when Congress pulled them into the committee hearings, right?"

"You're saying de Verro wasn't selling arms to the rebels in Africa?"

"No, what I'm saying is Mishkoph bought a senator to get de Verro pulled into trouble with his government contracts. Then he moved in, bought the remaining outstanding shares of DynBlack, deposed de Verro, and absorbed his company.

"I've been very strong and I've used my contacts to keep Mishkoph at bay. He's decided that trying to take my company a bite at a time isn't working so he's now going sub-legal, threatening everything and everyone I care about. When he touched you, whether he did it with his hands or with someone else's doesn't matter, when he touched you he touched me and I don't take kindly to criminal fondling." Marcus looked deep into his partner's eyes, "He forfeited his life the moment he told someone to hurt you. He's dead, he just hasn't gotten the notice from the Grim Reaper to fall down yet. No one touches someone I love. I promise you, he will only live long enough to regret it."

"Aren't you afraid" Marcus bristled at the word, "That you're going to be found out by the human authorities? It's getting harder and harder to keep them from finding out things, given DNA and computer records." There had to be a lot of evidence left behind in that alley where they found him, Jesse thought. He still couldn't remember everything but he knew there had to be something that might lead back to Mishkoph, which could, conceivably lead someone, including the police, right back to Marcus.

"Hell no, I'm not afraid." He blustered, "Between the vampires in the law enforcement area and the fact that I have nothing they can trace, it's all okay. You see, Mishkoph is at an extreme disadvantage. He has only one pathetic little human life-time to learn his dirty little tricks. I, on the other hand, have had many more lifetimes to acquire a veritable arsenal of strategies and maneuvers to deal with petty little vermin like him." He smiled. "I had Jorge Castro send my, shall we say, regards to Nelson Mishkoph and his lovely wife yesterday. I'm quite sure he got it."

"So, now we wait to see if Lilly turns Mishkoph's plant and then try to convert him to our side if she does? How will you insure his cooperation?" Jesse knew Marcus probably had hurt someone inside of the man's family, maybe more than one, he loved over-kill. In situations like this, subtlety wasn't his style. 'Nothing says success like excess' was one of Marcus's favorite sayings.

"Yes, we wait. Meantime, I have an idea, why don't we knock off some of this energy and pass the time getting reacquainted. Castro will let me know when things are finished and ready for my attention."

"I don't know, Marcus. I'm still not happy..." Jesse wasn't willing to give up a tactical advantage too soon, but he had to admit, he felt his resolution weakening.

Marcus caught himself before he started to plead. He wanted Jesse in the worst way, it had been too long since they had been together. But he stopped. He wouldn't beg, it wasn't a power position and the only thing Jesse respected was power. "I can't make you forgive me. So, we'll just go back to the penthouse and I'll get some work done. We'll do this some other time, I'm willing to give you time to get used to it." He turned to walk away.

Jesse rolled his eyes, "Damn it, Marcus. Let's go have sex." He took a couple of large steps to catch his lover and grabbed his hand. Together they walked into the elevator, the doors shutting on their kiss.

Chapter Three

THE ROOM WAS quiet, except for the sobs coming from the small woman sitting on the floor. Blood tears flowed down her face, falling on the hair of the man whose head she cradled in her lap. Her dark brown hair fell down across her shoulders.

The man did not move. His neck was a mass of bite marks, open, raw, still dripping blood onto the white tile floor. He was ashen, not breathing, no heartbeat.

Dead.

"Essex, what do I do? I know you told me that you didn't want me to turn you but I cannot allow Marcus to kill you, I can't just leave you to your death when I have the ability to make you live. What do I do?" Her wrists throbbed in pain where Marcus had broken them, although she could tell from the sharp twinges, they were trying to repair themselves.

She reached out and carefully ran the fingers of her hand through his hair, at least her left wrist didn't hurt as much as her right one did, she noticed. She looked at Essex's still face. Even dead, he looked so human, not at all like what she had always visualized angels looking like.

"*Lilly, do not do it.*" Baron whispered in her head. He was still on her bed upstairs where she had taken him after Marcus had tried to kill him by breaking his neck. "*You know the angels will mark you if you change him. You've been given a chance before, but this one, another angel, they will make sure you are punished. Do not change him.*" Baron's frantic pleading continued, "*Woman, are you listening to me?*"

"*I'm listening, Baron. You don't have to shout. I have to, he cannot die like this. It's wrong to kill an angel...*"

"*You didn't kill him, Lilly, please. You were just here. It's that damned man's problem he's dead, he ordered it done. He wants you to go to Hell, that would solve all his problems with the kitten and you both.*"

Lilly closed her eyes. Baron was still trying to recover from Marcus brutal assault, he didn't need to be involved in this. "*It's not a kitten, Baron. It's a baby...*"

"*Kitten, baby, puppy, pony, I don't care what you call it, you going to Hell would end the life of that one and you have to care about that. That means letting the angel die. He was stupid enough to come here, it's Marcus's fault he's dead. I'm going to be okay, he didn't kill me and he's not going to kill me. You need to listen to me, do not turn that man.*"

Lilly bent her head back to the prone figure, wiping the blood tears from his hair.

"*Lilly, darlin' listen to me.*" An Irish brogue intruded.

Sullivan. Just who she didn't need to hear from.

"*Lilly, you're hurt. What did he do?*"

"*I'm fine, I've got a situation here that I need to handle. Go back to whatever you were doing.*"

"*You're hurting, I can tell. Did he hurt you again?*" Sullivan needed to talk to her about Essex but the pain she was trying to shield was battering his mind.

"*He crushed my wrists. They're mending but it still hurts.*" She hated to tell him anything Marcus did, he got so angry every time.

"*I will tend to Marcus Lancaster for this and every other thing he has ever done to you. But right now, you need to listen. Essex is important. Mikhail sent him in to gather information on Lancaster. He's doing something important to Heaven and he needs to live, if nothing else but to report what he found to us, them, oh you know what I mean, Mikhail needs whatever it is he sent Ess in there to get.*"

"*Why should I care what this 'Mikhail' needs? It's enough that Essex deserves to live because he is someone. No one deserves death. Not a death like this.*"

"*Lilly, do it. If you think of him at all, do it for him. I will do what I can, he will do what he can, to intercede for you about any markings that you would get. You need to change him before the life light inside of him goes totally out.*" Sullivan sounded upset, she knew he would be, he and

Essex were good friends, as Essex had told her the night they shared the french fries in the building cafeteria.

"Life light?"

"Angels are of the light. You don't see it because you are not an angel. They have a spark of the divine in them. Once their shell is killed, the light only stays until the body cools, then it returns back to Heaven. You do not want that light to leave if you are going to turn him."

"You mean the soul?" Lilly wondered how an angel, who was divine to begin with, would have a soul separate from God.

"It's sort of a soul. Either way, you need to turn him. I'll try to be there to show him what to do, it's harder on us when we're turned, we get emotions we are not familiar with. It's why I acted the way I did with you, I wasn't familiar with the emotions..."

"No, do not try to pass that off as something out of your control, Sullivan. You knew, I told you not to drink that much. You are responsible. You need to come to understand that. Ask forgiveness to God for it. Maybe I should not turn Essex, I don't want him to do what you did. I would save him but I don't want him to turn evil. I just don't know what to do."

She sat back, closing her eyes, turmoil in her mind, indecision hammering at her.

"Don't do it, Lilly." Baron implored.

"Do it, please Lilly." Sullivan countered.

She sat, silently, trying to block both voices. She opened her eyes and looked into Essex's face, tracing it with her fingers.

She began to pray, "Mother, Mary, God, what do I do? Which way do I turn? I cannot think what should be done to help him. I need to choose right, giving him what he needs."

She heard another, quiet sound, like a song, a tune like a spark of music. It lifted her heart. She reached out to it, pulled it in closer, letting the feeling spread. Her fears calmed and she smiled.

She opened her mouth, opened her better left wrist and, opening his lips, placed the bleeding wound over it.

"Drink, Essex, drink and live."

The song blossomed within her.

SULLIVAN WAS MONITORING her thoughts, watching her struggle to find a way to save Essex without turning him. He tried to calm her but everything he said didn't seem to be helping. He despaired of ever getting her to save his best friend from the death that awaited him.

He found himself humming, trying to calm his own fears. The only song that would come to him was the one he was singing the night Essex came to him, a song that he had first heard in a concert hall in Calgary Canada earlier in the year as he, as an Enforcer angel, searched for a rogue vampire at the Canadian Juno Awards. He had been singing it, holding it to him as a talisman while he had toiled through the scrolls of the monastery, trying to find himself in the confusion of the turning he had undergone at Lilly's hands, trying to find forgiveness for his beating and rape of her during his blood madness.

His tenor voice burst into full words as he sang, singing for Essex, for only one of two angels he considered brothers, singing for his life.

I did my best, it wasn't much
I couldn't feel, so I tried to touch
I've told the truth, I didn't come to fool you
And even though it all went wrong
I'll stand before the Lord of Song
With nothing on my tongue but Hallelujah

He wept tears of blood, wishing for the forgiveness of Lilly, but also wishing for the life of his friend, a prayer in song and blood. He sang it over and over.

He heard her, over his words and the pounding of his heart, *"Drink. Essex. Drink and live."*

He sunk to his knees next to the table he had been working at, sobbing at the relief, and with the knowledge that he now had to teach his brother how to live.

ESSEX FLOATED IN the light above his body. He knew he was dying, dead. His light, his essence was retreating, beginning to leave the room in the tall building on San Felipe in Houston, heading home to Heaven. The life he had lived since his creation was over. Lilly had, somehow, found the strength to let him go.

He stopped his movement into the light, turning to look at her once again. She was crying, holding him in her lap, her broken right wrist held across her chest. Her left wrist hung at a weird angle, probably broken as well.

He felt sorry for Lilly. She was put into a position of no-win by that bastard vampire, Marcus Lancaster. She was struggling to find a way to save him, yet at the same time she was not only aware of him, but of the cat and of another...another voice...a familiar voice...Sullivan.

Sullivan. His friend was trying to convince her to turn him. He could hear him talking with her in her mind.

"NO!" He shouted at both her and Sullivan, trying to make his voice heard.

But he had no voice. He was light, pure energy. They couldn't hear him.

He could hear Sullivan singing, that song they had sung when Essex had visited him when he came to tell him he was going undercover in Lancaster's organization. He heard the pain and sadness in his friend's voice.

Lilly looked up, cocking her head, listening. He knew she could hear Sullivan's song. She smiled.

Then he saw her bite through her left wrist, crying out as she did. It obviously hurt her to do that simple action. She laid the wound over his mouth.

Essex could taste the blood, coppery and

warm. He tried to move, to move the wrist from his mouth, but he couldn't. He could feel his light being pulled back into the shell he had vacated, a wrenching feeling that brought back the pain of the wound in his neck.

An overwhelming need to drink consumed him. He knew he shouldn't but the compulsion was too strong. He took huge swallows of the life-blood offered to him. He could hear Lilly's heartbeat, strong in his ears.

He grabbed the arm, hanging onto the life it was giving him. Lilly let out a sharp cry of pain, he heard it but couldn't disengage. He needed, he _needed_ to continue to take what she offered. He knew he was doomed but he ceased to care. The energy of the blood giving him life was overwhelming.

Then he heard it. Faintly, he heard a faster pattern under Lilly's heartbeat. As he swallowed her life, he sought to find the sound.

A baby! She hadn't lied to him. Lilly was pregnant! The life he was taking was attached to the small life in her womb. He pushed his tongue against the wrist, licking the wound closed and pushed her arm away from her, causing yet another painful cry.

He opened his eyes, looking up into the smiling countenance above him. She was smiling at him, even through her own pain. Somehow, that made him feel worse, if that was possible.

He couldn't help the angry look he gave her, the anger rose in him like a monster.

"What the hell have you done to me?" He growled.

Chapter Four

THE WORLD CAME blazing back into focus and his memory of leaving his body receded. His chance to escape the situation had terminated when his essence slammed back into the body he was in when he was drained of blood.

He was trapped, and he felt like someone had stolen his one chance at freedom. His neck hurt, his head hurt, and he was lying on the floor. He looked up to see Lilly's blood streaked face above him. Suddenly it all flooded back, the draining, his trying to save Lilly from Lancaster, all of it. He felt a red-hot anger build inside of him as he realized the truth; he was now a vampire.

Essex yelled, "What the hell did you do to me!" It wasn't a question, it was an accusation, a defiant statement of his anger at finding himself back in his body. He pushed himself up and scooted away to the wall where he had sat when she first came in. He ran his hand through his hair, finding sticky spots from blood she had shed when crying.

"I saved your life. I gave you a chance to continue to live and maybe stop Marcus from whatever it is you found out he was doing." Lilly cradled the crushed wrists, holding them up against her to support them. She wished she could wrap her arms around her stomach, she needed to calm herself.

"Saved it? Are you fucking kidding me? I told you not to do anything. You didn't save me, you've doomed me to Hell, woman! I can no longer go into Heaven, which was my home! I cannot live as I used to. I'm not alive, I'm dead, or rather undead. A monster! You have condemned me and taken my soul." He ran his hand across his neck where Marcus and Jorge had bitten him, the wounds already closed and healing.

"I didn't want you to die. You were dead, I brought you back." she was confused, he was angry and she didn't understand it. "I didn't know what to do. Sullivan was begging me to save you."

"Sullivan? Bullshit. He's nowhere near here. You imagined it. You just wanted another vampire to serve you." Something in the back of his mind knew she might be telling the truth about his brother angel. Or former angel, or... His head hurt.

"What?" She pushed away from the place she was sitting, putting more room between them.

"You heard me. I didn't want to be a vampire. Sullivan didn't want to be a vampire. We knew vampires, we've marked more than you know, we've taken all of them, eventually, to Hell because they are wholly evil. Neither of us would want to become what we fought so long."

She couldn't believe her ears. Essex, the angel

who had been so gentle with her, who had felt bad about killing Baron and brought him back to life, the angel who had sat with her, shared part of his meal, and talked about Sullivan and Marcus. He had been so nice before. Now...

"You have nothing to say, you don't give a shit that I'm no longer able to be an angel. I got it. My soul is now in a little box in heaven, in the chapel of released angels. I'm forced to drink blood and live on Earth, waiting my turn to be dragged to Hell. And you have nothing to say about it." He was ranting. He knew he should have calmed down and talked with her, her confusion was apparent, but the anger at finding himself alive was still bright red.

"*Sullivan, help me. I did what you asked, he's so very, very angry with me. Please talk to him, calm him down. Tell him he's not going to go Hell. Help him, Sully.*" She reached out.

"*I can't get through to him. His mind is locked down tight and I cannot seem to push my way in. Talk to him and get him to calm down and open his mind.*" Sullivan replied.

She held her hand up to stop his ranting. "Essex, please. Sullivan is wanting to talk to you, he wants to help you with what you are feeling. Open your mind to him."

"That is so much bullshit. You know what you are? You're fucking deluded!" He shouted, "Not talking with Sullivan. We cannot talk to one another now. He's clear across the world in Norway. We don't have our rings. You're just trying to justify this mess." Essex yelled, he knew he was out of control but he didn't seem to be able to pull it back.

"You're wrong. I can talk with him. We've talked many times."

"Stop lying! Bah, You're a liar...you're evil...you,....you are a fucking vampire!" He stressed the word. "I don't know why we let you stay out of Hell, you should have been taken when you killed Sullivan. Just leave me alone. Get that vampire down here to let you out and leave me alone." He moved toward the corner, hugging his knees to him and closing his eyes.

"*Sullivan, he's shut down. He's not hearing you. He doesn't believe us.*" Lilly reached out to her progeny again.

"*I need to see him. I don't know how...*" He floundered in desperation, "*But I need to come...*"

"*NO! No you can't. Stay away! Marcus is doing something to the angels, he's trying to get angels to turn into vampires...*"

"*What? How do you know?*" Sullivan would swear the room just got frigid.

"*Castro said something when they were here to kill Essex that they were trying to turn angels into vampires. I don't know any details but I cannot imagine how they're trying to do this or why.*"

"*Lilly, you must get Essex to hear to me. I have to tell him what to expect, being a vampire comes with some major changes for angels, dangers we have encountered before.*"

"*I will try. But I also need to get out of here and go to the church to light some candles and pray for him. God needs to step in and stop this.*"

"*Lilly, spend some time talking to Ess first, I need time...*"

Lilly cut him off. "I've got to find a way out of here." She stood and walked to the door, trying the handle. It was still locked. "Damn it!" She shouted, kicking the door. "Marcus Lancaster, let me out of here now!"

She didn't want to be here. Not only in the room, not in building, not even in Houston. She wanted to go home. Her little home in the cemetery in New Orleans. Before she knew others, before she had turned Sullivan. She was happy, just her and Baron. It wasn't perfect, it was lonely, but it was home.

"Marcus!" she kicked the door again, harder, cradling her wrists against her to keep them safe. Small dents began to show on the metal door.

"You might try the camera, he's probably watching you and laughing." Essex spoke up.

Lilly whirled to face him and he pointed to the corner to the right of her. A small white box with a blinking red light caught her attention. "What is that?"

"That's a camera. It shows what's going on in the room. It probably feeds to the security staff but I bet Lancaster has the ability to watch it wherever he is. He's probably laughing at us right now."

Essex stood up and walked toward the camera. He extended his middle finger of both hands up, "Hey, Lancaster, Fuck You!"

Lilly closed her eyes and shook her head. She couldn't blame him for the outburst.

"Lancaster. Get down here and get her out of here, I am tired of her and her sanctimonious presence. She did what you wanted her to, she was a good little pawn. I'm a fucking vampire, asswipe. You come down here and let's fight, I need to kick your ass for getting me turned. I bet you're not man enough to face me, vampire to vampire. You know I can kick your ass. Come down, let her go, and face me."

Lilly stood by the door and just shook her head. She had no idea that Essex was capable of such cruelty and hatred. He had seemed nice when they first met.

She sat down next to the door, in pain from her wrists and overwhelmed by all of it.

Chapter Five

A S THE HOURS wore on toward morning, Lilly and Essex felt the pull of the dawn. Essex laid down and collapsed from exhaustion, Lilly had moved away from the door to the opposite wall, not wanting to allow Marcus another chance to grab her and hurt her. Her wrist throbbed, but it was less than when it first happened.

Essex had ignored her once his outburst challenging Marcus was over. He sat down and just glared at her, the camera, the door, everything. He had made his point vividly clear; he was furious at being turned into a vampire and everyone who was involved, and even those who weren't, were now his enemies.

Just as she started to dose off, Lilly saw a flash of bright light that blinded her. She blinked to clear her vision.

Two angels stood before her, their wings filling much of the room behind them. It was the severe looking woman with the grey wings who had come to threaten her with Hell once before. She was accompanied by the same, formidable angel with red wings and a big, flaming sword. They had been with Essex when he tuned her in the boat on the way to Houston from New Orleans.

They must have come to tune Essex.

He stood up to face them. "I wondered when you would show up, Nida. No time to waste, I have to be tuned, huh?" He didn't disguise his anger.

"Essexiel, you know why we are here." Nida's voice dripped with hatred, her use of his angelic name an indication of her contempt.

Helmut motioned to him, "Kneel, vampire," he droned in monotone.

Essex slowly sunk to his knees, moved by the angelic power wielded by the large Warror. It was then that he noticed something. "Where's your witness? You should always have the witness. What are you doing, Nida?"

The look she flashed betrayed her. Anger with him and his questioning of her. "Silence, vampire." She waved her hand, silencing him. Essex noticed Helmut raised an eyebrow in surprise but he quickly hid it.

The large angel turned toward Lilly, "Vampire, you will stand and stay quiet while we speak with your progeny." She was pulled to her feet by an invisible hand and she nodded meekly.

Nida smiled maliciously, "I am here to warn you about your new situation. You are now vampire, and with that comes your tuning. I will tune you so that we can, as you know, follow you. One violation and I will return to mark your hand. When you earn your three marks, as inevitably you will, we will escort you safely to Hell. You know the rules; you've given them out often enough so I will not repeat them." Essex knew she broke the procedure with that, even if the vampire knew the rules, they were always repeated. He forced himself to keep listening.

"But know this, we are watching you and you will not be given leniency just because you were once an angel. Quite frankly, I would say it would go harder on you because you know the rules. And once you finally do make it to Hell, you will undoubtedly be greeted by many of the malefactors that you have ushered to Hell. The reunion should be quite interesting." A contemptuous snarl twitched at her upper lip. "All vampires end up in Hell, eventually, and you shall be no exception."

She stopped and turned toward Lilly, who was sobbing quietly. "Do not shed tears for this one, he's guilty as you are. What I tell him is what I will tell you. Even without the mark, you are, in my eyes, two steps from Hell. You should only be one step from Hell because of what you did to Eistered..."

"Who?" Lilly asked.

"You know him as Sullivan, that silly name he took because he was with that family in Ireland too much. You were given mercy on his turning for some reason, but do not think it will happen again. I will see you taken to Hell. My only regret is that it's not my job to escort you, I would take great pleasure in that. Turning an angel into a vampire is the ultimate sin against Heaven." Nida stopped talking for a moment, her eyes sweeping over the standing vampire. "You're pregnant? How is this possible?" She paused for a moment then a sly smile crept over her face as she had a sudden revelation, "So, that is why Mikhail's stayed your marking. No matter, IF that abomination survives, you will still be marked and taken to Hell."

"What? No! I need to mother my child, I cannot go to Hell." Lilly was frantic inside, surely she would be allowed to raise the child before she was taken.

Her head reeled, heart sinking. Then she found the word. Abomination. That woman just called her child an Abomination. Suddenly the electric feeling of pure fury went through her. Lilly doubled her fists and straightened up, taking a step toward the offending angel before finding her feet fighting to glue her into a spot.

"My baby is NOT an Abomination. I will raise my child and I am not going to Hell." She spat as she shook with fury.

Nida took a step back as Helmut adjusted the sword, pushing it closer to Lilly, who could feel the heat of the flames, stopping her in her tracks.

"Well, if, and it's only an if, that spawn survives..." Nida resisted the urge to step up on the vampire, noting that the ability to move despite Helmut's force holding her was unusual, "Your child will be taken to foster, happens all the time. So typical of a prostitute, you have no idea who fathered that thing."

"I am not...I do know..." Lilly's bravado turned to impotent frustration, not able to move, keeping her from stomping her foot like a petulant child.

How dare the angel cast her in that light, "I am not a courtesan any longer. I know who the father is, he would protect the baby from you and your demon."

Nida threw back her head and laughed, "You don't know for sure. And if you are referring to Marcus Lancaster, he's even closer to Hell than you are."

She stopped speaking when a loud bang came from the door. Outside, a fierce growl sounded and another bang.

"Oh, good. Your protector is here. The cat should be in Hell already, he's an anathema. I think we will take him with us when we leave." Nida gestured toward the door.

"NO!" Lilly screamed. "He's done nothing! Baron, run!" She backed up the command in her mind, aiming the scream toward him.

"I will not run. She will stop her threats and leave, if I get into that room, I will shred her. I will show her what an accursed creature can do!" Baron hit the door again.

"No, Baron, stop..."

Nida slipped into both Lilly and Baron's mind, *"Oh, I'm terrified!"* Seeing Lilly's shocked expression, she snickered, *"I can hear you. Now, stop moving, cat. Sit quietly and wait while we mark her, then we will take you with us."*

Lilly started to scream in anger, trying to move from where she was, aiming for Nida. Helmut raised the flaming sword and strengthened its hold on her.

"Lilly, quiet. She's got her way, I cannot move

either."

"Now that I have that distraction dealt with, I need to continue with Essexiel." She turned toward him, "I have no need of a witness. I have been doing this since the first and Helmut is the only one I need with me. You will not question me or the rules."

Essex laughed, "The rules? The one you break coming here? That's rich, Nida. You believe you are a law unto yourself, that no one can stop you. You forget about Ranguel..."

"That weakling? He may be an archangel but he has never had to face a vampire, a malevolent paranormal, or angry spirit. He hides in the H.H.A.D. assignment room, and he believes he is in charge..."

"He is in charge, Nida. And if he's not, Mikhail is. You cannot make calls on your own, you have rules to follow and you have to answer for your actions."

"Mikhail," she scoffed, "He assumes he's in control but he has no contact with God. The only archangel with that access is Metatron. He's the real control in Heaven and he knows what we do."

"Metatron is not in charge, Nida. He cannot just give assignments without going through H.H.A.D., through Mikhail and Ranguel. Neither of them know you are here, do they?"

Lilly interrupted, "H.H.A.D.? What's that? Metatron, Mikhail are in charge, where is God?" The whole discussion was very confusing.

"Heavenly Host Assignment Department, Lilly. And God has moved on, leaving Mikhail to run things." Essex tried to explain quickly.

"Metatron is in charge. Mikhail has to answer to him. God, he is busy, too busy to bother about vampires and their insignificant matters." Nida countered.

"Go ahead and get the tuning done, I tire of your argument." Essex said.

"Tire? You just ran out of falsehoods to throw at me. You know the rules, break them and I will gladly take you down." She waved her hand and the room seemed to get very cold, then it heated up hotter than a mid-summer New Orleans day.

Lilly could feel the changes and remembered when Essex himself had done the same to her; Nida was giving him the tuning. It seemed to go on longer than it had when he had tuned her and Baron.

Baron. Her heart seemed to shutter, they were going to take him from her once they finished with Essex. She could not move, she could not fight them: they were going to take the one thing that she wanted, no, not wanted, needed in her life just out of spite. Baron never did anything bad. He never did anything wrong. Yes, he was mating with every little girl cat he could find but he was a cat, a Tom cat, it was part of his nature. Being a vampire cat didn't change him from what he essentially was.

"I'm not going anywhere." He said to her.

She didn't answer him, knowing that Nida could hear them. She didn't want to do anything else to antagonize the angel.

A small drop of blood sweat rolled down the

side of her face from her temple to her chin, dropping onto her shoulder. She looked at Essex. His face was contorted in pain, his blood sweat drenching his face, hair, and shirt.

"Stop! You're hurting him. You don't need to do it that long, it shouldn't hurt like that! You are killing him." She yelled.

Nida ignored her another few seconds, and then dropped her hands. The room temperature returned to normal and Essex let his head fall, his chin resting on his chest. He was obviously hurting, tired. Lilly's anger flared.

The angel then turned to Lilly, an evil smile on her face, "Helmut, make her kneel."

Helmut turned to look at her, his eyes seeking hers. She ignored him. "Do it."

Helmut pointed the large flaming sword at Lilly, "Kneel vampire."

Lilly sunk to her knees, fighting to stay standing.

"Raise your right hand." As Helmut demanded, her arm raised straight out, her hand flat despite the broken wrist. The vampire cried out as she moved, catching Helmut's attention.

As she complied, Helmut turned to Nida, "We do not have permission to do this." He objected.

"We do not need to have permission. She has made another vampire outside of the rules. She must be marked."

"Ranguel always assigns these: we do not do it without approval."

"We are here, the evidence is here and irrefutable. She will be marked."

"At least contact Ranguel and give him the information so he can make it official." Helmut countered.

"No. We do not need to waste time, we can do it, it's going to be done, and that is final. Now stop arguing with my word and do your own job, Helmut, or I will get you reassigned."

Helmut glanced at Essex, who had raised his head during the argument. He had never seen them do this; it was totally out of character as far as he knew. He shook his head and Helmut blinked slowly, concurring.

Nida did not seem to see the exchange. Her attention was totally on Lilly and the mark she was beginning to pull the energy to make.

MARCUS LEFT THE bedroom, heading for the kitchen to get a couple of beers. He had finally convinced Jesse to give in and, he had to admit, that bit of challenge made it extra fun. He missed being with Jess, their long love-affair had often been fiery and this time was no exception. Marcus could tell that his lover had still been angry at first; the energy he gave off was one of wanting to punish Marcus for turning him. Like all good make-up sex, it had ended up with both of them out of breath, sweaty, and totally satisfied. Jesse was now in the shower. Nude, Marcus headed to the kitchen to get them drinks. Maybe he would serve Jesse his drink in the shower and they could continue their make-up session. Marcus smiled at the thought.

He glanced at the monitors in the living room and something caught his attention as he walked past. He backed up and walked toward the wall.

He had left the CCTV feed on in the room holding the guy who was stealing his information and Lilly. He didn't see anyone but the two of them but as he watched, he saw Lilly sink to her knees and her right arm shoot out.

"God damn angels!" He yelled. Racing back to the bedroom, he grabbed the jeans that were crumpled on the floor and yanked them on. Snatching his cell phone from the dresser, he bolted from the room. Without stopping to tell Jesse where he was going, he slapped the elevator button. Punching the button for the 18th floor as he rushed into the elevator, he jabbed at the cell phone screen and held it to his ear.

NIDA RAISED HER hand and placed it over Lilly's, her first finger extended toward the top of the vampire's hand. The angel's hand seemed to glow with energy and then Essex could see a small red beam of light extend to Lilly's hand.

Sparks began to fly from Lilly's hand, lighting the area. Nida yelped and jumped back. Her eyes flashed as she looked in disbelief first to Lilly, then Essex, finally to Helmut.

"What the hell did you do, vampire?" She

stepped toward Lilly, challenge apparent in her stance.

Just as shocked as the angel, she stammered, "I...didn't do anything, I promise. I don't know what happened." Lilly added innocently, "I guess you aren't supposed to do the marking, if you didn't have the permission."

"No, you did something." Nida grabbed Lilly's arm and hand, pinching and pulling as she did.

"Stop it. You're hurting me, I did nothing. I don't know what happened."

Helmut stepped up and laid his hand on Nida's wrist, "Stop. Let's go back to H.H.A.D. and check with Ranguel about this. We can always come back and mark her later, she's not going anywhere we can't find her."

"No, we need to..."

The door handle rattled and then there was a pounding, "Unlock this door, you fucking angels. Now! Lilly, Lilly!"

Nida swung around, looking at the door, then to Lilly, who was still kneeling. "Helmut, open the door but bar him from entry."

The door opened and Marcus started to stride in but appeared to hit an invisible wall. The vampire growled, "Let me in."

Lilly could see how angry Marcus was and beyond him, she could see Baron, his head still sitting at an angle where her maker had twisted it until he broke it. Baron had not managed to heal before trying to rescue her.

"No. You may observe, vampire, but you may not come in."

Helmut stepped between Nida and Marcus. "Nida, let's go." He said between clinched teeth.

Nida started to shove him out of the way but then she stopped, her face turning red with anger as her eyes dilated. She stood, quietly appearing to listen to something. Once she stopped, she glared at Helmut.

"Fine, we will go. But," she turned to look first at Lilly, then Essex, and finally Marcus and Baron, "We will be returning to mark Ms. Marchantel." She turned to the door, "And Lancaster," She looked at Marcus with a self-satisfied smirk, "I get to finish your mark and will send you straight to Hell!" She laughed almost maniacally.

Helmut let the tip of the fiery sword drop toward the floor and a flash of blinding light, they were gone.

Chapter Six

PANGAIEL FLOATED THROUGH the aperture, heading for the Enforcer's station. She couldn't see Ranguel; one of his assistants was there instead. She needed to speak with the archangel directly, the news she had would not be pleasant and her orders were to report to Ranguel alone. Since he wasn't there, she thought she would give him some time to get back to the station, she really needed some ambrosia. She headed to the break room.

Most everyone was busy and she thought the room would be empty but Archangel Rafael was sitting in one of the chairs, his feet up on the table, reading something with bright colors on the front. She stared at it a moment, making note of the title, "Tales of the Teenage Mutant Ninja Turtles."

"Yes, it's a comic book." He said defensively from behind the book without looking up.

"Sorry, didn't mean to interrupt your reading, sir. I was coming in for some ambrosia." She filled the glass she had conjured from the air. "Sir, may I ask why you're reading a human comic book?"

"I find it interesting, amusing. I think it's funny that a character in the story is named Rafael. Do I look like a teenager? Or a ninja? Or a turtle? He shook his head, "I'm not even going to ask about looking like a mutant, that door needs to stay closed."

She smiled at him, "No, you have that one right, you're not a mutant." She drained the glass, tossed it up, and it disappeared. "I need to find Ranguel, enjoy the comic book."

"Haven't seen him. Will do," he chortled and turned the page as she walked out in search of the archangel.

Kozmiel was working on the request list for the Enforcers. There appeared to be an up-tic of vampires. He wasn't sure what was going on but he was going to have to let the demons know it was catching attention in Heaven. He needed to get away to do it and was reaching for the communications link when Pangaiel glided up.

"Hello Koziel. I need to speak to Ranguel. Do you expect him back soon?" She smiled.

"He's in conference with Mikhail right now and has left word not to interrupt them unless the universe explodes. You might come back later, I don't know how long he's going to be gone." Koz wondered why she wanted to speak to the Enforcer chief when she was a shadow and should be reporting to Uriel.

"I am on duty still and I need to get back. You have no idea when he's going to be back?"

"No idea."

Pangaiel looked around, wondering if she

could just leave the message with him. She had been told to talk to Ranguel, or Uriel, but both men were not at their station. She still needed to return to watch her angel and report at the end of the shift, an empty place for the time she was gone would be questioned.

"Koziel, this needs to go to Ranguel just as soon as he gets back. Since you're his second, I will leave it with you so I can return to my post." She whispered. He nodded.

"Okay, he needs to know that the angel, Essex, who is doing something for Mikhail, has been attacked by the vampire, Marcus Lancaster. He's being held in the Lancaster Industries building in Houston. Lancaster forced his progeny, a female named Lilly, to turn Essex."

Koziel nodded gravely. "I will make sure that Ranguel receives your message as soon as he gets back."

Pangaiel smiled, "Thank you." She turned and went over toward the Shadows station.

"Hi Gastiel, do you know where Uriel is?"

"He's up with Mikhail, so is Tamiel, that's how I ended up here."

"I need to speak with one of them as soon as possible. I am going back to work, please have them let me know when they return and I will come in."

"Can I ask what it's about so I can give them an idea?"

"No, this one is for them only, sorry."

"Sure, I'll let them know."

She called out "Thanks" as she glided up to the aperture and out.

Chapter Seven

A N APERTURE OPENED into the H.H.A.D and a pair of angels glided toward one of the assignment stations.

Negiel looked up to see Nida and Helmut approaching and waved his hand.

"Negiel, where is Ranguel?" Nida asked as she floated to the floor.

"He's in a meeting with Mikhail. All of the head archangels are there. Should I give him a message when he returns?"

Nida shook her head, "No, I need to...uh...we need to speak with him directly."

"I will tell him." Negiel stated, "Would there be anything else?"

"No, that's all." Nida turned to leave. Helmut turned to split off. "Where are you going?"

"I want to get some ambrosia and then go read for a while. I will come with you when we are needed." He didn't want to tell her he was very disturbed by her actions and needed to think about it.

"Yes, you will." She turned and floated away.

MIKHAIL'S OFFICE WAS loud with voices of the Archangels and their main assistants seeming to talk at once, very few were actually listening. The meeting had been going for a couple of hours. Mikhail stood behind his desk, some of his smaller red feathers ruffled. He focused on one and another of the discussions, it was obvious that this wasn't just a discussion session about the missing angels; this had the potential for an explosion.

"We cannot stop running our regular missions and just leave the humans without protection." Arael, Archangel Barachiel's assistant said, her blue eyes full of tears. "They depend on us to take care of them, that's what we are here for!"

But, we have to make sure that we don't lose any more, there have been 30 confirmed dead and even more missing world-wide, I've had to encase two-thirds of those into the boxes in the Souls room already, the others have just vanished." Kafziel said forcefully.

"And it's not just Guardians or Healers who are missing; we've got disappearances reported from every department." Shadfiel nodded, the golden wings of the Guardian shaking.

Mikhail held up his hand in an attempt to quiet the room. His quiet somber tone did not betray the extreme annoyance beneath, "I am well aware of the disappearances, however we need to keep our heads and investigate this properly. This situation must be analyzed, investigated, and evaluated. Then when we actually know WHAT is going on, WHY it's happening, and WHO is doing it, we can then formulate a plan. At this point, we don't even know if it is something we can subjugate.

Kafziel, his black wings suddenly popping out, causing the others around him to move, stepped in front of everyone else, his thighs touching the desk. "Investigate? You mean leave it alone. You are missing warriors, Mikhail. There are angels missing from all departments. And we know who is doing it, the demons are working with the vampires, obviously."

Mikhail raised an eyebrow. "You know this for a fact? What is your evidence, who are your witnesses?"

"We don't need witnesses, the evidence is clear. Who else would go after angels like this? Lucifer has been spoiling for a fight since she walked out after we beat her ass in the war. The vampires are her way of hurting the humans God seems to treasure more than the angels. She's trying to keep us distracted so we don't see what else she's planning." Tamiel added. Her boss, Uriel, archangel in charge of the Shadow angels glared at her. She shrugged at him.

"Now, everyone just calm down, we're all worried about this." Ranguel put his hands up, trying to quell the dissent.

Kafziel leaned over the desk, putting his face closer to Mikhail, "You have no plan. You expect us to keep throwing angels at the problem and letting them die, or worse. You're not doing anything to stop this. We need to gather the warriors and wage jihad on the vampires. Then march straight into Hell and end Lucy and her demons. But no, you are hiding up here in your office, shrouded from the terror and the pain we are going through."

Mikhail stood stoically still. His wings, half furled, ruffled a bit, the only indication of the mounting irritation caused by the insubordinate behavior from Azrael's assistant.

The rest of the assembly grumbled, mostly in support of what Kafziel was saying. Mikhail listened to all of them, his suppressed wrath smoldering.

"Well, don't you have anything wise to say, Mikhail?" Azrael put his hand on his assistant's shoulder.

Mikhail stared into his eyes, holding his gaze until the Soul Reaper looked away. He looked around the room, sizing up each archangel and their second individually. He saw that Koziel, Ranguel's second, was standing in back of the group in a corner. He hadn't given any indication where his sympathies lay.

Mikhail turned his gaze to Kafziel, his cold fury successfully restrained. He straightened to his full majesty. He leveled his unswerving gaze at Kafziel, coldly asking, "Can you do any better?" Mikhail's words were even, quiet, no emotion showing. He was angry, more than angry, and he would pull Kafziel's wings, sending him to earth to be part of the humans if he could.

Kafziel puffed his chest, emboldened by Mikhail's lack of shown anger. "I could do much better than you are. You are now weak and ineffective." A general shocked gasp rippled through the room.

Azrael tried to pull him back, placing both his hands on the junior angel's shoulders.

Kafziel shrugged him off, "I know what I'm doing, back the fuck off." Azrael put his hands up and backed away, thoroughly disgusted and not wanting any more connection. He shook his head, letting everyone in the room know that he didn't endorse or support his assistant's outburst.

Mikhail's eyes flashed, red, unseen by anyone. His gaze steady and unyielding, with a glow just flickering through his gaze at the angel. "Fine. It's yours." Cold shock immediately silenced the room. "The current situation as well as anything else that may crop up...angels, humans, animals, weather, trees...et al. I'm going on vacation. I may be back...I may not. Good luck." With that, Mikhail vanished.

The room erupted, everyone talking at once. Recriminations, blame, defense, statements staking out a position, and denials of positions all swirled together in a conflagration as those in position as everyone tried to make sense and plans in the wake of Mikhail's disappearance. Stepping around the desk, Kafziel took Mikhail's place with a cocky smug look on his face. Officiously, he began barking orders, pointing and talking to some of the assembled specifically about their jobs.

Next to the side of the desk, the remaining red-winged warrior angel, Simkiel, glared at Kafziel. He was hearing conversations critical of Mikhail and his stands on the demons, the vampires, even fellow angels. He finally had enough. He doubled up his fist, reached across the corner of the desk, punching Kafziel in the face. Kafziel staggered against the powerful blow. Simkiel raised his wings and started for the door, turning toward the group on his way out, "Mikhail's absence puts me in charge of the Warriors." He pointed at the visibly shaken Kafziel, who was staggering away from the wall. "You are not my boss and you can forget the Warriors coming to your aid." He pulled his wings down and glided out, heading for the aperture leading to the living quarters.

The stunned silence lasted for several heartbeats.

"Well, wonder why he's so testy. Must be off his ambrosia." Kafziel said trying to make light of the assault, rubbing his swelling jaw. "We need to get a plan to handle the disappearances. Let's adjourn to the conference room." Kafziel dismissed everyone and left the room.

Chapter Eight

T HE PRISTINE SNOW sparkled in early morning light in the wilds of Norway. A darkly shrouded lone figure trudged up to the shadowed gate in the towering monastery wall. He pulled the thick rope hanging beside the door and heard the clear tone from somewhere within.

He waited, glancing around at the massive St. Vigneous monastery. It had taken over two centuries to complete and continuously occupied since the early 14th century. What made it particularly impressive, besides the enormity, was the remote and treacherous terrain on which it stood.

Until recent years, within the last century to be precise, the existence of the cloistered priory had been fairly ignored by the Oppland region inhabitants due to its remote location and reclusive attitude of the inhabitants.

A small window opened in the door to a rosy-cheeked face. "Yes?"

"I am here to see Father Gudrun, I have a message from the Vatican for him." The man declared in English.

"Whom should I announce?"

"Brother Angelus. He knows me."

The little window shut and the door opened. The rosy-cheeked face belonged to a round little man in a brown robe, a rope securing it to the plump frame. "Come in, Brother Angelus. I'm Brother Thorbjorn. You are most welcome. Please follow me, I will show you to Father Gudrun."

With a nod, the monk wobbled toward the main building, Brother Angelus following.

Angelus followed, glancing at the heavily shadowed courtyard and thickly walled compound. He noticed curiously that there was no snow on the ground but what he had just walked through, outside the walls, was several feet deep. And there was plenty on the tiled roof and clinging to the eaves. Even at this early hour, just after dawn, there seemed to be lots of activity. The monks rushed with great determination to their tasks of the day. The rich warming scent of baking bread wafted through the crisp air. Angelus's stomach growled in response.

They reached a solid wooden door and Brother Thorbjorn turned, "Please wait here, I'll announce you." He turned and rapped sharply. He paused then entered, closing the door behind him. Seconds later, he opened the door and ushered Brother Angelus inside.

Father Gudrun came around his desk as Angelus entered, "Angelus! Good to see you, my brother. Come in, come in." The two men embraced. "Brother Thorbjorn, would you get us some tea, please?"

"Oh, and a bit of that wonderful bread that I smell, if it's ready, and some butter? If that's okay with you, Gudrun." Angelus took a chance, smiling.

"Of course, of course." Gudrun laughed, heading around the desk to his seat.

"What brings you to our monastery, Brother Angelus?" the abbot asked.

"I hadn't visited in quite a while and I felt the need to come and see you and how things are proceeding."

"We've added to the barn, not only raising reindeer but also some imported longhorn cattle, goats, and sheep. We have experimented with new seeds to try to bring more growth of vegetables, and we added a loom and are making cloth and blankets for sale. We have been cloistered for far too long. So we have made some tentative overtures beyond these walls and participated in the weekly market in the nearby village, quite successfully, I might add." Gudrun said, waiting on the food to be served.

"Sounds like you have been quite busy. Any new additions to the brotherhood here?"

"We've had a couple of newer brothers join the order, Brother Rikard came to us out of Denmark and Brother Hemmings is an American. Both came here about five years ago, a few months apart."

Angelus raised his eyebrows in surprise, "Five years? I had no idea it had been that long since I last visited. I'm sorry I've been lax in visits."

Gudrun laughed as Brother Thorbjorn brought

a tray with the tea service and the bread, setting it on the desk between the brothers. "I took the liberty of bringing some honey from the first harvest."

"Oh, how delightful." Angelus said, smiling.

"Thank you, brother. Please close the door as you leave. Angelus, don't worry about being lax, we always welcome your visits." The door closed and both men looked at it for a moment.

Gudrun sighed as he poured the tea, handing it across to the visitor. "Now, what brings you to visit us, Mikhail?"

Mikhail laid the cloak aside and took the cup. "I bear news that needed to be conveyed personally. I require some advice on a sensitive matter. And, finally, an update on the vampires in your care."

Gudrun didn't mask his surprise, "Advice? From me? What can I do?"

Mikhail moaned as he bit into the slice of fresh bread slathered with honey, "You still make the best bread here. This is so very good." He chewed. "I'm on Heavenly Hiatus." Mikhail licked a drop of honey from his thumb.

"Excuse me?" Gudrun's teacup rattled against its saucer.

"Seems some of the angels have decided that they can run the place better than I, so I just let them."

"What? Who?" The abbot's shock was evident. He placed his shaking cup on the table.

"It came out of some of the junior archangels, the big push was Azrael's assistant, Kafziel. I suspect that they have been talking with one of the other archangels and it has been brewing for a while."

"Really? I thought you had set up something that would keep them from having those types of emotions?"

"I did. But seems that adherence to the rules doesn't mean much nowadays. Some are curtailing their consumption and others have decided to go 'cold turkey'. I can usually tell when it's not being drunk, I keep an eye on the supply."

"That's why orders have fallen off recently. I was wondering. I still have several large barrels brewing for you."

"Just sit on them for the moment, one of the things I'm doing while I'm on hiatus is letting everyone just do what they think they will. Anarchy will abound, then I will see what is really going on." He held out his cup and Gudrun refilled it. "Tell me about these two new additions."

Putting down the teapot and re-covering it with the cozy, he picked up his slice of bread, gesturing with it, "You probably saw the reports about their activities inside and outside the monastery. Both are trying to work in all of the jobs, asking lots of questions, and getting scarce a few times a week, going for walks outside of the walls. I've had Brother Havvard shadowing them a few times and we've seen them with demons"

"Demons? Are you sure they are demons?" Mikhail stopped the cup mid-sip.

"We're sure. They are in the guise of humans, usually skiers in winter, but hikers in summer.

They have a 'shimmer' about them, I figure they're using some sort of cloak to keep from appearing as they do on the other side of the Hell portal. But they're demons." Gudrun shivered involuntarily.

"When did this start?" Mikhail prompted. He could tell Gudrun was not happy about the development.

"About a year ago. I am not sure why they are here or what it is they seek, but they come around here; they've also come to the village market and have been asking questions about our operations. Brothers Rikard and Hemmings usually come straight back and into the showers, trying to wash the demon stench off of them but I can always tell."

Mikhail nodded. "I can imagine. I need you to continue to monitor them. Lucifer's minions have been quite active outside of Hell recently." He took a sip of tea. "I need to know what is going on so I can plan accordingly."

"Do you know how the demons are getting out of Hell? You had the portal sealed eons ago."

"I did. They located a human alchemist from long ago and he managed to unravel the wards on one of the lesser portals. Lucifer knows the movements around Hell are carefully monitored. A demon or two come through at a time, only a few in total to lay the ground work. The idea was to keep me from knowing and now the covert plans are beginning to show, I just have to wait." He smiled and shrugged, wiping his hands on his robe. Gudrun smiled and handed him a napkin. "Thanks. I guess that was a bit rude of me." He laughed.

"No, I do it, just try not to, Brother Jorgen fusses when he has to soak them to get the butter stains out." Gudrun handed him another slice.

Mikhail took the warm morsel, nodding his thanks. "Well, I guess I need to ask the question of the day, how is Sullivan doing?"

"About as well as you could expect, I guess. He's still moody and sometimes brooding. He's trying to be better, working a lot in the scriptorium with Ragnavald."

"You think he's adjusting?"

Gudrun looked out of the window and then back to the archangel, "I think so. But it's slow. Today Ragnavald found him kneeling and crying just before dawn. I'm not sure why, neither is Ragnavald, he asked but Sullivan wouldn't say. He just retired to his cell."

"Hmmmm. I wonder." Mikhail closed his eyes a moment.

"Would you like me wake him for you?"

The angel shook his head, "No need to disturb him. I think I know what set him off this time; one of our angels was captured and hurt. One that Sullivan is close to."

"How did he know? He never gets mail and the only other outside communication is the satellite phone and it's locked in my desk."

"I think he has a link to someone outside, telepathic link. Is he still working on the scrolls?"

Gudrun nodded, "Yes, Ragnavald has him working several hours a day on them. He's making steady progress on them. He's got a fine hand; the transcriptions are very well done. Ragnavald wants to get Brother Matteus to teach him the illuminations to complete them."

"He must continue translating. Maybe after he finds the scrolls I need, he can learn that part of the process."

"I know you spoke with Ragnavald about that, may I ask what it is you are looking for?"

Mikhail set his teacup down. He debated whether to level with the abbot. "Okay, you know this goes no further. Not even Ragnavald or Sullivan need know."

Gudrun nodded, "Of course. Confession is good for the soul, Mikhail." He smiled.

"I'm looking for is a scroll that I transliterated during the first days of the Earth. God gave me the formulas for three things, I created scrolls for them. The Portal Scroll is the keys to making portals between the dimensions. The Originator Scroll contains the information to make humans and animals. The other, the one I really need, is the Restoration Scroll. That one contains the key to making angels or restoring one that has been transmuted."

"Restoration. I understand needing more angels, in the war with Lucifer; many were lost on both sides. Sending the apostates through the portal to Hell cut the census of Heaven back substantially. But why would you need to be able to restore an angel? What would they...oh." Brother Gudrun halted abruptly, realization dawning. "Sullivan."

Mikhail nodded, "Sullivan is not only one.

Lucifer has started a new campaign, in league with the vampires. The head of the project is a vampire named Marcus Lancaster and..."

"Lancaster." Gudrun's hazel eyes darkened, "That's the vampire that is causing much of Sullivan's grief, we almost lost him recently."

The look on Mikhail's face prompted the abbot to continue, "Evidently he has heard that his maker is pregnant with Marcus Lancaster's child, although how a vampire supposedly got her pregnant is uncertain. I sent the report to you when it happened. The angel, Sethiel, was the one who talked him down, he was so enraged, he tore up the building and headed out into the sun. Sethiel stopped him and talked."

"Report? I never got the report. How did you send it?" Mikhail adjusted in the chair, sitting straighter.

"Brother Lukkas hand-carried it to Heaven to give it to you directly. He indicated he did it."

Mikhail raised an eyebrow, "He told you that he gave it to me? Not to anyone else?"

"Yes, he did. You didn't get it?"

"No. I did not." Mikhail rubbed his hand through his hair, "I must find out who he did give it to."

"I will send for him." He raised the bell to call Brother Thorbjorn.

"No. We don't want to alert him that anything is amiss. I will find out. But I need you to keep an eye on him and, if you absolutely need to get something to me, send your most trusted angel to speak directly with Rangnel. I will check in with him. I know he can be trusted."

"So you're not going back to Heaven?"

Mikhail smiled, the look actually concerning Gudrun with its accompanying mischief, "Nope. They wanted it, they got it. I'm going to vacation, see a few friends, do some tourist-type stuff and just relax. They think they have this figured out, I'm giving them enough rope." Gudrun looked aghast. "Oh, don't worry my friend, I have my ways and I will know exactly what is going on."

"Now, I do need you to do something. Subtly encourage Sullivan to discuss looking through the scrolls with others in the monastery. Not so much the content but that he's on a mission for the Vatican. This information will to get to Lucifer surreptitiously to avoid the appearance of deception. This will pique her interest. Lucifer is always scheming and I want to find out the latest plotting."

"I can do that. If it comes to anything, I'll be in touch."

"Good, thank-you." Mikhail stood and put his hand out to shake, then pulled it back, reaching into his robes. He drew out a scroll and handed it to the abbot." This is for you. Only use it if you have to. If Sullivan goes rogue again, tries to leave, or take matters into his own hands, give him this. He must realize the consequences of his actions. He will risk harming the very ones he wishes to protect by leaving before the time is right. He must stay here until that time."

"How are we to know when that time is?"

"You will know, no doubt." He smiled reassuringly.

"Okay, I will give it to him if he insists." The monk took the scroll and placed it in a desk drawer. "Now, would you like to stay the evening, join us for prayers and a meal?"

"No, I have an idea to play some chess with an old friend. But thank-you for your offer and for the hospitality. Please tell Brother Hjalmar that his bread, as usual, is manna and most appreciated."

Brother Gudrun shook Mikhail's hand and opened the door to his office. "Thank-you, Brother Angelus. The information you brought was very welcome. Give our regards and prayers for the Pope." He smiled.

"I will. Goodbye, Brother Gudrun." He walked out of the building, across the courtyard and out of the gate. It wasn't until he reached the other side of the hill that he dropped the guise of the cloak, spread his red wings, and took to the skies.

Chapter Nine

T HE WEATHER WAS brutal. The Transylvanian mountains echoed with thunder, the lightning rippling between the mountains down the valleys as the wind howled, blowing snow in every direction. All contributed to making visibility very limited.

Mikhail had to stop flying, alighting on a rock under a tree to catch his breath. He could regulate his body temperature, however, flying and navigating in this blinding blizzard was definitely problematic. In addition, trying to locate familiar landmarks beneath a thick blanket of snow was a challenge. The result: he was wet and he could swear the tips of his wing feathers were coated in ice.

He shivered as another peal of thunder rattled the valley.

"Who goes on vacation in the winter to Romania?" He asked no one. "I have to be crazy."

He shook the snow from his feathers, extended his wings and launched himself once more into the storm. He flew low and close to the wall of the valley. "Why the hell couldn't he have a nice condo in Târgoviște or something? Why up here?"

He asked himself that every time he came up the valley. This was not somewhere anyone could just stumble upon, you had to know it was there.

Spotting the twin spruce trees with the beech, now bereft of leaves, standing just in front and between them, Mikhail fought to glide down to them without crashing into one of the trees. His left wing caught the tree in front, sending accumulated snow falling onto his head. He tried to throw up his shield but didn't make it before his head got wet and the snow trickled into his shirt.

Shaking the snow off him, he stepped behind the trees to a rock. He traced the rock with his hand and stepped behind it. Built into the face of the mountain was a door frame with a heavy wooden door in it. He made a fist and knocked on the door.

It seemed to take forever before he heard the sound of the lock bar being moved and the locks being thrown. The door creaked as it opened, Mikhail entered.

Warmth hit him, welcoming. The room was bright with flickering light from many candles; thick oriental rugs covered the floor under old, heavy furniture. He looked around, turning, to find his host standing behind him. He involuntarily jumped back.

His host smiled, white teeth with a pair of longer canine fangs greeting him.

"Vlad! Don't do that!" Mikhail exclaimed.

The man laughed, a deep sound that somewhat echoed in the room. "I do not know why you always fall for that, you have to expect I am the one who opened the door."

"Unless Claire is here, you mean? I expected her to be here with you so I expected her to open the door." Mikhail looked around for her, "I never expected you and that face full of ivory you sport."

"Unfortunately, the weather precluded her from joining me. I wasn't expecting you to be the one at the door." Mikhail shook his wings; the wet droplets from the snow were flung around the room.

"Hey, don't shake that everywhere. I don't want to have to clean it up." Vlad walked to a cabinet, pulled out a towel and threw it to the angel. "I guess you decided to come early for our chess match. You're that eager to get beaten again, right?"

"You realize that the law of averages is going to make sure that, someday I will make it into the winner's circle." Mikhail ran the towel across his head and then his wings, carefully drying everything. "I take it, since she's not here, you've not eaten today."

Vlad's dark eyes sized up the angel, "No, at least not the sustenance I prefer. I figure we'll eat the stew she made for me. It's in the freezer and I can warm it for both of us." He walked toward the part of the room that held his well-apportioned kitchen.

Mikhail never failed to appreciate the place. Vlad Tepes had taken an ordinary cave in the Carpathian Mountains and turned it into a richly decorated home. The entry through the door was into the living space, complete with candelabras full of candles, a roaring fireplace, and cabinetry. His gaze followed his friend into the kitchen area containing deeply stained wood cabinets, rock counters, and a wood-fed stove. Copper pots and pans hung from racks attached to the cave's ceiling. Behind that, Mikhail knew there were bedrooms with antique poster beds of wood, more fireplaces, and at least four deep pool-like bathtubs in private bathrooms.

Vlad had built the home after he was turned, carefully cleaning and fitting the layout into the cave so that it didn't take away from the beauty of the place but added to it. Mikhail always marveled at the way he had managed that. The other quality about it was that Vlad didn't have to worry about being incinerated by any errant sunbeams, he had a very secure place to pass the time.

Mikhail looked around, finally finding the remote control lying on a book next to the chair he knew Vlad loved to read in. He picked the book up, looking at the cover, and then opened to read the flap blurb. He started laughing as Vlad walked into the room.

"Seriously, Vlad? *Dark Lover?* A vampire romance? When did you start reading this stuff?"

Vlad set the tray with the bowls of stew and glasses of scotch on the table by the chess board. "I have always been interested in how literature portrays vampires. Sometimes it's interesting to see what the various authors come up with when they are working. This one..." He plucked the book from Mikhail's hands, "is by a woman, J. R. Ward. She's managed to find out, somehow, that we have vampires in Caldwell, New York but she's blown them up into some sort of supermen, all over six and a half feet tall, muscles on muscles, and such. She's writing fictional romance with guys who can keep on having sex all night long."

"Really? Why do you read that stuff?"

"I'm interested in the changing of the mythology around what we are. The closer they get to the reality, the more work the Council has to put out to information pointing to the book as totally fiction. I remember hearing about how they had to make sure that *Interview with a Vampire* was seen as a work of fiction. I heard that Xun about lost his mind over that one, he was insisting on finding her and stopping her from writing further books because she got too close to the way we are."

"Why does that not surprise me? So you go through all the new vampire books and try to figure out what to say to the author about getting too close to reality?"

"Not so much, I've learned to read and be amused. It's really not my place to judge the author, I figure Xun will be the one to deal with it. I am finding that vampire books are sometimes well done, others are just really drivel. I finish reading them and then donate them to a library somewhere, usually a library with a small budget that will appreciate it."

"Speaking of Xun, what's the old bastard up to now, anything special?" Mikhail asked as he sat down in the chair set up for the game. He pulled the bowl off the tray and ate a spoon full. "And Clare still makes some of the best stew I've had."

"You probably know more than I do, I'm retired, remember? I try hard to keep from having to deal with, or even think about him or any of the rest of the vampire population. I'm keeping to myself." Vlad put a little mental push toward the angel; it was not a subject he wanted to explore further.

"I need to catch you up on what's going on." Mikhail ignored the push.

"I really don't want to know…"

"Vlad, I need advice, it's why I came here. You know the vampires better than almost anyone else. Things are changing fast."

Vlad's spoon stopped the journey to his mouth, "You came here to ask my advice about vampires?"

The angel nodded. "Whose turn is it to be white?" He looked at the chess board.

"Mine. What do you mean you need advice; don't you have advisers up there to talk to? Why me?"

Mikhail looked deep into Vlad's eyes, "Your lineage is the main problem right now."

As he loaded more stew onto his spoon, the vampire moved his pawn from e2 to e4. "I have nothing to do with Drachenfeuer any longer. It's not my problem."

Mikhail studied the move for a moment, then moved his pawn from e7 to e5. "There's been a big change in what's going on, seems Marcus

Lancaster is working on declaring war on Heaven."

Vlad started to pick up another pawn, then put it down and grabbed the knight at g1, moving it to f3, "What's that bastard doing now?" Vlad growled.

Mikhail smiled at the name, knowing he had hit a nerve. "Are you aware he's made another progeny, a woman?" He moved another pawn from d7-d6.

"Really?" Sounding uninterested, he moved a pawn from d2 to d4 and took a bite of the stew. "I stopped worrying about him, or any of the other Drachenfeurer members when I stepped out of the Council."

"I, unfortunately have to pay attention to him." The conversation fell off as the men concentrated on eating and the chessboard. In a couple of moves, Vlad managed to take both a pawn and a bishop from the angel.

"Hey now, no reason to do that!" Mikhail objected, smiling. "Didn't we agree that I was going to be able to win this one?" He moved his pawn from d6 to e5, capturing the pawn that had taken the bishop.

Vlad smiled, fangs gleaming. "We did?"

"I never asked you, what happened on the Council that caused you to leave?"

Vlad moved his bishop to c4. "I objected to the affirmation of the new leader."

"Xun?" Mikhail countered with his knight to f6.

"Yes. You know he was the cause of my second mark, in a round-about way." The vampire raised his right hand and Mikhail winced, the burn on the top of the still-vibrantly young hand showed two marks.

"You got that one because you turned someone sooner than the rules allowed."

"Yes, but I did it to be able to get the angels to carry a message back to heaven about how Xun was planning to hunt down the Nosferatu and kill them." He moved the queen to b3. "I asked the woman, Nida, to take a message back to you about the Council debate." He laughed in derision, "She didn't want to be my 'errand boy' so she refused. I figured the genocide was going to happen so I just stayed away for a while."

With a move of his own black queen to e7, Mikhail countered. "I came to see you about that. The angel who was the witness for your marking, Sethiel, did come tell me your message. That's when I met you." The angel wondered where this was going.

The white knight was moved to c3, "You sent your second and the head of the Enforcers to speak with the Council, warning Xun to abandon the campaign to kill the Nosferatu. While Laertes, who was head of the Council at that time, didn't mind your presence, Xun was royally pissed off about it. And he made that attitude crystal clear with me."

"I had heard he was threatening you with a multitude of problems. Seems the guy knew you were the one who came to us about it." Mikhail tried to lighten the mood; he could feel Vlad's anger seething just under the surface. He picked up the black pawn, waved it around like it had wings, then set it down on c6.

Vlad smiled. "Somebody's been studying, I see. The only move to use is this one." He picked up the bishop and moved it to g5. "Not just threats. He managed to get several of the members of Drachenfeurer, progeny of my siblings, sent to Hell for various things. He just knew I was working for you, that I was pushing for things on the Council to make you happy."

Mikhail studied his host's face. "Xun didn't know the truth, he suspected. You are your own man, we both know that." As he engaged Vlad's eyes, he quietly made his move, pawn to c5.

The vampire smiled, "You realize that's a zugzwang play, right?" He moved his knight to b5, taking the black pawn.

"Zugzwang? You're making me move? Or were the angels forcing Xun's hand on your bloodline?" He moved his pawn, returning the favor and seizing the errant knight.

"Both. Your Enforcers marked Laertes for the third time and took him to Hell. This caused the vacancy in the Anführerüberlegen, the Council leader's seat. According to the rules we set up at the beginning, the oldest member of the Council takes the seat for 500 years, or until he is taken to Hell or dies. That rule gave the seat to Xun. That move by the angels on Laertes forced my hand and I could do nothing more than leave to stop Xun from hurting Drachenfeure worse. I named the oldest other active vampire in the line,

Marcus." He moved his bishop to b5, taking Mikhail's pawn.

"And Xun has kept Marcus off the Council. This issue is causing one with Heaven now, which is why I'm here." Knight to d7.

"Oh?" Vlad moved to castle the rook at a1 to d1, the king from a5 to a3, a move that Mikhail didn't anticipate, much like the moves Marcus was making. He hoped the information he had would change that.

"I'm here because I've left Heaven. There's a mutiny in the works and Marcus Lancaster is at the base of it." He moved his own rook to d8.

"You've left Heaven because of Marcus?" Vlad ignored the move.

"Lancaster is killing angels, then bringing them back as vampires. He's trying to raise an army to take on Heaven itself. I've lost many angels to him already, either murdered outright or turned. Some of my administrative angels are not happy with the moves I've made up there so they challenged me, told me they could do a better job, so I'm letting them handle it."

Vlad made his move, his rook moving from d1 to d7, he removed the black knight from the board. "I bet your leaving caught them off guard with that move. But, on the reason behind it, you are serious? Turning angels into vampires isn't possible."

"Oh, yes it is. The first one to be turned was done by Lancaster's progeny, a woman named Lilly. She turned an Enforcer angel named Sullivan into a vampire. She's also made a vampire out of a cat as well." He made the only logical move, his rook moving to d7 to remove the white rook.

"Impossible. Maybe not on the angel but animals cannot be turned. I've never heard of such a thing happening. Angels, well, that's your department, you can just get God to turn them back." Vlad slid his rook next to his king.

"Word is that he wants to turn the angels to get us to back off the marking and rules. Maybe get a few vampires out of Hell." He looked at the board, trying to figure out what his opponent was up to. It began to look like he was going to lose this one like he had all the others. He moved his queen to e6 to try to counter a lateral move by the white queen.

"Sounds like you have a problem, then. Why are you telling me this? Let me guess, you want me to stop him somehow." Bishop to d7.

Mikhail sat back a minute, not looking at the board but seeking out Vlad's eyes. He sat quietly looking intently at his opponent, friend. Taking a deep breath, he answered. "Yes, I do. I need you to go back and take the Drachenfeure seat so you can keep Marcus Lancaster off of it and provide some guidance to Xun and the others." He moved his knight to d7, seizing the white bishop, hoping that he could bring Vlad into the fray as the knight to upset the plans Marcus had for the world.

The vampire sat quietly, assessing the situations both on and off the board. He could think moves ahead of the angel from years of practice.

He could see that Mikhail wasn't concerned about him so much but more concerned about Marcus Lancaster getting control of the vampires. "You have got to be out of your mind coming here to ask me to do that." He moved his queen to b8, putting the angel's king into check. "I left the counsel. I don't want to return. I'm inactive, partially because of Xun and his machinations, but even more importantly, I don't want to get the last mark. I rather like it on Earth, I'm not willing for you and your minions to drag me into Hell where your ambassador of evil, Nida, says that eventually all vampires will go. No, I'm not going to risk it."

He held up his right hand again and Mikhail could see Nida's work on it. Some vampires deserved the marks, but not ones like Vlad, at least not since he left the warfare of his youth behind and the thousands of dead he created. He had, for all intents, been a model vampire since then.

"What if I can guarantee you that the third mark won't happen? That you will remain on Earth to do, within the laws, whatever you needed, and wanted, to do? You would be free of that threat, Vlad. I can make that happen." He moved his queen to b8, taking the white queen off the board. "I can keep Nida from you."

"I'm not willing to risk it. No." Vlad answered. There's no way you can keep your angels in line to not harass me and mine." He moved his rook to d8. "Checkmate, my friend. Just like in life, I win."

He saw the angel's eyes cloud over, staring at a point over his shoulder. He had seen it before; Mikhail was hearing something the vampire could not hear.

"*Mikhail, we need you back at H.H.A.D.*"

The angel answered both in his head and out loud, allowing Vlad to hear what was going on. "Handle whatever it is, or get Kafziel to handle it, I'm busy."

"*Mikhail*" the voice belonged to Ranguel, "*It's about Essex. We need you back here.*"

Mikhail cut the communication, groaning as he tipped the black king in defeat. "I am sorry, Vlad, evidently I have to deal with this whether I like it or not." The angel drained the last of the scotch in his glass.

"I understand my friend." He walked with the angel toward the door. "By the way, next time you memorize a chess game to take me on, try not to pick one of the most famous ones. You played the Night at the Opera game between Paul Morphy and the Duke of Brunswick and Count Isouard almost flawlessly."

Mikhail laughed, "Caught me, eh? I didn't know you studied the old champions."

"I don't. I was at that game in October of 1858. It is recorded as a game between the champion, Morphy, and the aristocrats. What they fail to mention in all the books is that I was sitting on Morphy's side, the white, just like tonight. And we won that game in seventeen moves. You didn't have a chance as soon as you made the second move."

Mikhail raised an eyebrow, "I will remember that. I can only hope I'm not that transparent to the angels who are opposing me. Thanks for the food and the game, Vlad. I will keep you apprised of what is going on."

He opened the door and walked out. As the door closed, Vlad said "I hope not, Mikhail, I don't want to know." Turning, he went to clean up the remains of their meal.

Chapter Ten

"I HAVE TO *get this to Lucifer a.s.a.p."* Koziel thought as he watched the meeting unravel into a shouting match. Mikhail's dramatic and abrupt exit had shocked everyone and the entire assembly had plunged into turmoil.

Once the meeting with Kafziel was over, Koziel waited until everyone seemed to be busy and he glided out of H.H.A.D. He had lots of information to pass along. He secreted himself into a remote corner. There he used a covert direct line to send a short message to Hell. It was a vague post, with enough facts to raise interest. The response was immediate and the directive emphatic "Come see Me Now." Go into Hell? He wasn't sure he wanted to go that far, meeting someone somewhere on Earth was the usual routine, many times in bars where the noise and activity would cover what they were saying.

Right into Hell. Holy. Shit.

He reached the coordinates he had been given. He was in the middle of the Indian Ocean, a small island that was manned only with a small group of scientists who performed geomagnetic, biological and meteorological studies.

He glided to the island's base camp, not bothering to hide his gray wings. A young woman noticed him and waved.

"Hello, can I help you?" She continued to look at the instruments on the panel she was working on.

"I need to see Lucifer. I have news, and an appointment." Koziel stared around him, not entirely sure he really had the correct location.

"Angels are not allowed. Go away." She never looked up.

"I'm a special case. I have some important information." Then he added, "I have an appointment."

"If that's true, who is your contact? Give it to them."

"This is privileged informa–"

"Are you deaf? Go away." She got up and walked to another panel with instruments, tapped on a few keys on the keyboard.

"No. I was told to see—"

She turned and hit a button, glaring at him, "Jon, we have a situation, send security."

"I'm not a situation, I am from heaven. I have information—"

Three big men walked up from the tunnel near the monitoring station and approached Koziel. One, the big man in the middle, had a gun in his hand. Like that would do a bit of good against an angel, yes, it would hurt but it...

"You need to leave. Now." He pointed the weapon at the angel.

"My name is Koz—"

"I don't give a shit. Leave, before you're dead."

Koziel looked at each man. All over six feet tall, muscles and grim looks on their faces. All wearing typical khaki military attire.

"If I leave, you get to deal with Lucifer, who will not be interested in your reasons for why you sent me away. If you kill me, well, I'm going to be happy to haunt your asses and watch you get tortured for eternity."

The radio squawked, pulling his, and everyone's, attention to the woman who had caused the little meeting with the charming gentlemen.

He could hear one side of the conversation and it was apparent that someone was not happy, if her immediate snap to attention and the number of "yes sirs" he was hearing was any indication. She finally laid the radio down and looked at the men.

"Lucifer wants him inside. Now." She turned around and went back to her dials and machines, ignoring the odor of fuming testosterone.

They stood looking somewhat confused.

"You heard the lady, which way to Hell." Koziel smarted off.

The middle guy gestured with the gun, "This way, to the left and up the trail."

Koziel followed the trail toward a cave, his gray wings ruffling in the wind being funneled between the trees. The closer he got, the more nervous he felt. It was one thing to meet up with a handler and spill the beans on what was going on "back home," it was entirely another to walk into the belly of the beast and make yourself available for whatever happened.

He could always fly off. Of course, the bully brothers could shoot at him while he did but he would be free.

He felt like he was walking the last mile to his own death.

He wondered if the feeling was some sort of a bottled security measure, something designed to make someone want to bolt rather than enter the cave. It felt like an itching powder had been poured inside his clothing.

It was working.

Inside the cave, the darkness was broken up by torches secured in sconces on the walls. The path went down into the earth, steeply, Koziel found himself wishing he had just given a note to his handler and kept his ass where it belonged, up in Heaven. Feathers didn't do well in hot areas and if any sparks from the melted magma touched them, he would catch fire. He didn't relish burning to death. He tucked his wings in a little tighter.

How the hell did the Warriors who brought the vampires to Hell do this anyway?

The path leveled out and he could see a door across a narrow chasm. The way between looked like it was two inches wide and he couldn't see the bottom of the gaping hole. If he fell, he couldn't raise his wings enough to fly because the walls of the chasm were too close. He took a timid step on the rock bridge and shuffled his feet to try to keep his balance.

He let out the breath he didn't realize he was holding as his feet passed the opposite edge.

Now to face what was on the other side of the door. He knew Lucifer. Koziel had been one of the combatants in the First War in Heaven. Well, combatant wasn't exactly the right word; he had been a spy for Lucifer's side against Mikhail. He had witnessed Lucifer's formal surrender, the sanction and penalty of banishment for the losing side had been handed down in a great ceremony with Mikhail and Metatron standing side by side. The choice of exile to a different dimension, which Lucifer had chosen to call 'Hell' was made. The angels involved were labeled 'fallen' and stripped of their rings and feathers. They were marched through a double line of their former peers to the portal and through it with Lucifer following after them. Then Mikhail closed the portal, sealing them out of Heaven forever. The only reminder of the fallen angel's existence in Heaven was a single, colored feather, left on the floor where the condemned stood, one feather for each fallen, which were quickly picked up and given to Zadekiel the Archivist, his yellow wings trembling as he took the feathers, placed them into a gilded box to be entombed in the Souls Room.

Mikhail had won that war, but the hostilities had never ceased. Koziel still believed in the cause, that Lucifer should have been the one chosen to rule Heaven and he had continued to work clandestinely, along with others, to unseat Mikhail and bring Lucifer back in triumph.

Koziel wasn't nervous about seeing Lucifer

again. What he was nervous about was the fact that he had no idea what was waiting on the other side of that door.

"Well, turn the knob and go in." The guy with the gun prodded him with it, hitting the muscle between his wings with the barrel.

"Don't touch me, asshole." Koziel growled as he reached out for the knob. Thankfully the man didn't have a snappy come back for it.

"Better the devil you know..." he joked to himself, trying to allay the fears he felt. He took a deep fortifying breath, painted on a confident smile and swung the door open. His eyes widened as he walked into the room of astonishing decadent grandeur.

It was about as far away from a cave as it could be. The color, after the dark grays and black of the cave, were dazzling. Bright reds and yellows mixed with browns and blues in the carpets overlapping on the floor. Large framed mirrors hung on the walls over small occasional tables and short embroidered stools. The lights, electric, he wondered how that was happening, were small spotlights around the edges with a larger round chandelier hanging in the middle. Billowy purple swags draped from the ceiling and trailed down onto the walls. It was all very Moroccan in style. Even the sweet, musky smell of incense almost masked the distinct fetor of brimstone.

The three men did not enter but one of them pulled the door closed, leaving Koziel inside the room.

"I suppose you made this trip to speak directly to me?"

Koziel turned quickly away from the tabletop statue he was examining to the voice; he knew who it was before he even looked.

Lucifer.

She looked much the same as he remembered. The last time he had seen her; she was drawing a line between her and Mikhail and declaring she would rather leave heaven than live under her twin brother's rule.

She stood in front of what had appeared to be a door-sized arched niche in the wall. She was still hauntingly beautiful. He stared at her, drinking her in.

Her skin was still alabaster, her hair, still red, was no longer confined to the conservative style she had worn in Heaven, but was loose, cascading past her waist. Her full, luscious lips now wore a coat of scarlet color. Yet, the most dramatic change...her eyes. Her eyes had been as crystal clear blue as the sky in Heaven. Now, they were black voids, frightening but hypnotic.

She had obviously given up all constraints of Heaven where her dress was concerned. Her bustier was blood red satin, overlaid with black spider-web lace. Her black leather skirt reached the floor.

The big shock was what was on her back. In Heaven, she had proudly sported beautiful red Warrior wings, majestic, grand, with the slightest sheen of gold. At the end of the war, mere formal surrender was not enough for Mikhail. Additional sanctions were imposed as with all victors, he insisted that she and all of her followers be stripped of any Heavenly visage. So, before banishing, each was stripped of their wing feathers that had indicated their status and role. Lucifer was the last. The delicate white skin beneath her feathers was streaked with blood as she disappeared through the portal to her Hell, her head still head high and proud, even in defeat.

Her wings were now intimidating sleek black leather, like her skirt, contrasting with the rest of her skin. The only reminder of her Warrior status was the slight dusting of red pin feathers across the shoulders of the wings.

Recognizing he was examining the changes, Lucifer pulled the wings up and out to full length, which took up almost the entire width of the room.

"Do you like them?"

Kozeil found his voice, "They are..." He searched for a word that wouldn't get him fried on the spot. "Interestingly beautiful."

Lucy laughed, pulling the wings down. "Diplomatic. Very good."

As she glided toward him, Koziel sank to his knees and lowered his eyes. That earned him another laugh. "Oh, get up. I don't want to stand on hypocritical formality."

Koziel stood and nodded.

"Well, go on. What was so all-fired important that you couldn't give it to your usual demon contact?"

Koziel fought the urge to smile.

"I have news. Mikhail has left Heaven."

"So my brother decided, finally, that he needs to take a vacation. He actually trusted someone to run things? Probably that ass-kissing Uriel, right?"

"No. It appears that the other archangels aren't stepping up, Kafziel, Azrael's assistant, is the leader right now." He watched Lucifer's changing expression, first mocking smile sliding down to pensive concern. "And Mikhail isn't off on holiday, he left. No one knows where he went or why."

Lucy stared at the Enforcer angel, was he running a scam on her at Mikhail's word? What was her brother up to?

"Oh really? Let's sit and you tell me everything." She indicated a couch. "Start at the beginning, what exactly is going on over there?"

Koziel smiled at this, it was what he wanted to happen, to get the attention of the next head of Heaven. He hoped it would allow him to move up into a more powerful position once she took over.

"No one is sure what he's been doing. It appears that the vampires are getting ready to challenge Heaven. Angels are missing, we know some are dead. No real pattern of abduction, every division has a few missing. Concern is mounting. There was a big meeting in Mikhail's office; the push came out of Azrael's Reapers. They interrogated him on the missing and Mikhail blew up, dumping everything, walked out, and no one knows where he is."

The unsaid support for Lucy to return was

glaringly obvious. Lucy ignored it for the moment.

"Everyone still drinking the Ambrosia?"

Koziel's smile faded. "Yes, why?" the ambrosia wasn't made a law in Heaven until after Lucy had walked out with her angels.

"Silly boy. You have no idea what that stuff is, do you." It wasn't a question. Lucy laughed again, even longer, her derision apparent. "Why do you think Mikhail made drinking it official and mandatory?"

Koziel frowned. Come to think of it, no one had seemed to question the drink or the rules.

"Of course you never questioned it." Lucy continued, reading his face, "The great Archangel Mikhail says jump and everyone jumps and just hopes that it's high enough. That story he told you, the one about the formula being necessary to combat a virus I had created is so much of a lie."

How the hell did she know that, Koziel wondered as Lucy snapped her fingers and a glass of what looked like ambrosia appeared. She held it out to him.

"Want some? This irresistible sweet beverage is a control device. Researched by my angels, it was supposed to be a liquor to calm the masses of humans, to make them docile and stop wars.

"When we had the war in Heaven, Mikhail's forces seized the laboratory. He had to torture my lead scientist to get the formula, then he killed him, and allowed his light to be released to the universe to keep me from being able to use it."

Koziel stared at the glass in her hand. "This isn't immunization?"

"No, silly, it's not. It makes the rank-and-file angels docile. How do you make angels not think for themselves? They were created to protect the humans and the planet, that duty breeds the emotions, you have to be able to weigh how things are going and make decisions.

"Mikhail wants total control. If angels think for themselves, they don't need the archangels, the hierarchy only exists if there are underlings that give away their own personal power. So Mikhail uses the ambrosia to insure that control."

"Not everyone drinks this as they should." Koziel placed the glass on the side table without taking a sip. "Many angels partake, in one extent or another, in human food and drink, only getting enough ambrosia out of the system to..." his sentence trailed off as the truth of her words dawned on him. "That's why the system triggers a personnel counsel if you don't withdraw enough from the system."

"Exactly. Big Brother is watching you. Every one of you." She looked into his gray eyes. "Now, for the other thing you came to talk about. Tell me about this situation with the missing angels."

Koziel managed to pull his attention away from the coal black eyes of the former Light Bringer. He rubbed his temples a moment.

"It started with the turning of Sullivan..."

"Sullivan? Not an angel?"

"You knew him as Eistered. He was an Enforcer and was allowed to take that ridiculous name from some poor human farmer. He got turned by a female vampire who also has a cat she turned into a vampire. Mikhail is very interested in this vampire and seems to be running some sort of interference for her for some reason. Then they grabbed Essexiel and have ....."

"Wait, go back. This woman changed both an angel and a cat and Mikhail is interested in her? What's so special about one former human?"

"We don't know. Mikhail is preoccupied with her and doesn't even seem concerned about the missing angels. That's what the uproar was about that ended with him leaving."

"So the woman is important and his very own angels aren't. Interesting. I need to know more about what the vampires are doing."

Koziel stopped, blinking. "You're not involved in whatever it is that the vampires are doing?"

"Why should I care what a few blood-drinking humans do? They are not my concern."

"You're not?" Koziel had figured that Hell was behind what was going on. "That seems like it would have interested you enough to be involved."

The fallen angel ruffled her leathery wings. "Who do you think actually came up with this plan? Those vampires couldn't think their way out of a spider's web; someone has to be the brains of the operation."

Koziel smiled, "Of course you are. Mikhail thinks you are safely tucked here in the dimension and neutral."

"My brother is, shall we say, less bright than you are." Lucifer purred. "So, anything else?" She laid her hand on his knee familiarly.

"So, if you are successful in helping the vampires turn enough angels to get rid of Mikhail, would there be a position for me, possibly a head of a department? I know the Enforcers will go away but…"

"Who says they will go away? We're going to continue the practice of finding, tuning, and removing vampires."

"Really? I thought vampires were somehow related to the fallen, that's the legend we are taught when we join the Enforcers." Koziel had wondered about that for a long time.

"Yes, vampires are distant relatives of the fallen, which means they are distant relatives of the angels as well. A demon bit a human and that human spawned a vampire, who then went on to make the vampires of today. But that won't stop us from continuing to deal with them as they are handled now; they are going to become useless once their use as a distraction is over." She smiled at him, "Do you have anything else for me, any little tidbits about my brother and what he's doing?"

"No, nothing else, yet. I may be able to find out where he is and I'll get that word to you."

"I don't want word. From now on, you are to come here personally and report to me whatever you find. I also need you to find out the names of the missing angels as well as the ones killed or turned. If you can also put together a listing of angels sympathetic to our side, I would like that."

"Yes ma'am. I will do that for you."

She rubbed her hand up his leg toward his crotch and purred, "Call me Lucy. Koz, I find you...interesting, and there is a reward ahead for you if you do well in this endeavor. I can make it very worth your while to work closely with me."

Koziel couldn't believe it but he was actually blushing. "Of course...uh..Lucy. I will report directly to you."

"Excellent. Now scoot along and find out that information for me. I will look forward to seeing you, very soon." Her hand landed directly on his cock, which was straining and threatening to break through his trousers.

He moaned as he stood and readjusted himself.

"See you soon...Lucy." He let his gaze linger on her for just a moment before he left the room through the door he had come through earlier.

After he was gone, she stood up, wiping her hand on her skirt, "Simpering idiot." She turned and left through the portal, heading back to rejoin Lillith and Stan, in their quest to find out what Mikhail was really up to.

Chapter Eleven

THE EXPLOSION OF light faded, leaving the vampires blinking. Baron wobbled his way into the room and plopped down next to Lilly, rubbing on her with his head. She reached down and ran her hand down his back, trying to get her eyes to work.

Marcus strode into the room toward her, reaching out to take her hand to pull her to him. As his fingers touched her, he was blind-sided and found himself sliding across the floor, punches raining down on his face.

Marcus reacted automatically, throwing the former angel violently across the room. Essex hit the door and slid down to the floor. Marcus carefully put a couple of fingers to his nose and drew back blood. Both men rose. Marcus growled his fury and Essex's gaze was fixed on the object of his intense hatred. They squared off in preparation for a brawl to end all brawls. Lilly shouted for them to stop.

Stop? Marcus thought. Not hardly. He was going to pummel that angel into dust for daring to steal from him, for bringing the angels to his building, and for causing Lilly to be marked. He took two steps toward the man and launched himself into the air, crashing down, battering him with his fists as they landed on the floor, punching, kicking, and cussing.

Lilly watched helplessly, bloody tears falling again. The savagery before her almost made her forget her own pain. She wanted to separate them, but even greater was the desire to flee. To get away from Marcus Lancaster and the chaos around her.

The sound of the crushing blows and breaking bones was exacerbated by the snarling and growling of the two combatants. Four big men Lilly didn't recognize rushed in. Two pulled Essex off of Marcus, who had suffered a well-placed vicious knee to the groin. The other two helped their incapacitated boss from his crouched fetal position that Essex's kneeing had placed him in. Staggering to his feet, Marcus snarled and wiped the blood from his face, slinging droplets everywhere. The two men stepped back, respectfully flanking their boss as he swayed precariously, but close enough to steady him if needed.

"Take that miserable son-of-a-bitch to the training facility and lock him down tight. I'll be up, later to deal with him."

The men hustled the former angel out the door. Marcus turned to see Lilly doubled over, hands on her abdomen.

"Lilly, what the hell?" She looked up at him and he could see the fright in her eyes. She had been screaming at him and that bastard angel before the security made it in, there was no sign of fear before. But now?

She curled in on herself again at the feeling that something was very wrong. "Marcus, get Dr. Young. I think it's the baby."

He pulled out his cell and hit a button. The ringing continued without picking up. Lilly looked up just in time to see the cell phone hit the wall and shatter into a million pieces.

Marcus scooped Lilly into his arms and ran out of the room, ducking into the open elevator and pushing the button for the clinic, Baron following, mewing his concern. Lilly clung to Marcus for support in her fear, closing her eyes and letting him move her while she tensed against the pain.

The doors opened and Marcus charged into the clinic, yelling for Dr. Young. He looked into rooms as he dashed toward the exam room he had been in with Lilly on previous visits.

Nurse Reba King came out of a room, pushing her strawberry blond hair out of her face. "Wha...?

"Dr. Young...Now!...Lilly!" Marcus hurried into the exam room and gently laid Lilly on the table.

The doctor rushed into the room, "Sorry, what seems to be the problem?"

Lilly started to say something but Marcus ran over the top of her words, "She's in pain. Something's wrong. Fix it."

Jack looked up at his employer. In a calm, reassuring voice, born of years of facing families of trauma victims, said, "I need her to tell me what's going on. You need to sit back over there and allow me to do my job."

"I am responsible..." Marcus started.

"And I am going to take that into account, but right now I can't help her if you are in my way. Now please, go sit down."

Marcus thought better of hitting the man, now wasn't the time. He would address the insubordination later, he backed off. Not watching where he was going, his gaze fixed on Lilly and the doctor, his legs hit the chair and he collapsed into the seat.

Baron crept under next to the examination table. He wasn't sure if she could hear him through her pain, so he purred as loudly as he could to let her know he was with her always. Just like in the little house back in New Orleans. *"I will always take care of you, Lilly."*

Jack Young turned back to his patient, his entire countenance slowing and a smile crossing his face, "Now, Lilly, tell me exactly what you are feeling and where."

"Something's wrong, doctor, I'm hurting in my stomach, can't make it stop." The words tumbled out so very fast that Jack almost missed them.

"Lilly, take a deep breath through your nose and hold it." He breathed with her as he laid his hand on her abdomen, feeling for the contractions. "Now, blow it out through your mouth, slowly. Good. Again." He waited as she did it again. "One more time." He could see her relax down a bit. "Very good," he cooed, "Now, breathe slowly, that's it, show me where the pain is the worst."

Lilly tried to keep her breath slow, raising her right hand. She groaned and lowered her hand back to her chest, then raised her left hand and very gently rubbed the area around her navel. "Here. Is it the baby?"

"What happened to your wrists?" The doctor reached out and gently cradled her wrist. She winced and let out a tiny groan. Even without the x-rays, he could tell both wrists were broken. He shot a dark questioning look at Marcus, who merely shrugged. He turned back to Lilly, "Did you fall?"

"No. The baby? She whispered.

"I need to check a few things to determine that. Try to stay calm. I'm going to need to get you into a gown. After we determine how the baby is doing, I will x-ray those wrists." He noticed Lilly's look of concern, "Oh, don't worry, it won't hurt the baby, we have ways of protecting babies." He smiled reassuringly. "Reba will help you. Marcus and I will go out and talk while you change." He looked to Marcus, who nodded his head.

The doctor then caught a glance at Baron and stopped, noticing the head was laying on the cat's shoulder at an odd angle. "What's wrong with the cat?"

"It's nothing, doct..." Marcus started.

"Marcus broke his neck." Lilly said defiantly, rising to a sitting position. "I need to feed him again so he can heal."

"He..." Jack looked toward Marcus, "...you broke his neck? Why?"

"Never mind the damned cat. Pay attention to Lilly." Marcus growled, turning and walking out of the room.

"Good, let's get you changed." Reba began to pull out cloth from drawers as the doctor followed Marcus out, closing the door behind them.

AS THE DOOR shut, Jack led the way to his office. The doctor shut the door, taking his seat behind his desk, leaning forward on his elbows "You wanted to explain?"

Marcus sank into the guest chair. "As I said, I am responsible for this one. Lilly was involved with someone who was stealing information from my company..."

"Lilly? I don't believe..."

"She is, was, friends with this spy. I had isolated him so that we could ascertain what he had taken. She discovered that we apprehended him and came to his rescue. I interrupted their little scheme. The spy and I got into a fight. Lilly tried to intervene and he violently pushed her. Lilly was upset, I believe the stress and his shoving her so violently probably caused this. Is she in labor?"

"It may be Braxton Hicks contractions or she may be trying to go into full-fledged labor, I'll know more after I examine her. This is a high-risk pregnancy. There no precedent for a vampire pregnancy; therefore we must err on the side of caution in all things. High stress is not good during any pregnancy and from all appearances, your business dealings are extremely...demanding. For Lilly's health and the health of that baby, you must keep her out of your business dealings."

"I don't want her anywhere my business, it's none of her concern. She inserted herself. And now she's having trouble with the baby. It's her fault she's in this situation."

"You took responsibility..."

"Responsibility is not fault, Jack. I am responsible for the dealings I have, but that does not include her interference. Her meddling is something that was none of her concern and is what caused the problem. Therefore, it is her fault." Marcus wasn't going to explain his motives further and signaled that by crossing his arms.

"Ok, I get it. What did she do that I need to know? Did she do anything that might show up in the tests when I do them? You're leaving out something, something important to her health and I need that information."

Marcus's gaze narrowed, "I did nothing. She ended up giving the guy her blood..."

"What???" Jack Young struggled to stay professional but feeling his anger rise, "She's pregnant, Marcus. If she exchanged blood with him, and we have no idea what he has in the way of diseases..."

Marcus cut in, loudly. "He's not diseased and there was no exchange. I had someone drain him and she chose to donate to him rather than watch him die. She gave him blood but did not take his.

And anyway, he's an angel and doesn't have diseases so she would have been perfectly safe anyway."

Jack Young sat quietly staring at his boss in shock and disbelief. Maybe this wasn't a plumb assignment after all. Marcus Lancaster just admitted murdering the man. Angel? "She saved his life by giving blood? That may be why she's hurting, she needs every bit of the blood she has to support the baby. That's the nutrient system for a baby of any kind. She gave up blood; she took it from the child. I now need to give her blood to get her back in stasis." He tapped the desk with his fingers, trying to relieve the urge to hit Marcus. "I guess you also take responsibility for those broken wrists she has?"

"She was fighting me on draining the angel and ended up hurting herself. Give her some blood, those will heal rapidly. No need for casts."

"She broke her own wrists?" The urge to pummel the vampire surged higher. "I will still need to x-ray them and see if we might need to intervene with surgery..."

"No, you don't. They will heal up just fine after she feeds. I want you to find out if there is anything wrong with the baby."

"She's my patient, Marcus, I'll treat whatever I need to in order to make her comfortable. And that will mean getting her blood as soon as my tests are over."

"I can donate..." Marcus also stood.

"No, you need to let me handle this. I will donate, or I will get Reba to do it. We could get her, the word is ghoul, right, to donate to her if you can get him down here fast."

"No, Gregory is in San Antonio with Isobel, visiting with his grandmother, moving more of his things back here. We're here, let's just do this and get her on her feet." Marcus turned to go.

"There is no 'on her feet' for her now. She's on strict bed rest until the baby comes. No stress. No arguing, nothing. She can move into here or we can set up round-the-clock nursing for her in her apartment but she is not going to be up and around." Jack stood, opening his door, an obvious sign of dismissal.

"She will be moved to my apartment, I will arrange for the staffing."

"That's up to her. You aren't in charge on this, she is. Whatever is less stressful for her. I will ask her." He walked out, leaving Marcus to follow, or not.

Chapter Twelve

D R. YOUNG RAPPED on the door, pushing it open when he heard Reba call come in.

Lilly lay on the table, legs in the air but covered demurely with a sheet, a tray table next to her feet, the instruments covered with a sterile cloth. Reba let go of her hand and stepped back, "We have had two contractions since you left. She is calmer but still experiencing pain."

Dr. Young noticed that Reba had also managed to wrap both of the wrists with a bandage to give them support. He nodded and smiled. "Good. Lilly, there are a couple of things we need to do. I need to check your cervix to see if labor is progressing. We need to get some blood back into you, and you are not to donate any longer while you are pregnant. I can donate or Reba can, if she's willing. You must, first and foremost, think of the baby."

Reba smiled at Lilly, "I would be glad to donate. Here sweetie," she proffered her wrist, "It's okay, go ahead."

Lilly looked into the nurse's kind eyes, "Thank you," she said weakly, taking Reba's wrist and pressing it gently to her mouth. Dr. Young put his stethoscope on her belly, listening for the sound of the baby's heart. It was quiet in the room so he could hear. Without the fetal doppler it was hard to find the heartbeat without quiet. Once he found it, he counted out the beats.

"The heartbeat is a bit sluggish, which concerns me." As he was relaying that information, he felt the muscles in her abdomen tighten. He looked at his watch and counted. "You also have had a contraction just now.

Lilly released Reba's wrist long enough to look disparagingly at the doctor, "Really?"

"Yep." He said with a chuckle, "Not really strong, hopefully it's just Braxton-Hicks, or what you might call "practice" contractions. But just to be sure, you are now on total bed rest, young lady. I can set you up down here and keep an eye on you..."

Lilly pulled away from Reba's arm and licked the holes to seal them, "Do I have to stay here? I would much rather be in my own room and bed, it's not far from here, it would be safe."

"I want you where we can be there within a few seconds if necessary." The doctor moved down to her legs and reached under the drape, checking for further signs of labor. "You have dilated to about 2 centimeters. Not bad, given the recent circumstances, but not great. Just another reason to put you on bed rest."

Marcus appeared in the doorway, having followed the doctor to the exam room unnoticed, "So, she's going to have the baby when?"

Jack looked up, his smile melted and his demeanor cooled as he addressed Marcus. "Not yet. We need another month if we can get that much. Since we have no data on how long the gestation is, I want to make sure that she has all the time she needs to bring this little miracle into the world. She needs total bed rest and round the clock nursing care."

Marcus balked, he didn't want his privacy invaded, especially now that he and Jesse were getting acquainted. "Well, I want her up in Isobel's apartment, she can take care of Lilly up there and you can go up daily. She will be easier to contain that way." Marcus dictated abruptly.

"Contain?" Lilly sat up part way, "I am not a zoo animal to be contained," she said indignantly. "I am going to follow the doctor's orders, not yours. I am not going to do anything that will endanger my baby." She fell back on the pillow.

"That's not what I meant..." Marcus countered.

Reba interrupted in a cheery helpful tone, "Why don't I go up with her and stay. I can sleep on the couch and be close when she needs me. That way I can make sure she gets the proper monitoring, nutrition, and care 24/7."

"Okay." Marcus barked grudgingly. "You will move into the office—your belongings will be sent from the tower, 24/7 for the duration." Marcus didn't ask, and Reba knew he probably wasn't in the habit of asking, he expected unquestioned obedience.

"Ok, we can do that." Reba shot a smile at

Lilly and winked, "It will be fun." She tried to reassure the vampire.

Jack helped Lilly put her legs down and sit on the side of the table. "I'll come check on you a couple of times a day, just to make sure." He patted her hand, "It will be okay."

"Since this is solved, for the moment, I've got work to do." Marcus said abruptly, "See Lilly upstairs. I will have the other arrangements taken care of." Marcus got up and started to walk out. He turned back, "Of course, all of this is, as usual, privileged information and you won't be discussing it outside of this room." He turned and left.

Jack watched the door to the clinic shut behind Marcus and then turned to Lilly, "Is there anything you want me to know, Lilly?" When she didn't respond, he continued, "There's something called doctor-patient confidentiality. It means whatever you tell me, I cannot tell anyone else, it's our secret. Whatever has happened, you can confide in me," he looked at Reba and back to vampire, "And that goes for Reba too. You can talk to us about anything...anything that is bothering you." As he waited for her to talk, he gently took her left hand and looked at her bandaged wrist, then switched to the right one. "These seem to be healing. I'm amazed at how vampire blood works so fast. Do they hurt?"

Lilly bit her bottom lip. She wasn't sure if she should say anything to either of them, Marcus could kill them if he didn't like what she said. "Not so much now, thanks to Nurse Reba. I can't talk about what happened, I am fine. Just worried about my baby. Can we go back to the apartment now?"

"Of course. But know that, if you need me, I'm just down here and can come up to see you, any time," he emphasized, "Reba will be with you until the baby arrives and we know everybody's ok."

Reba helped Lilly dress and then into the wheelchair, tucking a blanket securely over her lap. Baron, his head still lying to the side, jumped up in her lap. She put her arms around him.

"Baron, do you want to drink on the way up or wait until we are home. You need blood to heal."

"Well, you're not going to be the one to give it to me Remember what the doctor said...no donating. I will drink from the nurse once we get upstairs. You have to take care with the kittens." Baron's eyes sparkled at her.

"You are a scoundrel, you know that, right?" She smiled at him, ruffling his fur the wrong direction.

"Watch it, woman, or I might have to tattle on you to Isobel."

"Marcus sent her to San Antonio with Gregory. I wondered why she didn't come to get us when this thing started."

Baron's demeanor changed, *"He sent them after he locked you in the room with that angel. He didn't want them interfering with his plans. Both of them argued with him, not wanting to be away but he insisted they drive there and back."* Baron's tail flipped in aggravation. *"I just checked, they are about half-way back, she tells me. I've told her to come quickly, we need both of them here soon as possible, I want to get you out of here."*

"Baron, no. We cannot leave. Not until the baby is here." Lilly knew there was nowhere to turn while she was pregnant. *"Once the baby gets here, I will take him and leave. We'll go somewhere we can't be found. He will not raise this child or have anything to do with him"*

"You could go before. This woman helping us is...interesting. She can protect you. And Isobel and Gregory can as well. We need to go before he kills you."

Lilly thought about it, it was what she wanted to do; leave and hide from the man she used to think of fondly. Now, he was just Marcus, someone who had hurt her and others without any sign of conscience. He could hurt, or kill, without a second thought, how safe was a helpless child around him?

The elevator dinged for the floor and Reba wheeled Lilly down the hall and into the apartment she shared with Isobel. Looking around, she knew they could comfortably fit another person, or even five, inside the massive home. Reba locked the door behind them.

"Thank-you Nurse King, I..." Lilly started.

"Reba, please. Do you have a favorite nightie that you would like to put on before I get you settled in bed?" She asked as they headed into Lilly's room.

"There's a pink gown in that top drawer," Lilly pointed to a large wooden dresser. "Ummmm?"

Lilly's voice trailed off, she wasn't sure if she

was imagining things or not.

Reba stopped looking through the drawer, "What is it, Lilly? Are you feeling worse?"

"Oh, no, I'm feeling fine, just a little tired and sore. I guess bed rest is what I need." She paused thoughtfully, chewing on her bottom lip. "When you shared your blood with me..." she paused, uncomfortably again.

"Just say it" Reba smiled as she walked across the room and handed her a pink cotton nightgown.

"Okay, your blood tastes different."

The nurse laughed, "I didn't know blood had anything except a coppery taste, I did have Mexican food at Ninfa's last night. I love their green sauce!"

Baron jumped up on the bed and plopped down between Reba and Lilly.

The nurse pulled up a chair and sat down next to the cat. Unbuckling the watch she wore, she laid her wrist next to the cat, whose head was still lying sideways. "Here you go, boy, go ahead and feed."

Baron didn't need any further prodding; he opened his mouth and bit down hard, causing Reba to yelp.

"I'm sorry, he does that, he has the manners of an alley cat where feeding is concerned." Lilly ran her hand down his back.

"*I'm not an alley cat, woman.*" He growled at Lilly.

"Oh, he's a sweetheart. I like him." Reba stroked his head as he fed, he answered with a purr.

"*You're right, she does taste sweet, like the other one. I can feel my neck healing faster than usual.*

"*I wonder, could she be an angel? Don't talk to her yet, we don't know what we are dealing with here. Promise me.*"

"*Ummmhmmm.*"

Lilly paused, she didn't know how much to reveal. "*There's only one way to find out*" she said to Baron, then inhaled deeply. "It's not Mexican food, I remember someone else's blood tasting like yours."

"Oh? Who?" Reba kept petting Baron as he drank.

"His name was Sullivan...." She hesitated and then blurted out, "He was an angel."

"Men like that are really rare."

"No, I mean a REAL angel...like from Heaven." Reba looked askance. Lilly suddenly had an overwhelming peaceful, safe feeling. A feeling that she could tell, that she needed to tell this woman everything. She continued, "He was hurt, I thought he was dying. I shared blood with him so he would heal. It turned him into a vampire. His blood tasted like yours, ...sweet, and..." she got a puzzled look on her face, "...and kind of, uh, ...sparkly."

"Really? You turned an angel into a vampire?" Reba knew all about what happened; the talk about Sullivan's downfall was the favorite subject around the ambrosia-cooler since it happened.

"Yes. I really didn't mean to, I just didn't want

him to die. Are you an angel?" Lilly pushed gently to try to get the nurse to agree to it.

"My granddad thought I was an Angel, but that was just a pet name. I'm a nurse, just here to help..." her words trailed off as she looked down at the cat fastened to her arm. As she watched, his neck seemed to repair itself, his head going from laying askew on his shoulder to upright. As he continued to drink, he stretched his body out and back. He drank for a few more seconds and then pulled his fangs out of her arm, licking the wounds with his rough tongue. She saw them close as he finished and turned his head, looking around the room. "It looks like he has recovered. I'm glad, I hated to see him like that, it had to hurt."

Lilly smiled and ran her hand down his head and felt his neck, "I think you're right. It feels like he is healed up, no thanks to Marcus. Are you feeling better, Baron?"

The cat turned to look at her, *"I'm fine. It fixed the break faster than your blood would."*

"That's because she's an angel, I'm certain of it." Lilly said aloud for Reba, who gave her a puzzled look.

"You act like he can talk to you. He's a cat."

"Yes, he's a cat, he's a vampire, and my progeny. Because I am his sire, we have a special connection and can mentally communicate."

Reba studied the cat a bit closer. There was something else, more than just a cat, or a vampire. Almost...what? More sentient than either.

She looked back at Lilly, "We all have our secrets. We all hold things close to our hearts that we do not, or cannot, share."

"I can respect that. With the limited experience I have had with angels, ...they can be a bit unpredictable and violent at times. I am very wary of them, one in particular. A female, she is really nasty and just down right mean."

"Nida." Reba mumbled quietly to herself.

"Wha....?" Lilly cried, a little louder than she meant to.

Busted.

Reba gasped. She didn't realize that she had uttered that hateful name audibly, forgetting that vampires have exceptional hearing. She took a deep breath and closed her eyes for a moment, then opened them and fixed them on Lilly's brown eyes, "Okay, I will explain, but you cannot share this information with anyone."

Lilly frowned, "Only with Isobel and Gregory, I have no secrets from them."

"No! Not even them. If anyone," she stressed the word again, "Anyone found out about me here, they would kill me. Or worse, make me like Essexiel."

Lilly looked quizzically at her. "You mean Essex? You know him?

"Not well, he is...was...in a different department."

"Oh, but I must tell Isobel and Gregory..." as Lilly started to get excited, Reba frowned. Lilly noticed, "I trust them, both. Isobel has saved me more times than I can tell you and Gregory is totally loyal."

"And I'm not going to swear not to tell, but Marcus will be the last human to know, probably when he goes to Hell." Baron purred in Lilly's head. She nodded.

Reba looked at him, "You can't tell anyone either, pussy cat."

"She did not just call me a pussy cat!" Baron growled, showing his fangs to her.

"Uh, he doesn't like being called a pussy cat."

"I'm sorry Baron. But please don't tell anyone. My life, and my assignment's life, depend upon it. Yes, I am, indeed, an angel. But not an Enforcer, I'm a Guardian. I protect certain individuals from impending harm.

"Me?"

"No, right now I'm assigned to your friend, Gregory."

"Do I have a guardian?" Lilly asked.

"You don't have one right now. Not officially. The Guardians are assigned when someone needs them, for a period of time that they need one. Most humans only need one a few times in their lifetimes so they are assigned as needed. You had one when you were about 10, someone kept an eye on you until you were old enough to deal with things you were involved in..."

"That was when my father took me to New Orleans."

Reba nodded, "Until your becoming a, uh, one of Miss Lulu's ladies. At that point, you didn't have one until the night that you were bitten by Mr. Lancaster. I'm not privy to how that happened or why but you had one until you came to Houston. I can't tell you who, and it wouldn't make any difference anyway but you did have one."

"That's sort of comforting, someone in Heaven thinks I matter enough to have a guardian." She smiled, "So you guard Gregory. Were you there when he got shot?" Lilly remembered sitting in the emergency room after Gregory had tried to get to Ace, the driver they had when they went to find Jesse at the hospital.

"No, I wasn't. I missed him at the elevator after I got to the hospital and changed clothes, it closed before I could get in it. I got to the garage just as the car with the assassins pulled away. He wasn't in danger from the shot, he was just needing help at that time. My boss..."

"God? You know God?"

"No, no one knows Him. My boss is Barachiel, she's the one who assigns the Guardians."

"Is there any way you can help Essex? Marcus has turned him, used me to turn him, and he's now, like Sullivan, fallen. Can you get this, Barachiel, to ask God to change him back into an angel?" A red tear left her eye and rolled down her cheek.

"Oh, sweetie," Reba reached out and wiped away the tear, "I wish I could, I don't know of any way to change them back. I will report his turning to his boss, hopefully there's something they can do to help him. Please, don't worry, it's not good for your baby."

"Please, find out if there is anything that can

be done. It's my fault about Sullivan and Essex...they shouldn't have to pay for my sin."

"*You didn't hurt me, Lilly, nor did you hurt
Essex. Both times you were set up, I don't know
why but there is someone else's hand in this.*"
Sullivan's Irish lilt came to her over their link.

"*I wish I could believe that, Sully. I really do.*"
She thought back to him.

"Lilly, are you okay? Feeling bad?"

"I'm tired. I'll try not to worry but it will be
hard."

"Well, let's get you settled for the day, you get
some sleep."

She helped Lilly lie down, Baron settling
against her stomach, guarding the baby. Kissing
her forehead she walked to the door, opened it,
shut off the light, and whispered, "Sleep well, let
that baby grow."

Just as she closed the door behind her, an
insistent rapping came from the entry. Reba raced
to the door to quell the pounding.

Reba open the door and four burly men stood
there. "Mr. Lancaster sent us. We have some
furniture and stuff to deliver and some other stuff
to remove," said the muscular leader of the group.

"Yes, of course. But can you come back later?
Miss Marchantel is resting."

"No," answered the leader. "Mr. Lancaster said
now and what Mr. Lancaster wants, Mr. Lancaster gets."

Reba frowned, "Okay then. But," she stressed,
"You must be very quiet. Doctor's Orders ... and
that over rules even Mr. Lancaster!" she huffed
and led them toward the office.

Chapter Thirteen

M IKHAIL COULDN'T WAIT for the meeting.
Normally, the thought of a meeting of the Archangel Synod would make him want to run away. It was just not his favorite activity. Most of the archangels were even tempered, but there were pockets of contrary assholes that seemed to live to give him shit.

"I have to moderate my language." He said to the reflection in the mirror. It would just cause more trouble if he used foul language with the said assholes, er, archangels.

He had to admit, if he was going to throw them off their game and get into their heads, this plan was probably going to do just that.

Mikhail smiled broadly and did a bit of preening in front of the full length mirror in the hotel room. He started at the floor, admiring the heavy pair of black leather knee-high boots with stainless steel buckles. Above those was a pair of skin-tight black leather pants, a black t-shirt with "Hog Heaven" on it—a pig with wings wearing leathers and riding a Harley Davidson, and a black leather vest with "Mikhail" on the front left.

As he turned, he could see the back of the vest. A large red and black embroidered patch read "Archangel Synod Motorcycle Club" was sewn on the back.

He had to admit, it was an inspired plan. One of his warrior angels, Asaeil, or Asa as he was known, had been the model. One day the angel wandered into the break room in Heaven while Mikhail was there talking with Tamiel about the Shadows rotations. He was dressed in black stone-washed jeans, black boots like the ones Mikhail was wearing now, and a black shirt with "Schitt Creek Paddle Club" on it. Over the top, Asa wore a black leather vest with patches, including one that said, "Angelic Warriors Motorcycle Club" on it, tucked between his red wings. The look was topped off by a bandana printed with flames that hid the mass of curly black hair Asa sported. Mikhail had spent some time talking with Asa about how the Warrior angels would take time out to go riding the motorcycles they kept at a "clubhouse" somewhere in the wilds of the New Mexico Mountains. Mikhail had envied the fun and freedom his Warriors got to experience.

Well, at least he got to play at being a motorcycle club president, at least for a while tonight.

He checked his watch. The rest of the archangels would be arriving soon. Looking outside, he laughed.

Snow. It had been snowing for about six hours, the wet white flakes piling up on everything, the grass, the trees, rooftops, and...roads.

Late February in upstate New York was not kind to people who were riding motorcycles. The last time Mikhail had seen the local news, early that morning, it was 25 degrees and the area expected an additional 3 feet of snow on top of the 27 inches that they had gotten over the weekend.

Served them right, most of them.

He didn't want to go back to his job. He wasn't ready. But whatever was going on, Ranguel was adamant that it needed Mikhail's voice. And his voice had to be in the room, still attached to his body.

Nope, not happening.

So he cooked up a plan.

Each archangel was given notice of the meeting happening on earth. They were to report to a location in New York City to pick up a package. The instructions were included in the package.

"You will put on the items in this package. Stow your wings, you won't need them. And don't bring your assistants, they aren't welcome. This one's strictly upper management. Once dressed, the good looking redhead at the counter will bring you to the garage where you will be provided with your transportation. You will have a map to guide you to the meeting. I do not advise messing around trying to figure out another way, you will be timed. We will begin promptly at 8 a.m. Eastern time. Everyone needs to bring drinks and snacks, you can work out who will bring what, but everyone brings something."

Mikhail laughed. That was going to drive the other archangels crazy. Their clothing would match his, black leather motorcycle gear, except they would get the vest and a black leather jacket with the patch on it, black gloves, and a Bell full-face helmet. They would be given Harley Davidson motorcycles to ride the almost 300 miles to the meeting place near the Great Lakes.

In. The. Snow.

And. The. Cold.

Their arrival will be spectacularly funny. At least to him.

He ran his hands through his hair, pulling the curls out to a very messy, spiky style. Then he grabbed his room key, a six-pack of Foster's Lager, and headed to the lobby on the way to the meeting room.

"Hi there..." He checked the name tag of the older woman desk clerk on the morning shift at the hotel, "Beatrice, I just want to give you a head's up. I have colleagues coming into the hotel for a meeting this morning. They're supposed to be here soon. They'll probably be wet and cold. Make sure they wipe their feet and not track that snow inside, will ya? Then, please, would you direct them to the meeting room. I'm going to get down there to set up."

"Sure Mr. Angelus." She gave him a smile, "Will you need anything else down there besides the water? Maybe some hot coffee?"

"Nah, we're good, they're bringing snacks and drinks. I don't want to be disturbed when we meet, it might get loud but I promise, no furniture or walls will be harmed in connection with this meeting. We'll be good."

"Oh, I'm not worried, sir. You have a good meeting." She giggled as he dropped her a quick bow before striding off to the meeting room.

He didn't have to wait long, about twenty minutes after getting to the room, he began to hear the low rumbling of the motorcycles coming into the parking lot, and soon he heard them shut down and voices started filtering inside and down the hallway.

The first to open the door was Ranguel. If looks could kill, Mikhail would have been a little pile of ashes on the floor.

"Hi Ran. You managed to get here okay..."

"Stuff it, Mikhail. You planned this atrocity, I'm calm compared to Metatron and Azrael, they're looking for your head and I may just let them have it."

"You're damned right you'll let me have it." Azrael pushed past Ranguel into the room, carrying a helmet like a Halloween treat bucket. "You did this on purpose! Do you know how bloody cold it is out there? Or how far it is from New York to here?"

Mikhail just smirked, not saying a word. The head of the Soul Reapers pitched his helmet across the room, it bounced once and rolled into a corner.

"Don't get too comfy, you have to go back out and get the beer and snacks." Mikhail said as Az began to peel off the jacket he wore.

"Nope, you can go. I'm not going back out in

that weather. Or starve, I don't care which."

"No, I'm not. You were the first to walk in here without food or drink, so you're going to make the food run." Mikhail said as the rest of the "gang" came in, some carrying beer, others carrying bags of chips and other items.

"Get comfy, pull up a chair, we have some work to talk about." Mikhail snagged a beer from a six pack that Barachiel carried in and leaned on a table facing the rest of the archangels. She pulled the bandana off her head and ran her fingers through her blond hair.

Gabriel took off his jacket, hanging it on the back of his chair, sat down and put his feet up on another chair. Azrael found a corner where he could watch the door with his back to the wall and planted himself on the floor. Uriel and Rafael moved two chairs closer together and sat down, whispering between them.

Her hair somewhat combed, Barachiel dragged a chair up next to the boys and tried to get between them. Uriel pointed to his right side and she moved the chair to that side, plopping down wearily. She always seemed to get the feeling that the most of the boys resented a girl in their midst, Uriel and Rafe always seemed more like big brothers and included her.

Ranguel pulled a chair up closer to Mikhail so that he could advise his boss like he normally did in Heaven. Faranel parked himself in a chair closest to the snacks, which made Mikhail chuckle. Faranel had a habit of snacking whenever he could. Uriel finally picked out a chair, slung it around and sat down with his chest against the back, cradling his head on a hand.

Mikhail noticed Metatron didn't take off his jacket, didn't spend time picking out a spot in the room, he walked up to the first chair he came to and sat down stiffly, back straight and posture perfect, folding his hands in his lap. Prim and proper, that was the definition of Metatron in the Heavenly Dictionary.

"Ok, now that we're all comfy, I need to know what is going on up there. What's Kafziel doing in my name and do you have any concerns about it?" Mikhail took a swig of the beer.

Everyone looked at each other, not saying anything.

"Let's not stand on ceremony, people. It's just like in my office, except with beer and pretzels. What's happening?" Mikhail prompted.

"Kafziel isn't changing anything except making people sign in and out when they go out on duty. He wants to know where each angel goes, who they see, what they are doing, when they are back. He's trying to micromanage everything and there's chaos in the departments as this is implemented." Gabriel commented.

"No, he's doing a good job, he's managing to make things work well." Azrael defended his junior manager.

"Says who? You would say he was doing a good job if he was raping babies up in that office, Az, you don't need to defend him with lies." Gabriel snarled.

"Now wait a fucking minute, Gabe, you calling

me a liar?" Azrael began to stand up, hands clenched.

"Gentlemen, stow it. I don't want you brawling here. Az, you have a right to back your boy, but if Kafziel is doing things he doesn't need to, there needs to be a meeting by you guys to tell him to make the changes." Mikhail didn't need the added cost of fixing a demolished hotel meeting room, besides, he had promised Beatrice that they would be good boys and he had spent a load on this whole thing already.

"Like he would listen to anything we had to say? Yeah, right." Rafael said. "He doesn't listen to us any better than he listened to you when you were there. He thinks he knows everything."

Mikhail pinned Azrael with a look designed to stop him from moving further. "What else is going on?"

"We're missing more angels. Last count was about 300 world-wide." Rafael said. "I think Az can tell you how many soul boxes we have of those 300, but I know it's not even as many as we have lost."

"We have 75 in reliquary. That's it. I don't know what happened to the remainder of the souls we should have gotten, the last count I have is 321 missing, 75 confirmed dead. We've tried tracking down how this is happening and I have a few theories, but they are just that, theories." Azrael reported.

"Theories equal wild-assed guesses." Faranel said. "Of course, none of the human media is talking about this but there's some mysterious traffic on the internet about "collecting fighters" coming out of some of the communication and even Live Journal posts discuss the possibility of vampire connections to these disappearances but we have no solid proof of that."

"I've got Shadows out watching the major vampire house centers," Uriel spoke up, "I'm getting reports of vampires gathering in the main cities and a possible spike in turnings. Currently, there are at least 40 Shadows MIA. They are discovered, apprehended, or forced out of concealment, and then...nothing. We never hear from them and there's no trace of them. We can extrapolate that they have been corrupted or captured."

Mikhail knew Uriel, if he was complaining about this, he was understating it. That concerned the archangel.

"Thing is, I think this is coming out of House Drachenfeur, Marcus Lancaster's organization." Gabriel added. "I am not so sure about why."

"We need to go into those nests and clean them out." Ranguel commented, "We can't monitor them like we need to, I'm having trouble keeping up with the tunings. There's been an uptick in vampires going to Hell, courtesy of Nida and Helmut. These 'third-strikers' are very crafty and good at hiding. They know we are looking for them. They are mere hired guns and their influential bosses are keeping their hands clean. They are running this operation within the rules, but just barely."

"Are you admitting that your Enforcers aren't

up to the task they have created?" Azrael pushed. "I thought the Enforcers were the golden boys and girls of H.H.A.D."

"Muzzle it, Soul Eater. We're up to the task. The rule is that we mark on second turning or if a child is turned. They are turning one, then using that one to turn the next. It's like an assembly line. We can't mark them because the sires are adhering to the letter of the law but flaunting the intent. I can't change the rules on them and mark them for the first turning. We didn't set a limit on the number of members a vampire house can have. This limits our ability to step in to stop them. Therefore, we have to operate with the constraints of our own laws." Ranguel shook his head.

Mikhail was thinking about the implications of this when Faranel opened a beer and poured it over ice.

"Uh, Fare, you might not want to do that, tastes...." He started.

"Oh wow, why haven't I tried this before now?" Faranel smiled, a suds mustache decorating his upper lip from the foam in the glass.

"Maybe because that isn't the way it's done?" Gabriel made a face like he knew how awful iced beer was. He learned to drink beer in Germany.

"You put ICE in that beer, what are you, a Neanderthal?" Rafael chimed in, making another face.

"Hey, everyone has their way, this is mine." Faranel drank more of the beer from the red Solo cup.

"All your taste is in your mouth, obviously. Beer is best cold but never, ever with ice." Barachiel chimed in. "Or warm if it's a European brand. What are you drinking?"

"One of those big cans of Fosters, which is hot. I'm cooling it off, leave me alone." Faranel took another big gulp of the liquid, groans sounding around the room.

"You realize that putting ice in your beer is canonically considered as a valid instance of 'the angel needed killin' defense in New York, right?" Rafael said, affecting a New York accent.

"You mean Texas, don'tcha?" Uriel drawled with a fake Texas accent.

"Try it, cupcake. We can have it out right there in the snow...just as soon as I finish my beer." Faranel lifted the can into the air in salute and took another big swig.

"No, it goes 'Hold my beer and watch this' and then I reach over and clean your time piece." Uriel said.

"Clock, dude, clock." Rafael corrected.

"Clock, time piece, whatever" Uriel shrugged.

"In Texas, the phrase 'Hold my beer and watch this' never ends well, something stupid always happens," Gabriel offered.

"Okay, bring it back in and leave Iceman alone." Mikhail stepped in. "What makes you think Lancaster is doing this?"

Gabriel groaned at the next sip Faranel took and purposely turned his chair where he could not watch the sacrilege continue. "Rumor has it around the ambrosia cooler that there have been calls from Drachenfeur to several others around the world. I've seen a few new vampires in places where we have Vampire Council-affiliated house headquarters. I don't know if the Council is involved in it..."

"I don't think so." Mikhail countered.

"They would be stupid to, quite frankly, but it looks like they have a renegade problem. That usually means Drachenfeur. Marcus Lancaster is a malcontent. Since Vlad left the council and Xun has blocked every attempt that Lancaster has been made to ascend the Drachenfeur throne, it's always been Lancaster at the center of any upheaval" Gabriel continued.

"I will see if we can get information from the Houston area and see if we can trace down the source." Mikhail turned to the media coordinator, trying not to watch him shove a couple of pretzels on top of a gulp of the watered down Fosters.

What a waste of Fosters...

"Fare, you need to try to monitor the communications from the main Vampire Council leadership and their immediate family members. Pull a few angels if you need to double up on some of the help in your department." He wasn't surprised when, instead of a verbal answer, Faranel gave him a thumbs up as the pretzel dust fell from his lips.

"Okay, now, Ranguel, what is going on with Koziel?"

The Enforcer Archangel scowled, "He's continuing to meet with people we would rather not have him meet with. I'm not giving him important information and I'm not allowing him to monitor most of the more important missions with the Enforcers. We have definite information now that he's dealing with the Fallen Ones." Ranguel paused briefly. What he said out loud expressed the nauseating thoughts that had plagued him for days. "I strongly suspect that Koziel has somehow contributed to the detriment of our angelic forces."

As Ranguel spoke, Mikhail glanced at each of the archangels, trying not to let them know that he was watching their faces. Everyone looked surprised to hear that one of their own was dealing with Lucy and the demons.

All except Metatron.

Now, was he being stoic or was he really not surprised that the assistant to the Enforcer Department Head was a mole?

Mikhail filed that little piece of information in his head until he needed it, it would probably prove to be very useful.

The rest of the meeting went pretty much according to the way it always did in his office. No one questioned him on where he had been or what he was doing, just dropping reports and making sure Mikhail was up on things.

Finally, he looked up and the clock on the wall of the meeting room read 4:45 p.m. and a glance out the window told him the sun had set. Snow was falling, again.

"Okay, you guys need to get back and I need to relinquish the room. Take the drinks and food with you, the staff will probably appreciate having the munchies in the break room. Make sure, of course, they still get their ambrosia as well.

"The bikes need to go back to New York. The Harley store will be closed, but there will be a staff member to accept their return."

"Wait, what? We can't keep the rides?" Barachiel complained, "I was looking forward to getting some time off and riding the mountains..."

"Stow it, Chiel. You can get your own bike; these are slated to be auctioned off for a wounded warriors charity next month, each and every one of them. There's a group of actors that are going to sign them and help with the auction. So, they must be returned in pristine condition. No off-road detours, No wet work. No Evel Knievel antics. If, perchance, something untoward happens, you will get to buy a replacement for the auction. But you can keep the spiffy motorcycle gang duds. Later." He said with a dismissive wave.

"You coming with us, boss?" Rafael stood up, stretched, and started to pull on his coat.

"Nope, you're still in Kafziel's keeping. I'm still on vacation."

"Oh, please, we want you back." Barachiel protested.

"Eventually, Chiel. Right now, you need to get back and check on things. Keep your eyes and ears open for anything that can tell us what is going on with our MIAs."

The group gathered up the snacks and cleared out. Mikhail walked them to the lobby and even collected a couple of hugs as they filed out.

He walked back to the meeting room, steeling

himself for the coming confrontation.

Metatron. Who did not move, even after the rest of the archangels left. He sat, still rock straight and stiff, where he had for the entirety of the meeting.

Mikhail walked in, but didn't pull up a chair, opting to stand in front of the Guardian of God's Throne.

"You stayed. What do you want to say that you couldn't do it in the middle of the rest of the archangels?"

Metatron stood, stiffly moving first up, then forward to within a couple of feet of Mikhail, like a black Bishop rolling up to a trapped white Queen, a threat.

Mikhail raised an eyebrow but stayed silent, not moving away from the obvious intent.

"You need to relinquish the office since it's obvious that you have no intention of doing the job." Metatron's deep voice was low, he had no need to shout, the force of a whisper could reduce angels to their knees in fear when he wanted.

All but Mikhail, who was not intimidated by the archangel in the least.

"And nominate who? You?"

"I'm senior to everyone but you, and therefore the logical, only choice."

"And who would you put in your position? Azrael? Barachiel?"

Meta's mouth twitched, catching a smile before it broke through, but the twitch was enough to cue Mikhail's notice.

"No, really, Meta, you need to think about this,

who you would pick to take over your job, who is qualified. Who would God approve of? Of course, you haven't had the position for the entire time, you actually got it because your predecessor, Ishiel, died defending the throne during the war. So, yeah, you need to figure out who is next if you make a try for my job."

He turned his back to the archangel.

"You think you can stand if I challenge you?" Metatron questioned.

Mikhail stood, back turned for a long few moments, then stepped forward and whirled around, "Not only yes, but you would not be taking back the job you had should you challenge me. I will not merely send you to Lucy, I will end you once and for all."

"And God will end you." Metatron's voice went up a few notches, the words beginning to echo in the meeting room.

"You think? If you come at me for me doing my job, you think he would take me out? No, I'm in control of Heaven, even when on holiday, and if you try it, you will be the one who makes your exit."

Metatron studied Mikhail's eyes, looking for a tell of a bluff.

He found none.

He was not the warrior that Mikhail was.

After a moment, he stepped back, retracting the threat.

Mikhail nodded. "I thought that might be your best option. Go home, Metatron. Do your job. And leave me to mine."

The archangel, still stiff, nodded to Mikhail and turned to go.

"Don't forget, return the motorcycle."

Metatron raised his arm in acknowledgment as he left the room, headed out.

"Queen takes black bishop." He said to the empty room.

Chapter Fourteen

S ULLIVAN COULDN'T SLEEP. He had awakened out of a fitful sleep, crying out for Lilly as he did. He had helped her with the decision to turn Essex before he had to retreat to the need to sleep. He had fought the pull of the sun; there was no way he was going to allow Essex to die.

He knew what his best friend was going through, the crushing weight of the realization he would never go home to Heaven. He was now an abomination and, as a result, would be going to Hell. The emerging emotions were overwhelming him. The only saving grace of this whole thing was that Essex had been working in the human world and was familiar with how life would go from then on.

But there was something else, not Essex, who he couldn't feel. Something was wrong, he could feel it but he couldn't quite identify what it was. He reached out to her. "Lilly."

No answer came. He could feel her connection, she still lived, but he was also feeling the edges of panic, her panic.

"Lilly, please, let me know you are okay. I am

here for you." He tried again, beginning to pace small circles in the small cell-like room.

The quiet of the connection scared him.

"Baron?" He tried the cat.

"Yes, I'm here. You need to come here. Lilly needs you. That bastard hurt her, forced her to turn that angel, and now there's something wrong with the kittens."

"I don't know that I can come. There are problems, people who are in control."

"You want to save her, you have to come here and take her away from that bastard. He hurt her, he hurt your angel, and I cannot protect her from him. He will kill her. You have to come." Baron's voice sounded tired.

"Are you okay, my friend?"

"I am healing. This time he broke my neck. If we hadn't had an angel near us, neither of us would be recovering like we are. Her blood is strong, Lilly's wrists are healing from the breaks, the kittens are now in danger."

Sullivan forced down the impulse to punch a wall. He didn't need another set of broken knuckles. "He hurt my angel, Essex?"

"That was the name Lilly said. He took his wings and took his blood. He made Lilly turn him or he would die. Then the big angel and the mean angel came here and they..."

Sully's heart began to pound. There was only one set of angels that matched that description and it had to be Nida and Helmut.

"They marked her, didn't they? That hurts badly and she's probably in a lot of pain from it."

Sullivan couldn't help but wince at the thought.

"*They had her kneel and the mean angel pointed her finger at Lilly's hand. I couldn't get to her to stop it.*"

"You couldn't stop her, my friend, no matter how much you wanted to. What has Lancaster done with Essex?

"*I don't know, they took him out and I don't know where. I will try to find out where but if we don't find him, we will have to leave him and come back for him.*"

"That's fair. I will try to..." Then his mind grasped what the cat had said earlier about angel blood. "Wait, an angel gave you blood? Who? What did this angel do to get near you? How do you know it was an angel? What color were the wings?"

"*Oh meow, slow down! The angel doesn't have wings so I don't know. She said she's Gregory's guardian. She is working for the doctor. The bastard hired, a 'nurse.' She fed Lilly, then allowed me to feed. I know that taste, it's stronger than humans, a bit on the sweet side, and the healing is very fast. She's an angel. Your blood tasted the same.*"

Sullivan tried to think. Thoughts rushed through his head, '*A guardian was with Lilly? He needed to get to Lilly and get them out of there. He needed to go to Gudrun, talk the abbot into allowing him to leave and make arrangements to fly to Houston. He needed to get Lilly to a good doctor to check the baby, he had to find them a place to live, he needed to find Essex and get him out of there, he needed to...'*

"*You need to get here first. Everything else can be done after she is away from that vampire. She needs you here.*" Baron put everything so simply, he was right; Sullivan had to get there first.

"Thank-you, Baron. I'll go talk to the priests and see about getting there. Please, watch over her, keep her safe until I can manage that. If anything else happens, let me know. Try to find Essex, but Lilly is your priority. I'll find a way to get there."

Throwing on the plain brown robe he wore at the monastery, he opened the door and stalked down the corridor toward Fr. Gudrun's office.

Chapter Fifteen

T HE MONASTERY WAS humming with activity as
Sullivan rushed down the hallway. He could
hear talking in the various rooms, smell bread
baking and the stew Brother Hjalmar was
cooking. Brother Nicholaas was sweeping the
lobby floor. Sullivan jumped over the small pile of
dust as he continued toward Fr. Gudrun's office.

"You're up early, Brother Sullivan, is everything all right?" Nicholaas called after him.

"No but it will be." Sullivan never turned back
but waved one hand in the air.

Stopping outside the door, he wiped his hands
on the robe. That small gesture made him stop,
since when did he get nervous trying to talk to the
abbot? His stomach was in knots and he was
sweating profusely. Knocking, he wiped his hands
again, pushing the door open when he heard the
voice bid him to enter.

Fr. Gudrun was sitting behind his desk, papers in front of him, three books open with notes
in the margins. As Sullivan stepped into the room,
the abbot took off his heavy black rimmed glasses
and looked up. "I didn't expect you to be the one

at my door. Sit down, son, what's troubling you?"

Sullivan took the chair in front of the desk, "I have had word from Houston. Lilly's in trouble, Essex has been turned, and there's another angel there who can be discovered and is in trouble. I need to leave and go to them."

Gudrun laid his glasses on top of the notes, "You are asking for permission to leave the monastery? I cannot grant that request, Sullivan. I have been told you are to remain here."

"Who has told you that? Do they know or understand that Lilly is in danger? I need to go to her and get her out of Marcus Lancaster's clutches. I was just told that she and the child she carries are in danger, that she was forced to turn another angel and the angels have marked her for it." Sullivan held up his right hand, the burned-in marks for his own transgressions very visible. "I have to get her out of there."

"Sullivan, Mikhail himself has sent you to me; he has told me that you are to remain here until he gives the word."

"Mikhail? What does he care about me or the situation? He's in charge of Heaven and I'm no longer an angel. I am asking you, Father, out of courtesy only, to allow me to leave here so I can go to Lilly. I could have just left without asking but I do respect you more than that."

"I know what you feel you need to do but I also fear there's an ulterior motive for this trip, you believe Lilly's in danger so you will go to kill Marcus Lancaster. Is that not truth?"

The flare of Sullivan's nostrils and the tightening of his jawline told Gudrun that he hit the main point, even if Sullivan wasn't consciously aware of his desire to kill.

"You do not need that last mark, Sullivan, and that's what would happen to you if you went in anger to Houston. You would kill Lancaster and in the process, you would end up with the last mark and be dragged into Hell. I do not want to see that happen."

"I would not get the mark for killing him; the rules don't object to vampire-on-vampire killings, the angels could care less about another dead vampire."

"Really? You know the rules that much that you can allow your life and your soul to depend on the whims of Heaven? Are you so sure that the rules you once enforced haven't been changed, given the circumstances?"

Sullivan ran his hand through his hair. "The rules haven't changed enough to worry about the death of a vampire that I know."

Fr. Gudrun shook his head, "Your place in all of this is not to rid the world of Marcus Lancaster and your place isn't to rescue Lilly. There is one thing Mikhail has asked of you and that is why I am denying your request. Your mission is far more important than you realize, you must continue your work. Those two scrolls are critical."

"Scrolls? Lilly's life, and the life of her child, is going to be traded by Heaven for scrolls? That's ludicrous, Father. I could, if nothing else, bring her and the child here. Keep them safe. Then I will find those bloody scrolls for Mikhail, I promise. Please let me go. I can't let that fucking bastard hurt her with impunity."

Gudrun's demeanor changed, his eyes growing hard, "Watch your language, Kilcoan. You are still required to conduct yourself in a polite manner befitting this sacred place. I will accept nothing less." He leaned back, "Now, since you have been shouting and not listening, I will repeat." He slowly stood, leaning across his desk, he leveled his gaze. He spoke with a slow, quiet, deliberate intensity that startled Sullivan into silence. "It is Mikhail's orders that you find those scrolls. The rediscovery of them is imperative." He paused to let the intensity penetrate. "In terms of the situation with this woman, your sire, and her maker, it is being evaluated and handled."

"Handled!" Sullivan yelled, "She's still in his hands, how is that handled? Heaven is not interested in individual people unless they have something Heaven wants or needs. She's just a vampire. Nothing different or special to them, to anyone but me..."

"I don't know why, but I do know there are others around her, insuring her safety. If the situation becomes too volatile, she will be taken to safety."

"You don't know that!" Sullivan raged, standing up and pulling his hand through his hair. He made a fist and turned toward the wall.

"Sullivan, sit down." It wasn't a request. He walked around and sat on the edge of his desk.

"Why?" Sullivan continued to pace. You're not

going to do anything but tell me no. I cannot stay here while Lilly is in danger." Turning to plead with the abbot, "That baby could be mine, but even more than that, Lilly doesn't deserve what that mad man is doing to her."

"You are right, she does not, but you cannot go to her. Allow those who are there to deal with the situation, monitor it from here if you must. You have your mission, get those scrolls."

"Scrolls, scrolls, fucking scrolls!!" The look Sullivan gave the man froze him. Sullivan was out of control, again.

"I warned you, Sullivan Kilcoan. I will not tolerate that type of language." He repeated, "It is Mikhail's orders that you find those scrolls. The rediscovery of them is imperative. The reason is 'need to know' and you do not need to know, just do it."

"I don't care, can't you get that through your thick head? I must get to Lilly, and I'm leaving tonight." Sullivan turned, walking to the door.

"Sullivan, wait." Gudrun's voice stopped him; Sully didn't look back but left the door knob in partial turn.

"I have something for you." Sullivan heard a desk drawer open. He spun partially and watched the monk slide the desk drawer closed and walk to him holding up a plain envelope. "Read it before you go."

The vampire cocked one eyebrow up as he took the envelope. He noticed a red seal with Mikhail's imprint in the wax. It was from the archangel. Pulling the end off, he pulled out the

letter. He recognized the precise script.
Mikhail.

Eistered,

I know you are angry and concerned about Lilly's well-being. She is being protected. I know it's not to your liking, but too much interference on our part would alert Marcus Lancaster to our presence.

<u>Please</u> <u>stop</u> *and* **<u>listen</u>**—*this is* <u>*Very important*</u>.

You have a larger mission right now, something that <u>only</u> *you can accomplish. This mission will mean everything to the entirety of Heaven.*

Because of your special knowledge, **<u>you</u>** *are the only one that can do this. The* **<u>only</u>** *one who can accomplish it is* **<u>you</u>**!

The two scrolls that we seek are written in Enochian, the obscure and ancient dialect that you can translate.

I know, I know, there are thousands of scrolls in the Scriptorium, to be precise, 7987 of them. Most are very simply the accumulation of esoteric learning since the First War, histories, biographies, and such.

But, and get this exact—The scrolls you are looking for are the Restoration Scroll and the Portal Scroll.

Make no mistake—you are **Not** the only one looking for this, the demons are also seeking them. Be assured, they will be coming for them, either to find them before you or to destroy them to keep them from getting to me.

<u>This Cannot Happen!</u>

If you do not find them before they get to them, you **<u>must</u>** destroy all of the scrolls to keep them away from Lucifer by whatever means you can.

But, I **need** those scrolls, If Essexiel and the others are to have any hope of regaining Heaven, I must have the Restoration Scroll. I need not tell you what that scroll can do for the Fallen, turning them from Demons back to Angels to be able to retake what they lost. And the Portal Scroll will allow them to leave the dimension of Hell.

Nothing, no one, is safe if this happens, **especially Lilly** and her baby.

Lucifer knows of her and her baby and will, if liberated from Hell, come after them. You only believe Marcus Lancaster is her problem—he is the lesser problem, believe me.

Eistered—you are the only one who can save her, save Essex, and save Heaven from Lucifer.

Is this dramatic? Is it over the

top?

Am I lying to keep you from her?

Simply: **No**.

*The trumpets heralding the Second War in Heaven are about to sound and without you finding those scrolls, the war **will** happen.*

*Yours is the only action to stop it. Your burden is great. **YOU** are our salvation.*

Trust me—find those scrolls.
Mikhail. \/

He crumbled the papers in his hand. "You think this is going to change my mind? Does Mikhail think he's going to stop me with this? Absolutely not. I'm out of here. He can send some other idiot in to try to find these things, I have responsibilities elsewhere."

He stepped out and then made his point by slamming the door behind him. Grumbling under his breath, he walked back to the small cell he had called home for months.

Once inside, he looked through the austere wardrobe that held everything he owned. Four more robes like the one he wore now hung next to a hanger with his only pair of jeans and t-shirt he owned, the ones he was wearing when he was brought to the monastery. The ones he was wearing the night he went in search of Lilly after his attack on her. A sharp stabbing pain of regret filled his chest, attack wasn't the right word. He had raped her. A horrible word for such a vile deed. He could not forgive himself, how could she ever forgive him? He had to try. The blood stains were gone, thanks to Brother Ingvar who had managed that miracle. He picked up his Air Jordan's and pulled the clean pair of socks out of the left one. Yanking off the brown robe, for what he knew would be the last time. While he appreciated everything the abbot had done, he had to get to Lilly. He pulled on the shirt and jeans, noticing with some horror that he had managed to gain some weight while here. He barely got the 501s buttoned. He sat on the edge of the cot and struggled to put his shoes on.

Spying the crumpled letter on the floor, he retrieved it and smoothed it on his knee. He reread the words. This time it wasn't just words on paper, he could hear Mikhail's urgent and serious voice. The statement about Lucifer knowing about Lilly and the baby made his nerves twist into knots. She wasn't safe, not with Marcus Lancaster and certainly not where Lucifer could get her. He had to protect her, grab her and run, find somewhere that the bitch-ruler of Hell and that evil vampire couldn't find her. He couldn't bring her here. He was sure he had burned his bridge with the abbot. Besides, he couldn't endanger the brothers if Hell came knocking. He needed a place away from everyone.

But where?

He would figure out that as they traveled. Right now he needed to get her.

He stalked out, closed the door to his cell behind him. He had begun to see it as home. Stopping at the cloister gate, he looked around, saying a silent goodbye to all the men he had made friends with.

He unlatched the gate in the high outer wall and stepped through it.

Gudrun watched the gate close from the entry outside his office. Shaking his head sadly, he started to retreat into his office; the feeling of failure overwhelmed him. What would he tell Mikhail? The creaking of the front gate sounded again. The abbot turned quickly to see Sullivan reenter.

Sullivan kicked the gate closed, more in frustration than anger. He glanced up to see Gudrun smiling in the window. Walking back into the abbot's office, he sighed deeply and growled, "God damn it. Okay, I'm staying here for the moment. But if anything happens to Lilly, I will hold you and Mikhail personally responsible and I will NOT be kind."

Gudrun nodded.

"I'll be in the scriptorium, after I change. These jeans are killing me."

The vampire walked back down the hallway, disappearing into his cell.

Chapter Sixteen

I T WAS DARK and he couldn't move. He knew the beating was going to continue. He felt like his knees would give way any second but the two faceless thugs had pinned his arms back and held him tightly, ready for the next blow. He couldn't move his jaw, he could feel it was broken. There were holes where teeth should have been and his mouth was full of blood.

Blood. He craved it.

Every shallow breath was excruciating. His eyes were swollen almost shut. He could no longer see the details of that brutish face that loomed before him, smiling viciously. However, he could still make out the blurred splashes of the garish colors of that tacky Hawaiian shirt worn by Fat Magnum.

Ralph, Fat Magnum called him, was sending the message with his fists by pummeling every inch of his broken body. If nothing else, he would remember that name. If he survived. Another agonizing punch tried to push his stomach into his spine, expelling what air he had managed to suck in.

Somewhere to his left, he heard his name called and he tried to swing his head toward the call. His eyes focused on a figure at the entrance to the alley and he watched as Duncan's head exploded and the bodyguard's dead body toppled over. There would be no rescue. He was going to die in that alley with his pants down. He screamed in frustration, in panic.

"Jesse?" He could hear Marcus's voice. He looked up and Fat Magnum now wore his lover's face. "Jesse! Wake up!"

What was Marcus doing in this alley; he was in...wherever he had gone. No, it was Fat Magnum, he would never see Marcus again.

The fat man stepped up and threw his arms around Jesse, reaching for his hair. Jesse felt his arms go slack and he could move. He grabbed the man holding him by the hair and swung his right fist hard into his nose, once, twice, and then shoved him away.

Why was he lying down? He had to get up, he could see Fat Magnum begin to pull himself up off the...floor? He shook his head, trying to clear his mind and his eyes as he stood up, wobbling.

He needed blood. He felt...fangs, his fangs punch down from his gums and he growled, descending on the staggering man. He could smell his blood, coppery sweet. He would stop Fat Magnum. Punish him for killing Duncan and beating him, he would drain the bastard.

He staggered to the man, grabbed him, and sunk his fangs into his neck. He took long, strong pulls on the blood but the man didn't fight him, instead he started running his hand up and down Jesse's arm, talking softly.

Why isn't he fighting for his life?

MARCUS HELD JESSE with one hand, rubbing his arm while he held his bleeding nose with the other.

"Jesse, it's Marcus. Baby, wake up. It's me. You're safe. Take what you need. I've got you, you're safe."

He hoped he was safe, Jesse wasn't showing any signs of knowing what was really going on. Marcus didn't want to pull his lover off his neck, the fight that could sever his artery and let him bleed out. Not that it would kill him, but he would go into stasis and need a lot of blood to recover. He needed to slow down the bleed and get through to his lover to release him.

"Jesse. Jesse, you need to slow down, stop feeding." He pulled away slightly, testing the hold on him.

He was jerked back hard into Jesse's chest, a growled warning him to not try that again. Okay, this was going to have to be done the hard way. He moved slowly, pulling his legs under him while reaching up and behind him with his free right hand, his left pinned under Jesse's arm. He just hoped he could pull off the maneuver without having to hurt him.

"Jesse!" He yelled, startling the vampire attached to his neck. As the man moved back, Marcus shoved up and tucked, pulling the naked man over his shoulder, his head, and he felt the fangs leave him, blood running down his silk robe and down into his crotch as he backed out away from Jesse, who was lying on his head and upper back, his feet on the wall.

"Jesse, it's Marcus, damn it, pay attention, it's okay!" He continued to back up; putting the most distance he could between him and his lover. He licked his fingers and rubbed his wounded neck, trying to use his own saliva to close them. Flesh and artery had been torn; he could feel the jagged cuts under his fingers. He needed Jesse awake so he could close them.

As the new vampire righted himself, he shook, the tremble apparent in his hands. Marcus watched him carefully as he rolled onto his ass, rubbing his lower back. "Damn, man, what the hell?"

"Jesse, who am I?"

Jesse raised an eyebrow, "You're the damned idiot who threw me against the wa..." His voice trailed off. "Where's Fat Magnum?" He looked around the room. He was home.

"You were dreaming, Jess. I heard you scream. Who is this 'Fat Magnum'?"

"You're bleeding, come here." Jesse reached out, his hand doing an imitation of a hula dancer in the tremors.

Marcus eased over and sat down, facing him. Jesse pulled him to him and carefully laved the shredded punctures closed. Then he reached down and kissed Marcus deep, losing himself in the feeling.

As he pulled off, "Sorry. I didn't know..."

"Shhhh. It's ok." Marcus reached up and traced a lip with his finger. "You were dreaming. I didn't expect you to grab me. I'll be more careful. Damn, you've got a great aim and my nose seems to be your favorite target," he tried to laugh, choking on the blood flowing down the back of his throat in his attempt to add levity to the situation and failing. "Now, tell me, who is Fat Magnum?"

Jesse let his head fall back against the wall, closing his eyes. He took deep breaths, fighting off the panic he felt rising in his chest. He could see these men in his mind's eye, almost so real he reach out and touch them. He shivered, the reality twisting back and forth between his room and that alley. He felt tears begin to form, to fall down his face.

"It's ok, Jess, you're safe here. It's okay."

Jesse's eyes snapped open, the blue washed out to almost white around the blood tears. "No! It's not ok. It's never going to be ok ever again. Not until they are dead by my hands. Promise me, Marcus, if I tell you who they are, I will be able to kill them myself. You can be there, but I want to be the one..."

"Absolutely, love. Absolutely. But I need to know who we're going after."

"I thought you said Castro found out that Mishkoph was behind my beating?"

"Ultimately, yes, But we haven't found out who the individual corpses are that actually did this. But, mark my words, we will."

Jesse chuckled, a pained laugh. "I remember a heavy man in a loud red Hawaiian shirt being the one who was giving the orders."

"Fat Magnum. No real name?"

"Not that I remember."

"What else? Anything else? Other names of anyone else who was there?" He wanted anything he could get to give Castro a hand with tracking down the bastards.

"Umm...Ralph? The hitter. Magnum also said two other names, the guys who held me, but no..." his voice trailed off as he tried to think.

"It's okay, it will come. Anything else?"

Jesse opened his eyes, the haunting memories seeming to float in front of him. "Nicholas. That was the guy in the bar who lured me outside. We had gone out back to..." Jesse shivered. He had placed himself in that situation, no one forced him. He wrapped his arms around himself and rocked, keening in fear.

Marcus leaned in and held his lover, whispering that it was ok. When Jesse slowed to a series of hiccups, he let go.

Jesse took a deep breath and looked up at Marcus.

"They shot Duncan. Marcus, they shot him in the head, I saw his head...explode. He was coming to help me and they......oh God!" Jesse fell into another fit of screaming and crying, allowing his lover to hold him and comfort him as he lost control.

Marcus knew how it felt, even after waking up

as a vampire, the blood and sounds of the battle of Towton during the War of the Roses had been horrible to get through. Hand to hand, everyone had a good look at the other person's eyes as they fought and the men he had killed haunted him even to this day when he was tired or stressed. The subsequent deaths in the next several wars he was involved in, the stress on the human men he had seen had resulted in shell shock, drawing in on themselves as they relived the horrors of battle, the sounds and the smells...that sickening stench of death and dying. Marcus never really got over all the death and fear himself.

Jesse was going to be having these nightmares again and Marcus felt the rage rising again. For months after he had plucked Jesse out of Camp Douglass, the man would wake screaming from things he had seen while a soldier in the Civil War. That was what had turned the sweet man he had met in a Chattanooga bar into a haunted wretch who saw ghosts creeping in to torment his sleep. It took him a long time to save Jesse's sanity from that, much longer than it took to rebuild his health.

The so-called War To End All Wars, that first world war, gave him some nightmares but it was World War II that restored the screaming night terrors in full force. While Marcus had worked with the British Special Air Services, or SAS, behind the lines as a spy in France and Germany, he had arraigned for Jesse to stay at home in London, supposedly unable to serve due to an old hip injury. However, there is no safe place when the war is on your doorstep. The German blitz of London brought back all of the fear and terror to his lover once again. It had been years before he got over it enough to sleep peacefully again.

All the torment and terrors returned pulling him under, drowning him in the memories and fear.

As he kept holding Jesse, rubbing his back and his arms, he vowed that each of the men who had done this would die, slowly, painfully, and at Jesse's hand if he wanted.

But, they were all dead.

Including Nelson Mishkoph.

Chapter Seventeen

T HE BLACK RANGE Rover followed the black panel van loaded with what little Gregory had left in his grandmother's home in San Antonio. The third car in the caravan contained a security detail sent to watch over the occupants of the Rover.

As the Rover drove through the dusk, music could be heard.

"Shot down, in a blaze of glory." The duet rose over the road noise in the SUV's cabin. "Take me now, but know the truth."

The passenger, Gregory had a great voice, Isobel thought. He was kind, he didn't even react to her singing off-key. Try as she might, she knew she couldn't carry a tune in a bucket. He also had a good taste in music; he hated rap music as much as she did. In the end, they had settled for '80's pop music, easy to sing to.

"I'm going down in a blaze of glory."

She wondered if the lyrics had some strange prophetic meaning. Was it why Marcus had set up this little trip to get her out of the building, to distract her? Marcus never did anything without a selfish reason. What was he up to? Nothing good, she would wager. She would find out soon, Flatonia was in their rear-view mirror and they should make it home to Houston around 9pm. That was if Eddie Garcia, the bodyguard in the cargo van made it past the ever diligent Texas Department of Public Safety patrol units. It was not unusual to spot marked and unmarked vehicles representing the DPS, various County Mounties, and even the Texas Rangers since I-10 was an infamous drug and human smuggling corridor. The chances of a Hispanic man driving a black, cargo van, driving toward Houston at dusk might as well have been a big old "Trooper Target" painted on the side. Yeah, there was an almost certain chance of being stopped, which would be a larger delay.

"You stopped singing."

Gregory's words shocked her back to the present.

"Sorry, just trying to figure out when we will get back and why Marcus sent to us to do this right now."

"You think there's an ulterior motive in this?"

"I'm certain of it. He was way too insistent about us going on this trip right now for it to be just about getting your stuff and meeting your grandmother."

Gregory frowned. "Is he always that manipulative?"

Izzy let out a snort and a long laugh. "You could say that. Marcus is a force of nature, doesn't have an altruistic bone in his body and he never does anything unless it will benefit him. He is, after all, the center of the universe." She said, laughingly but serious as well.

"And that other guy, Jorge? He seems to be grumpy all the time."

Another chuckle, "Castro's good people. He was a Gunnery Sargent in the Marines. As long as you do what he says, you'll do fine."

Gregory nodded. "What I find amazing is the history vampires have. It still amazes me that I've actually met Jean Lafitte, The Jean Lafitte."

"I know, right? They talk about knowing people that we studied in history."

"*Woman, where the hell are you?*"

The sudden intrusion of Baron's voice made her swerve the Rover, causing it to sway violently.

"Baron! Don't do that when I'm driving!" She cried aloud.

"*I don't know what you're doing and frankly I don't care, you have to come back. Lilly needs you.*"

"Baron?" Gregory mouthed. He hadn't learned all the finer points of being a ghoul yet, forgetting that Baron couldn't hear him when someone was communicating with the vampire cat telepathically.

Izzy nodded, "What's wrong?"

She could swear she heard him growl, "*Marcus Lancaster is what's wrong, again. My neck is better. But this is about her. This time he tricked her into turning an angel, the mean angels showed up and she's going to have the kittens early. She is stuck in bed; you have a new house guest. You*

need to be here. Bring her ghoul, he's needed too."
The words just tumbled into her head. She had never heard Baron talk like that; usually it was a short few words.

"Wait! Your neck? Wha...?"

"It is broke, um...healing...never mind. Lilly needs you now, not me." He stressed.

Izzy shot a look at Gregory. He had a strange look on his face; he wasn't hearing the conversation on Baron's end. "He said his neck is broken? And we need to get to Lilly, something's very wrong."

"How far out are we?" Gregory looked around; he still wasn't sure where he was, never having driven to Houston before.

"Far enough." She responded and reached for the microphone of the radio system and keyed it. "Garcia, Kennedy, there's a problem back at HQ. I need to either step up this caravan or I'm going to have to ditch and run fast. It's up to you, Kennedy, but one way or another; we need to get back fast."

The reply came in two voices, each keying at the same time.

"I didn't get that. Come back Kennedy." She said.

"I said, you have to stay with us, I can't guard the truck and run with you at the same time." Kennedy's voice repeated.

"Let her go, Bry, go with her. I'll bring the truck in as soon as I can." Garcia spoke up.

"NO! We go together or not at all. I can't cover both of you if you take off on me. I have my orders."

"I don't give a crap about your orders, Bry, I am needed back. I'm going on, stay with the truck, I'll be okay, I'll step it up and head in on 10." Izzy pulled into the passing lane, stepped on the gas and the Rover roared to life. Thankfully, Marcus didn't believe in small, 4-cylinder motors in his vehicles. She passed the van and waved to Garcia as they passed.

"Aren't they going to be pissed off if we just take off like this? We got the lecture before we left about staying with our security." Gregory asked.

"Let them get bent, I don't care. Lilly needs us and we're going to get there as soon as we can."

"Okay."

"Great, grab the phone and check the local traffic for Houston. There's an app on it that Marcus had designed that gives us the local news and any traffic changes, it's that one with the wheel on it."

Gregory pushed a couple of buttons. "Looks clear. How far into Houston do we need to go?"

"Just to 610, that will be the fastest way back."

"We're clear that far in, looks like. There's a part of the road just before there that is marked with red..."

"How far before?"

Gregory enlarged the picture to get the names of the streets, "It's somewhere near a street called Silber."

"That might be trouble." Isobel scanned ahead of them for the glow of brake lights, trying to figure out just how far the backup was. "Do me a favor, get into the contacts and click on "Gilbert", then hit the speaker so I can talk to him." As she moved closer to the lights, she pulled across the lanes to the far right so she could exit if needed.

Gregory found the contact, putting the ringing phone on speaker.

"Gilbert, what do you need, Izzy?" A deep voice boomed from the phone.

"Hey, Gil, I need a favor, can you pull up the Tex Dot site and check for a wreck on 10, around the West 610 interchange? I am running hot coming in and I want to find a way off this highway if they've got a problem." She could hear keyboard clicking over the phone.

"Yeah, looks like a big one. Cows."

"Cows?"

"Yeah, cows. One of the people coming in for the Houston Livestock Show and Rodeo evidently lost it on 10 near some of the construction and the cows have escaped. They've closed the highway, rerouting people to Campbell and Gessner because they're bringing in cowboys and horses to rope the cows and put them into another trailer. Looks like you need to pick another route back."

The entire freeway shut down and Isobel frowned, slowing to a stop with the rest of the universe that seemed to be wanting to go to the same place she was, although this traffic was probably on the way to the rodeo. The stranded multitude in the sea of cars were going to be late for the George Strait concert on the first night of the rodeo.

"Gil, you're a life-saver. See you soon." She nodded and Gregory closed the connection.

"Looks like I'm going back-road to the office now." Izzy looked around, trying to find a way to pull off the highway, not finding one. The entire freeway was under construction; again, all she could find were barriers, tore up concrete, and blocks. Gone were the days of just hopping off the road, crossing the grass, and going down the frontage to escape.

She pounded on the wheel, "God damn it, we're stuck dead in traffic." She took a deep breathe, settled, "Baron, there's a problem."

"*What now?*" the growl was evident.

"We're stuck. Some cows are on the road and..."

"*Cows? Cows don't belong on the road, they belong in a pasture...*"

"Focus, Baron, I'm stuck, we can't get off the highway and the cars are all stopped while they try to round 'em up."

"*And what, exactly, do you want me to do, chase the cows?*"

She rolled her eyes and Gregory stifled a giggle at the face. "No, you can't chase the cows. I need you to stay with Lilly until we get there, this may take a while."

"*I need to get out or we're going to have little piles of shit on the carpet again.*"

"Baron, don't you dare! Use the toilet."

"*No way, last time I fell in.*"

If you are that bad, go on. I'll radio back to HQ

and get them to send up a guard for Lilly..."

"*She doesn't need a guard, she needs her lunch and she needs you to calm her down.*"

"Ok, Baron, I will get us there as fast as we can. You run out, do your business, and come back."

"What happened? How did he break his neck?" Gregory looked around, trying not to be spooked by the people in other cars looking toward them. He wouldn't know if one of them was going to do something to them until they were on top of them, but he wasn't going to tell Isobel that.

"I don't know, but evidently Marcus has something to do with it. Listen, depending on what we find at home, you may need to stay close to her, keep her calm and fed. I don't know what I'll be doing; we may have to pack and move; even though I work for Marcus, I'm going to make sure she's safe from him and anyone else."

"Do you think he will hurt her? I mean, he loves her, she's carrying his baby."

"I really don't know anymore, I would hope he wouldn't. I don't think Marcus loves anyone but Marcus. Maybe Jesse, but no one else."

"You've been with him for a long time, right?"

"Since I was 20, you were two when I first started with him. I have had to re-think my priorities a few times, knowing who he is and what he is capable of, but I've stayed..."

The conversation died off as the traffic began to creep forward ever so slowly. Isobel was lost in thought, worried about Lilly and how things were going. Marcus had rushed them out of the way so fast, she knew he had something going on; she wasn't going to pry, but when it hurt Lilly, there were questions that were going to have to be answered. He was up to something big, there were people coming and going in the building that she didn't know and when she asked Castro about it, he gave her a verbal pat on the head and asked her to go find out how many apartments were available in the towers across the street.

She was paying attention to not running into the bumper in front of her when she heard a noise that sounded like it was coming from beside her. She looked to the side of the car, scanning for trouble.

The sound of rapid gunfire sounded. Gregory was turning around in the seat to see what was happening and Izzy grabbed him screaming "Down NOW!"

The gunfire sounded louder and louder, pinging on the body and glass of the Rover. There were motorcycles passing between the stopped cars, one on either side of their lane. Once past the Rover, they sped up and raced between the cars.

Isobel looked around as the noise ended, cautiously poking her head up. The glass had spider webbed but held. There were no holes in the body of the vehicle. "You ok?" she asked Gregory as they sat up.

Pounding on the car and shouting startled her, she screamed and pushed away from the door. Through the ruined glass, she could see a man frantically trying to get into the car.

"Hey Lady! Are you okay lady? Lady, are you

okay?"

She could hear screaming from somewhere. It sounded close.

"Isobel, are you hurt?"

The sound of a voice, Gregory's voice, sounded over the screaming.

She was screaming. That sound was her...

Isobel shook, tears forming. Did she...did they just come close to dying? Who the hell was that? What the hell just happened? She felt tears forming in her eyes, threatening to fall.

"I called 911. Help is on the way." The man yelled through the glass.

911....

Her brain struggled to figure out what was going on, how they had survived an ... attack?

"Isobel? Are you all right? Are you hurt?" Gregory's voice broke into the fog she felt like she was in.

Was she hurt? She quickly let her mind run over her body. Nope, no pain.

She found her voice, "I'm okay, um, we're okay, right?" She looked to Gregory who slowly nodded. She closed her eyes and tried to slow down her breathing.

There was a growing crowd around their vehicle, faces peering through the cracked glass. She could hear screams from somewhere outside of the Rover, lots of voices yelling.

"I didn't know this was armored, we didn't get any holes, in the car or in us." Gregory observed.

"I didn't either, but it makes sense, Marcus is thorough about security. Saved our lives this time."

Her cell began to ring. She searched for it, following the sound until she found it on the floor. "Hello?"

"Kincaid! Are you okay?" Brian Kennedy. How did he know....? She looked at the phone, the tears falling.

Gregory reached out and took the phone from her, putting his other hand on hers. "Hello, this is Gregory."

"Freeman, you two okay?"

"Yes, sir, we're not hurt. We got shot at, two guys on motorcycles. None of the bullets came through the glass or the body, I don't know how we're not dead..." his voice trailed off.

"Armored car. I heard the police are on the way. Don't give them anything more than your driver's license and a statement that you have no idea why you were targeted. It's the truth but we don't want anything else said, got it? You've got to help Isobel calm down and understand. Stay with the vehicle if you can, we're trying to get to you."

"Ok, sir. How did you know...?"

"The media already knows, one of the TV station helicopters was covering the cow crash live and they saw the attack. The video is already hitting the internet. Our media monitor saw it and Jorge radioed. Stay inside unless the cops want you out of the car but do not go anywhere until we're there, got it?"

"Got it, sir." Gregory looked around and saw police approaching, maneuvering through the stopped traffic.

"Call me if you need to, we are trying to get to you." The security chief paused, "Hey…"

"Yeah?"

"Glad you guys are okay." Brian hung up.

Gregory turned to Isobel, "Hey, we're alive, it's okay." He unhooked his seatbelt and leaned over to Isobel, who was staring at the faces outside the car. He put an arm around her and gently turned her head toward him, "Izzy, it's okay. We're okay. The police and Mr. Kennedy are on their way, you have to pull it together so we can talk to the police when they get here. We're supposed to just tell them our info and what happened. He doesn't want us to go anywhere else until he gets here."

Isobel turned her gaze to him, nodding. "They were trying to kill us, Gregory. They meant to kill us. Who…? Why did they try to kill us?" She searched his eyes for an answer he didn't have. She tried to quiet her mind, to try to figure out what was going on and to try to remember what happened exactly. The police would need the statement, they would want to know. She closed her eyes and sagged onto the ghoul's shoulder.

They lived through an ambush.

They lived.

That was the important part. They lived.

She could hear sirens coming closer. They would have to answer a lot of questions and she didn't have any answers. She had more questions than they did. Who were they? Why were they targeted? Had they been tailed since San Antonio? Did they know who was in the Rover? They must have, but what did she or Gregory ever do? Her mind swirled with unanswered questions and the echoing the rapid fire spray of the bullets that tried to end their lives.

Marcus would be mad that someone shot ....

Marcus.

Did they think it was Marcus in the car? Were they targeting him? Who would be trying to kill the man she worked for?

Could it have been the ones who nearly killed Jesse and did kill Duncan Morrison a few months back?

Could it be the same people or person? Who was it, she couldn't remember, maybe if she heard it again, she would remember...

She sat up, "Give me the phone." Gregory handed her the phone and she hit the name on the speed dial. It rang three times, then picked up, "Hello, you've reached Marcus Lancaster. I am not able to answer right now, please leave a message and my assistant or I will return your call as soon as possible. BEEP..."

Of course, he wouldn't be bothered to answer; he was too busy with his life to answer a call for help. She hung up and put the phone down as a police officer tapped on the window.

She unlocked the door and tried to put the window down. Even with the car still running, it didn't move. She opened the door just a bit and saw the officer move to pull his gun. She put her hands up and glanced at Gregory, who did the same. "Officer, I'm glad you are here. There's been an incident..."

She laughed, an "incident" indeed.

"Step out of the vehicle, ma'am, slowly with your hands where I can see them. Your passenger needs to do the same, slowly." The officer said.

She pushed the door open and stepped out, hands in the air, glancing back to see Gregory doing the same on the other side. She was grabbed, spun around, and her hands placed on the hood of the car. As she tried to adjust, she heard screaming and loud talking somewhere behind her. She was patted down hard, closing her eyes as the hands hit places she didn't want touched without dinner. Once they were through, she was told to turn around. The officer was looking at her like getting shot at was her fault somehow and she finally felt herself getting angry.

"Now ma'am, what's your name?" He asked.

"Isobel Kincade, I live at 5151 San Filipe, 24th floor. My friend is Gregory Freeman, he lives at the same place. Yes, that is the location of Lancaster Industries, the car is registered to Marcus Lancaster, who is my boss. And I have no idea why we were attacked."

The policeman nodded. "That jives with our records. You have no idea why you were shot at?

She shook her head, "We've had threats over the last few months from someone, that the security detail knows about, and that's why I had a team with us coming back from San Antonio. But I'm not privy to that information."

The officer raised an eyebrow, "You have a security team? Where are they?"

"We cut away from them, I have an emergency to handle back at the tower and they were behind us. I know they're on the way but with the traffic…"

"They may not make it until we get both your shooting and the mess with the cows cleared. The entire freeway is being shut down until we get things settled." The officer said while she looked at his uniform and saw his name was "Campbell".

"Have you caught the shooters? And who has been screaming over there?" She pointed across the lanes of cars.

"We have officers all over looking for them and handling other things. A stray shot, probably ricochet, caught the person in the car in the next lane, the bullet went through the window and killed a man who was driving. His wife is bleeding and hysterical right now. Another occupant is also injured."

"Oh my god! Anyone else hurt?" Izzy felt sick.

"Not sure. We're bringing in Life Flight for them, do you or your passenger need medical attention."

As much as she wanted to get out of the traffic, the noise, and everything else going on, she shook her head, "No, we didn't get hit. Once Brian gets here, we'll go with them."

"You and your passenger need to go to the station and give us statements. Since there's a fatality, you are central to the investigation. We will want to talk to Mr. Lancaster as well, he can come down and give us the statement and he can pick you up as well."

That was the last thing Isobel wanted to do. She wanted to go home, get something to drink—

maybe even more than one, and then punch Marcus in the mouth for this one. She and Gregory weren't involved in whatever Marcus was up to and whoever the person was who shot at them. They were just innocent bystanders. Then she wanted to check on Lilly and try to figure out her next move.

Which, if this bullshit kept up, would be made without Marcus Lancaster.

She seemed to be pulled back into the now with a shout from a familiar voice and she looked up to see Brian Kennedy jogging between the cars, Stanley Moore and Peyton Naismith following him. Neither man had bothered to put on a suit coat, their shoulder holsters with their nine millimeters clearly visible.

Officer Campbell also turned at the shout, his hand on his gun.

"No! They're my security detail." Izzy grabbed the officer's arm. He glared at her quickly and then turned back to the men, who had stopped a few feet away, Naismith peeling off to go to the other side of the SUV.

"Officer, I am Brian Kennedy, the leader of the security team for Ms. Kincade and Mr. Freeman. We got separated in the traffic." He looked past the officer at Isobel, "Are you all right?"

As Isobel nodded, Kennedy handed his ID and security license to the officer. The officer checked both and handed them back to the man. "We had an incident; someone shot at your client's vehicle and took off. I need answers and we're going to need to go downtown to get them once we can move."

"I understand, we can....." Kennedy's words were drowned out by the sound and wind of a Life Flight helicopter landing in the west-bound lanes of the freeway. Izzy turned to look, watching the paramedics that had come in on foot to the car next to hers. They moved a woman to the helicopter, coming back to pick up a child, who looked like a bloody rag doll in the arms of the man who carried her.

As she watched the helicopter lift off and race toward the medical center, Isobel tuned out the conversation between the police and her bodyguards.

She was definitely going to have to punch Marcus Lancaster right in the mouth.

Chapter Eighteen

I T WAS ALMOST 4 a.m. when Isobel pulled the SUV into the circle drive, slamming into park. The interrogation at the police station was long, longer than she ever thought it would be. It seemed like the Houston Police and the district attorney thought they orchestrated their own hit by the way she and Gregory were questioned. It wasn't until Assistant Chief Robert Harvey and the corporate lawyer, Javen Federman came in and put a stop to the harassment that they got to finally go home. Both men, vampires and obviously called by either Jorge Castro or Marcus, had cut everything short and escorted them out to the SUV.

As they exited the car, Gregory pulled the suitcases out of the back and they walked up to the front door and were buzzed in.

Jackson Davis was holding the security desk and waved to them.

"Hi Jack, can you get one of the guys to park the beast? I need to get upstairs." She flipped the keys across the room to him. "Oh, and the rest of the crew will be here later, just have them back the van into the loading dock and Gregory will get things out tomorrow."

"Sure thing Ms. Isobel."

As the ghouls rounded the elevator towers, a voice called out, "Kincade, Freeman, get your fucking asses over here."

Castro.

Gregory shot a look to Isobel, who shook her head.

"Jorge, I have to get upstairs to..."

"You have to get your ass into the security offices."

Isobel stopped. Her first instinct was to just tell him no, but she knew the Gunny wasn't going to take that well. So she changed tactics. "You know my 'little voice', Gunny. I got a feeling that there was something wrong and I need to check on Lilly."

"Your little voice isn't wrong;, she's been in the sick bay. But that doesn't mean you can ditch rank and come back on your own. We set these regs for reasons..."

"I know, Jorge, but if she's been in sick bay, that means she needs us, especially Gregory since he's her donor. You know I don't make a habit of it, we're just been gone too long and she's due another donation soon. I'm tired, I've been shot at, scared and then interrogated, and all I want to do is go upstairs. We can argue this another time, or not, you know I won't do it again."

Castro pulled the chewed cigar from his mouth, waving it in the air to punctuate his words. "You're damned right you won't. I will handcuff the security detail to you next time, they will be with you, in the car, and you will sit in the back seat and behave yourself, is that understood?"

"Yes, sir. Can I go now?"

Gregory watched the conversation with interest. Isobel had been standing, essentially toe-to-toe with the former Marine, hands at her sides, back straight, never turning away. As she asked to go, it was like she let go and deflated, she looked down, chastened.

"Get outta here." Castro waved them toward the elevators. As they turned to go, he added, "And Freeman, don't copy Kincade's mistakes, learn from them. I'll kick your ass so fast you'll think someone punched your momma."

"Yes, sir." He bristled but turned and disappeared into the elevator.

As soon as the doors closed and they were on their way up, Isobel laid her hand on his arm, "Don't let the old bastard get to you. He's mostly harmless."

"I won't. But it's the 'mostly' that I'm worried about."

Isobel laughed, "Smart man."

The elevator opened and Isobel exclaimed, "What the hell?" She threw her arm out to stop Gregory. The apartment door was open and there was a man holding a stack of books, walking toward her living room.

"Let me," Gregory pushed past her and walked into the apartment, "Just what the heck are you doing?" His voice loud.

"Shhhhhh!" Reba hissed as she turned around from putting books into a bookcase.

A bookcase, Isobel noted, from her own office. "Reba? What's going on, what are you doing?"

"Let's go into my room and I'll explain." Reba stood, laying the books on the shelf.

"Excuse Me?" exclaimed a flabbergasted Isobel as she followed the red head back to what used to be Isobel's office.

Izzy stood in the doorway taking in the mass of boxes piled on a bed, clothing in the closet that stood open. Everything looked different than she had left it two days previously.

"Sorry, it's obvious from your reaction that neither Mr. Castro nor Mr. Lancaster told you what is going on."

"Apparently so." Isobel said, scanning the room, stunned.

"Lilly needs round-the-clock care. She refused to stay in the clinic, so Mr. Lancaster had all my things moved over here so I could be close if I am needed. I'm really sorry, I thought he would have warned you. Returning to this mess must be quite a shock."

"Yeah, it is." She sighed, resigned. "Marcus has a habit of making snap decisions without advising the person effected. If she needs you here, we're going to keep you here until she's okay. But I don't understand, she was fine two days ago when we left. Otherwise, we wouldn't have gone." She looked at Gregory, who was standing behind her nodding in agreement." What happened?" Her serious tone and stern expression only accentuated her concern.

"I really don't know what 'excitement' caused her to go into premature labor. Mr. Lancaster brought her to the clinic. We got the contractions stopped but the doctor ordered complete bed rest. No excitement of any kind. And that's why I'm here. Sorry your stuff is just piled everywhere."

"Not to worry," she said dismissively, "I have somewhere I can move it. The second walk-in-closet is big enough for an office. It'll be more convenient anyway. I'll have Castro send the guys back up tomorrow and we'll settle me in..."

A scream split the quiet.

Gregory scrambled out of the room with Isobel and Reba trailing, dashing to the door and throwing it open.

Lilly was sitting up, crying, pale and shaking, holding her right hand. Her eyes didn't seem to see Gregory as he stopped and put his hand out.

"Lilly. It's Gregory. You're ok, I'm here. Lilly?"

She seemed to calm at his voice, then blinked a few times, brushed away the tears and looked up at him, "Gregory. Yes, okay, uh...yes. I'm ok." Her confusion was clear.

"Do you need to feed? Let's calm you down and let you feed, then we can talk." He walked to her side and sat down, offering her his neck.

She didn't comment, her fangs punching down and she tapped the vein, then struck. She closed her eyes and gently held his hand. Isobel stood nearby, watching her feed while Reba stepped behind them to fluff and position the pillows so Lilly could recline a bit when she was finished.

Isobel turned as she heard her front door open, stepping back to close the bedroom door to shield Lilly's feeding from whoever was there.

"*I'm here, woman, let me get to her.*"

Baron. She should have known he would come in running. He streaked between her legs and jumped onto the bed, setting in Lilly's lap. Lilly stroked the cat's fur as she fed.

After the feeding concluded, Lilly licked the holes in Gregory's neck closed, hugged him, and then lay back onto the pillows.

"Lilly, honey, what happened, did you have a nightmare?" Isobel asked.

Lilly's eyes glistened with the blood-tinged tears she had yet to shed, "Marcus. He has forced me to turn Essex, he broke Baron's neck…"

"What!?" Isobel shouted, looking at Baron, moving to check him.

"*I'm fine, woman, I'm healing. We've got to get Lilly out of here.*" The words were accompanied by an audible growl from the cat.

Isobel turned to Lilly, "He forced you change someone without your permission, or the person who was turned's permission?"

She nodded, her eyes downcast, a blood tear dripped onto Baron's head. "Yes" she groaned, looking up, the blood tears streaking her face. Gregory handed her a tissue. "Essex was an angel, he was working at Lancaster Industries and was discovered. I am not sure how Marcus found out that Essex was an angel, I don't know why he was working here but something is going on. I was trying to protect Essex from Marcus."

Lilly rubbed her arms, a motion that Isobel had noticed she did when she was upset.

Isobel shook her head. "The angels will be coming soon to mark you for that turning. We have to hide yo..."

"No," Lilly interrupted, "They've already been here. Something went wrong with the marking, I'm not marked. But they will be back. That woman angel was very angry. She said she would be back to take me to Hell" Lilly's tears flowed at the thought, "I don't want to go to Hell. I did the wrong thing for the right reason, I didn't know what else to do, I couldn't let him die."

Isobel stared at the vampire. Nida's marking hadn't taken, that was a surprise.

"She can't be hidden." Reba spoke up, "She's tuned, the Enforcers will find her, no matter where she goes. I'm surprised that Nida wasn't able to do a marking, I've never heard of such a thing happening before."

Isobel's gaze immediately jerked the nurse, "You have never heard....wait, you're not a vampire, how do you know about the vampires and the marking?"

"She's an angel." Lilly said. "Like Essex and Sullivan. I'm sorry, Reba, I can't keep it a secret from them. You see, Reba fed me when you two were gone. Her blood tastes like Sullivan's did before I turned him." Lilly said, trying to sit up in bed.

Gregory helped lift her and plumped the pillows for her to lay back. "I knew we shouldn't have gone. I'm sorry Lilly."

Isobel reacted to the news very differently. "Really?" She folded her arms across her chest.

Reba knew there was no way to deny it "Yes, I'm an angel. I'm Gregory's guardian angel. I had to move to work with Dr. Young to keep up with him. It wasn't supposed to be known but Lilly figured it out and I couldn't lie to her."

"My guardian angel?" Gregory turned to look at Reba. "How did that happen?"

"You're my assignment. So I'm here to work as a nurse so I can be close to you. Mr. Lancaster had me moved up here to take care of Lilly so now she's my charge as well."

"Ok, so you are an angel. Marcus cannot know this. He's been determined to build an army against the angels, which, by the way, I think is insane." Isobel said, "So now he has made his own vampire from an angel. But why did he want you to do it, he could have just as easily turned him himself."

Lilly sighed, rubbing her growing abdomen. "He didn't want to be marked again. His first marking was because of me."

Baron growled, startling Gregory, who had been petting the feline. The ghoul pulled his hand away, hoping not to get bit.

"That's not fair. Did he order you to turn the man?" Gregory probed.

"No, he had Castro drain him and then locked us into a room. He wanted me to decide to turn him or not. I couldn't let him die! Sullivan even said to change him." Tears started rolling down her cheeks, "I did and now Essex is angry with me. He said he would rather have died."

"Oh honey," Isobel sat on the edge of the bed and hugged the vampire.

"And they came and tried to mark me, but somehow it didn't work." Lilly rubbed her right hand where the mark would have been. "The lady angel with the gray wings and the tall male angel with the red wings and the large sword appeared in the room where Essex and I were. The woman tried to put the mark on my hand but it didn't work. She accused me of doing something to stop her. She was very angry and said she would be back. I didn't have a choice, I had to save Essex, but she wouldn't listen. Essex wouldn't either!" She began to hiccup.

"Shhhh, it's okay." Isobel soothed, "I'll try to find out what Marcus is doing, but you need to calm down for the baby's sake."

"What did the third angel look like? Did he, or she, have gray wings?" Reba asked.

Isobel shot her a look to silence her but Reba shook her head.

"There were only two this time. When I was tuned, the woman and the man came with Essex to do it but this time it was only two." Lilly drank from the glass of water Gregory brought.

"That's odd..." Reba mused.

"Oh?" Gregory asked.

"That is not proper procedure. The rules say there has to be three angels at a marking, a judgment or a tuning. They never do it without a third. Never. Nida goes to do the sentences, Helmut is the guard, and they send another

Enforcer to be the witness and do the tuning. They never do it without a third." She paused warily, "Or at least they are not supposed to..."

"What does that mean?" Isobel asked.

"I am not sure, I've not been told of any procedural changes, but Enforcement isn't my department. I think I need to go to H.H.A.D and find out what is going on."

"H.H.A.D.?" Lilly hiccupped again, then let out a large burp, "Excuse me!"

Gregory stifled a giggle, a little too late.

"Heavenly Host Assignment Department, the area of Heaven that keeps up with all the working angels on Earth."

"That sounds like a company bureaucracy." Isobel quipped.

"I guess it is," Reba said, "If you're here for a while, I will go on my errand. I will return shortly." She turned to Isobel, "Can you stay with Lilly? If anything happens, call Dr. Young. You can tell him that I went out for some medicine if he questions my absence."

"Sure, we'll be here. Do you need a car or anything?"

"No, I have my ID. I'll tell the guard on duty that I'm going over to the Randall's grocery store. I can take off from the alley."

As she left, Reba hugged each person in the room. "I'll be right back. Lilly, rest well." She reached out to pet Baron, who rubbed her hand with his head, purring. She kissed him on the top of the nose and then left the room.

"Don't forget your coat, it's cold out there,"

Isobel called after her.

"You're right, must keep up appearances." Reba grabbed her cloak from the back of the chair and closed the door as she exited.

"Come on Gregory, let's let Lilly rest and we can move stuff into my new office."

"Isobel," Lilly called out as the duo turned to go to the door. Isobel turned back, "Can you find Essex and check on him? Maybe let him know we will try to help him?"

"Sure, sweetie. I'll see if I can find him. You relax and I'll be in to check on you in a bit."

"Thanks."

Isobel closed the door as Lilly settled down to try to sleep.

"Oh!" Lilly suddenly chirped.

"What?" Baron opened one gold eye and looked at her.

"The baby just moved!" She rubbed her belly.

Baron got up, and walked across the bed, lying down against her. *"Shhh, kitten. I'm here."* He purred and Lilly felt the baby settle in response.

"How odd." She thought as she drifted off to sleep.

Chapter Nineteen

R EBA WAVED AT guard Jackson Davis as she exited the elevator area. "Hi Jackson, errand for Lilly. Need anything while I'm out?"

Jackson Davis smiled at the pretty red-headed nurse, "No ma'am, I'm great, thanks. Do be careful, I don't want anything to happen to you."

"I will. Thanks."

He buzzed her out and she hurried down the sidewalk toward the parking garage. Looking back, she didn't see Davis, he must have been called away. She quickly turned into the alley leading toward Sage Avenue and out of sight of the security cameras. She knew as soon as she spread her wings, she would become invisible but a sudden disappearance on-camera might be a bit suspicious. Unfurling the wings, she launched toward H.H.A.D.

JOEY MASON CROUCHED in the shadows, watching the traffic in and out of Lancaster Industries parking garage. He had been sitting in the cold, wet air for weeks it seemed like. Dressed like a homeless person, his job was to monitor the activities in that part of the alley. Another person monitored the front of the building from the parking lot across the street. Mason brought along a fifth of Jack Daniels to help with the look of being homeless, but it also kept the mid-40s air a bit warmer.

He looked up to see a woman come out from beside the garage and walk down behind the strip center that housed the grocers and other stores. That was unusual, people usually didn't walk in the alley at night, even in the Galleria area, it could be unsafe, especially for women.

To relieve his boredom, he allowed a bit of fantasy with the woman play out in his mind, thinking of how she would react if he stepped up behind her, grabbed her, and pulled her into the darkest corner of the garage. Would she fight him? Nah, he could hit her hard enough to take the fight out of her and then he could fuck her without worry.

As he was getting to the good part of the rape fantasy, she dropped the cloak from her shoulders and giant shadowy outgrowths seemed to erupt from her back. They unfurled to reveal enormous white wings, the tips of which touched the sides of the alley. With a single flap of those massive wings, she propelled upward—and disappeared.

He shook his head to clear the cobwebs. This must be a bourbon-induced Victoria's Secret fantasy. He looked at the last third of the bottle of

Jack and shook his head again. He may have to switch to vodka, the whiskey was giving him hallucinations and those weren't covered by the insurance that his boss, Nelson Mishkoph, carried on his crew. No sense in wasting a good fantasy, he swallowed the last bit of the amber liquid and threw the bottle against the fence, breaking it.

Someone's tires would go flat if they hit that glass, which was fine by him.

THE PORTAL OPENED and Reba glided toward the Guardian's station in H.H.A.D. She wasn't sure why, but the vast room felt...weird. There were still plenty of angels coming and going but she usually could see several of the Archangels working their department boards along with their assistants.

Her own department, the Guardians, was being manned by an assistant as well. Arael looked up from his report as she landed and walked up into the operations area. She folded her white wings, not bothering to pull them into the pouch in her back where they normally were when she was walking around humans.

Arael flashed her a smile. "Rebangiel, I didn't expect you in today. What can I do for you, girl?"

"Hi, Arael. I have some news for Barachiel, is she up with Mikhail?" Reba looked over her shoulder toward the head Archangel's office.

"Oh, you haven't heard the latest then. Archangel Mikhail has left Heaven."

"What?! When is he coming back? I've not heard of him leaving, not since…"

"Shhh." He shushed her, "We don't know when, or if, he is coming back."

"So who is in charge now?"

"Kafziel is running things.

"What? That pretentious prig?"

"Believe it or not, he was insubordinate and challenged Mikhail over a situation. When Mikhail asked if he thought that he could do better, Kafziel, the arrogant idiot, said 'Yes.' Mikhail said 'Fine, Show me!' and left, we've not seen or heard from him since"

"That's not good. So where is 'Chiel?"

"The Archangels are out of the department, I'm not sure where they are meeting. Is there anything I can do for you?"

Rebangiel looked around, taking note of where other angels were, lowered her voice and leaned toward Arael, "I have some information for, well, someone who can get it to Mikhail and Ranguel, concerning one of the Enforcers."

Arael kept his voice low as well, "Ranguel is with the rest of the Archangels. You might check the meeting rooms, I know that they all left earlier today."

"What's going on?" Reba felt like she was out of touch with everything in Heaven.

"We're missing angels. Many have disappeared, some have turned up dead. We're not sure what is going on, but the Archangels are very upset."

"That's what I have information about. I know where one of the angels is. He's one of Ranguel's Enforcers. I need to report directly to either Chiel or Ranguel."

"If I see them, I will let them know, but you really should check the meeting rooms." Arael said as another Guardian glided up. Reba waved to the newcomer as she thanked Arael and started off toward the conference center.

THE CONFERENCE CENTER attached to H.H.A.D. was huge, even by Heaven's standards. Reba had to search through several halls before finding the room the Archangels were using. Of course, she would have found them easier if she had been looking for two very tall muscular red-winged Warrior angels in full silver and gold battle armor.

As she came up to the door, the angels dropped their swords, crossing each other, blocking her entry.

"I am Rebangiel, I must speak with both Archangel Barachiel and Archangel Ranguel.

The red-headed warrior on the right spoke, "No Entry. No Disturbance. Come back once they are finished."

"I know they are not expecting me, however, I have information about one of Ranguel's angels, information he needs to know now, not later."

"No entry!" the red-winged angel said.

"Okay, you need to tell him I'm here, that I want, no, I *need* to speak with him."

"No entry. Go wait in H.H.A.D."

She saw that this wasn't going to be easy. She began to turn to walk away, then she turned back and, raising her voice to as loud as she could shout, "*Look*! I must speak with Ranguel, it is a matter of life and death and you need to tell him that. I will not be responsible if someone dies because you are being stubborn and..."

"Angel, you are to be quiet and leave." The red-winged angel raised his voice to match hers.

"I will, as soon as you allow me audience with Ranguel."

"Leave now, before we are forced to apprehend you for disrupting the peace."

Reba raised her voice louder and more shrilly, "All I need is to speak to Ranguel for three minutes..."

The door opened behind the swords and the gray-winged head of the Enforcers stepped out.

"What is going on out here?" The angel glared first at the two Warriors, then at the Guardian angel. The Warriors snapped to attention, their swords pointing toward the ground at chest height.

"Archangel Ranguel. Please forgive me for disturbing you. I have vital information. Enforcer angel Essexiel has been taken by a vampire named...."

"Marcus Lancaster. Does he live?" Ranguel's anger was apparent in the force of his clipped words.

"Yes and no, sir. He has been turned."

Ranguel closed his eyes and rubbed the bridge of his nose. "Did Lancaster do the change?"

"No sir, he forced his progeny, Lilly Marchantel, to do it. She is the vampire's mistress of my charge, Gregory Freeman."

"So Nida has marked her?"

"She tried, sir. But something went wrong and it didn't happen. Also, Nida was there with Helmut but no other Enforcer."

"Who did Essex's tuning?" Ranguel asked.

"Lilly didn't say, sir, I would guess Nida did since there was no witness Enforcer present."

"I see. You did well coming to me. Please keep me, or Barachiel, apprised of any further actions in Mr. Lancaster's operations and no one else." He glanced at the guards. "Report directly to us."

"Yes, sir."

Ranguel turned to go, he paused. With a mumbled invocation, he swept his hand in the direction of the two guards as if he was shooting a fly.

"Sir, is Archangel Mikhail really not in charge of Heaven right now?"

Ranguel halted in mid-step and turned. "That is untrue. He has appointed someone to hold the position while he is away on business. The Archangel Synod stands in support of that decision."

"Oh. Okay." She swallowed, nerves flaring, "Thank-you, sir."

Ranguel walked back into the chamber and shut the door. Reba noticed the rather vacuous gaze of the two guards as she walked away."

Chapter Twenty

"I CANNOT DO this again." Sullivan stood in front of the wall unit that contained the library scrolls. He felt like he was going blind while killing massive amounts of brain cells after reading the first 500 of the thousands of scrolls in the unit.

"Find the scrolls Mikhail said. They are important he says. He needs to come find them himself, I'm tired." He rubbed his eyes. "That's it. I'm taking a fucking break. I deserve it." He said to the air.

Sullivan took a scroll and dropped it on his table on his way out of the scriptorium.

The abbey was quiet, which was normal for 3 a.m. The monks wouldn't be up until 5:30, so there would be no one to tell him no as he crept down the hallway and opened the front door.

The frosty cold hit his face, clearing his head. It was just above freezing. The air was brisk but he didn't have to wear a coat, the vampire blood kept him warm enough, even in the freezing temperatures of Norway.

He closed the door and looked up. The usually bright dancing ribbons of light, the Aurora

Borealis looked dim. Maybe it was the small amount of light coming from the electric candles the abbot kept in the windows.

Sully walked around the outside of the building, searching for a way up to the roof, above the lights. He found the rain barrel on the northern side of the building. Scrambling up on it, he grabbed the downspout and began to pull himself up toward the slate roof.

Creak....

Snap!

The metal screws came loose and he was unceremoniously dumped on his ass on the ground, the robe he wore riding up over his hips so that his bare ass made contact with the snow. He stood up, shook the snow out of his robe and looked around for another way up.

"I guess I can go get the ladder out of the shed." He said to no one in particular.

"Or you could hitch a ride with your friendly, neighborhood angel."

Sullivan whirled around, he knew that voice. "Seth! What are you doing here?"

"Beware of angels bearing gifts, or rather angels bearing beer and food." The gray-winged angel held up an insulated bag, smiling. "Grab on, I'll take us up."

Sullivan linked his arm in his friend's and with what seemed to be an effortless flap-of-those giant grey wings, both men rose from the ground and onto the steeply pitched roof of the abbey.

"You gotta lay off the bread and beer, Sully, I swear you've put on weight since I was here last."

"Don't start, I have kept my angelic physique, that's about the only thing I have retained." He made a grab for the bag, but Sethiel pulled it away.

"Hey, we're sharing up here, okay? I stopped by the Brazen Head in Dublin, picked up Beef and Guinness stew and a couple of thermoses of Guinness, cold and just pinted. I figured you could use a break and we can catch up."

Sullivan laughed, "You, kind sir, are an angel and a gentleman! I've missed going to the 'Head and partaking of their great fare while singing bawdy songs."

"I'm not singing with you, vampire, you still can't carry a tune in a leaky bucket."

"Hey, hey, I'm not the one they asked to stop singing, that was you, son. I got asked to solo several times."

"Because the barkeep was smashed on his own mash. Otherwise you would have been out in the lane singing to the horses."

"Whatever. Break out that food and give me a thermos." Sully looked up at the sky, "Damned shame that the lights are so faint tonight, I wanted to sit here and just let them wash over me."

"Sunspots are non-existent right now, we're at that phase of sun flares. But I know I can still see them, what about you?"

"Yeah, just not too brightly. I sometimes go out on the glacier and just stand, watching the lights dance. The gentle undulating colors are hypnotic and calming and today I really needed it or I was going to lose my mind"

Sethiel passed a thermos to his friend, then a container of stew and a spoon. "What are you doing right now, still copying books?"

"Nah, His lordship, the Most High Muckety-Muck Archangel Mikhail has me going through the entire library archives looking for a couple of "vital scrolls." He made the air quotes. "I'm going blind trying to find them."

"Mikhail is looking for scrolls? That's what he's doing down here?"

"He's not here, if that's what you meant. I was told he came by briefly, it was daytime so I was asleep. Apparently it was all hush-hush because he came in disguise, dropped off something with Father Gudrun, and then left. Went back to heaven, I guess." Sully sipped the Guinness "Oh wow, I haven't had this in … forever. I forgot how much I love this stuff."

"Glad to bring it." Seth paused between bites of stew. "Oh, you haven't heard?"

"What?" Sully looked up from his bowl.

"Mikhail's not in Heaven."

"Where is he?" Sully asked, dropping the spoon into the bowl to look at his friend.

"Dunno. There was a big meeting in Mikhail's office with the archangels and their seconds about the missing angels. I don't know the details, but apparently things got pretty ugly. Kafziel, you remember him, Azrael's assistant?"

Sully rolled his eyes and nodded.

"Kafziel got up in Mikhail's face about how he was handling things."

Sully's mouth fell open in disbelief. Sethiel continued, "So, Mikhail said, 'Fine, if you can do better, have at it,' and dumped the whole thing on Kafziel and left Heaven entirely.

Sullivan closed his mouth, opening it again, "Whoa. It must have been really bad for Mikhail to leave Heaven in the hands of that pompous ass. Where would he go?"

"No idea." Sethiel took a big swig of the Guinness.

"Mikhail isn't that thin-skinned."

"No, there has to be some method to his madness. No one has a clue, no one that's talking anyway."

"What does the Archangel Synod say?"

"I'm not sure, they've been meeting for the better part of a week and they aren't allowing anyone into the conference auditorium where they are meeting. There's no word about what they think of all of this."

Sullivan took a large swig of the stout, "Missing angels? Like when we would go AWOL for a day or two?" Sullivan smiled, sipped his stout and remembered the good old days.

"Unfortunately not. This has them seriously concerned. So far, about 30 world-wide. Some are confirmed KIA and the others are listed as MIA. But we don't know."

"Essex got turned" He said solemnly. "Lilly had to turn him or he was going to die."

"Wait, Ess got turned, by Lilly, your maker Lilly?"

"Yes, she was trying to decide whether or not

to do it and I told her to do it, I didn't want him to die. Vampirism isn't fun but it's not bad either. Not nearly as bad as being boxed."

Sethiel stared at his friend, his mouth gaping, his brain obviously trying to make sense of it.

"Seth?"

He shook himself, "Wait. You...*told*...Lilly to turn Ess? How is that possible? She's in Houston, you're in Norway. Essexiel's dying in Houston? He probably joked that the humidity was a killer, you know Ess." Seth forced a laugh but looked unsettled. He was hoping that Sully would crack that infectious grin of his and reassure him that it was all a typical Sully-prank. He didn't, Sully just looked up with a sad, haunted gaze.

"I've discovered that vampires can talk to each other, telepathy. It works on ghouls too, I've been able to talk to Isobel, the ghoul assigned to help Lilly. I can't talk to anyone who blocks it or hasn't learned to 'open up' yet. But if you're the least bit receptive, or open, you can communicate with others in your lineage.

"You mean you can communicate with Marcus Lancaster?" he said, aghast.

"No He's so closed off and secretive, I don't think anyone knows his secrets. I can get through to Lilly, sometimes. She hasn't learned how to shut me out completely."

"Ok, go back. Lilly was trying to turn Essex and you told her to do it?"

Sullivan nodded his head and took another bite of stew. "Essex was on assignment to Lancaster Industries, a mission Mikhail had him doing. Evidently the bastard found out Essex had infiltrated and decided to have him turned. Lilly was crying and scared. She wavered between turning Ess and letting him die. I had to push her to get her to do it. Of course, Ess is raging and angry enough to beat her..."

"Sully! You could have left that part out..."

"No, I couldn't." He shook his head, "I had to learn to handle the overwhelming flood of emotions and I didn't do that well enough until I landed here, after hurting Lilly and killing someone. Essex will be feeling these same things, as will any other angel who is turned. Blood lust, rage, anger, depression, happiness, it all happens all at once and it's an uncontrolled explosion of emotion to an angel's system."

"It's obvious that angels don't handle intense emotions well." Sethiel said, "I guess it would be easier to see suicide as an option if an angel was used to having more dealings with humans. You're coping now, but it was touch and go there for a while. What about Essex? Do we know how he's handling being turned?"

"I don't know, he's shut me off or he's not learned to open to that sort of communication. You've heard of 'blind rage?'"

"Yea."

"Well, that's what it is, I don't think being around humans would make suicide easier or more of a choice. We've had to deal with more emotion when we're down here with people, some angels don't get that much live contact, they do their jobs and that's it. Even some Enforcers don't have that sort of contact, preferring to deal strictly with the paranormals and not humans." He got quiet to let Sethiel wrap his mind around that concept. "Our love of humans may have, in a way, saved us from greater harm in the face of having to become vampires."

"Interesting. I hadn't thought about that being an asset to us. So, do you have any ideas as to what to do about this situation, you're a vampire, does making angels into vampires make any sort of sense to you?"

Sullivan looked out over the landscape, the faint green glow of the Aurora lighting the glacier a pale gray. "Lancaster's making angels into vampires. Maybe revenge for our taking vampires to Hell? Trying to make an army to go against angels? But that one doesn't make sense, how would former angels go against their own kind without having to pretty much rewire their DNA to make them hate angels...?"

"Revenge I can see, an army...not so much. Is Lancaster working alone or is the Vampire Council doing it? So many questions and no answers."

Sullivan finished off the stew, dropping the spoon into the sack with the container. "Damn that was great. Thank-you for that one."

"You're welcome, I guess I could become your source for better food, show up here to talk more often. I also have another topic for you: have you had any trouble with Nida and Helmut?"

"Other than them marking me and Nida gloating about seeing me in Hell?"

"She's never been too friendly about vampires, true. But there's some scuttle-butt going around about her going rogue and doing things without Ranguel's assignment. Helmut isn't happy but he's not requesting a change in assignment either, yet. I wanted to talk to Mikhail about it but he's been gone. Ranguel is..."

"Tight lipped as usual, I bet. Yeah, Nida's been strange for a while now but I didn't think it was anything more than just doing the job."

"Yes." Sethiel finished off his Guinness. "Strange woman. She definitely has an overly inflated-estimation of her own importance. I guess I will try to talk to Helmut, see what he thinks..." his voice trailed off and he stared off into the green sky.

Sullivan knew that look, Sethiel was getting orders from H.H.A.D. Draining the last of his own Guinness, he put the lid on the thermos.

"I gotta go, Sully. Ranguel wants me back." He took the proffered thermos, "I'll bring more next week, any requests for food?"

"Believe it or not, I'm wanting haggis."

"You cannot be serious. I guess this means a trip up to The White Hart in Edinburgh for it, yes?"

"Oh yeah, and can you bring a really nice Dalmore Selene with it? I'll share if it's over 25 years."

"Really? You know what that costs, right? Why don't I just pick up the whole pub, dart board and all, and bring it to Norway for you."

Sullivan laughed loudly, then covered his

mouth, remembering he could wake up the monks even up on the roof. "You do that and I'll spring for dinner, but I want the whole pub, even the basement. That's where they keep the back stock." Sully flashed the electric grin he wore when they were out to have fun.

Sethiel missed that smile. "You are incorrigible. I'll see you next week then. I've missed our pub crawls. Stay safe until then." Sethiel popped his wings out, ruffled the feathers, then lifted off. "You need a ride down to the ground?"

"I'm good, I can get down easier than coming up. Thanks again. Stay safe, and out of the hands of the vampires."

He watched his friend until Sethiel disappeared behind the green Aurora and then slid down the roof, jumping to the ground and going back in to work again on the scrolls.

Chapter Twenty-One

A LONE ANGEL glided down from the portal and stopped before the massive golden doors. The angel guards standing on either side were in full red and bronze armor with flaming swords, their red wings partially furled. As she reached, opening the door, a deep bell sounded somewhere above her.

Every time she came here, she marveled at the structure. It was the largest, most ornate one in heaven, designed for the visitors to marvel at as they walked the very long gilded hallway to visit the owner: God.

Not that he was ever there. God had made the world, and the heaven, and then, after installing the angels and humans they took care of, left to make another galaxy, another population with more angels. Of course, the humans didn't know that God was gone, the only thing they would find would be a large cavernous room. Against the opposite wall, high on a plinth was an ornate throne and sitting on the red velvet cushion was a crown. Off to the side was an empty room with an ornate crown on the equally ornate throne and a large male angel with gold, red, and white wings sitting at a magnificent gold carved desk.

The walls behind him were covered with an immense bookcase lined with leather-bound tomes. A large ledger lay open on the desk but the angel wasn't looking at it. Instead, he was reading a book with a black leather cover and the words 'The Odessey' and 'Homer' emblazoned in gold.

Nida stood in front of the desk, waiting for the angel to put the book down and notice her. One just did not interrupt the great Archangel Metatron, even if he was ignoring the person standing in front of him.

Finally, with a sigh, Metatron folded the corner down on the open page, closed the book and laid it aside. He looked up at the waiting Enforcer angel.

"The dog dies." Nida quipped.

Metatron's eyes flashed with anger, something that anyone else would not catch but Nida had a long-standing relationship with him and knew his emotional tells.

"Indeed. Is that why you've come, to ruin my reading time?" Metatron's voice was deep with what could be described as a British accent, oddly familiar.

"No, we have a problem." The archangel raised an eyebrow, "Something odd happened today and I'm not quite sure why. I went to mark a vampire for making another vampire outside of the rules."

"That your job, Nida. For this you interrupted, and spoiled, my novel?"

"The transgressor, the victim, and the…" she

paused uncomfortably, "...incident."

Metatron leaned back in his chair and stee-pled his fingers, "I take it was not business as usual. Go on."

"No, it wasn't. The vampire turned another Enforcer angel... Essexiel." Metatron sat straight-er and leaned forward as Nida continued, "She is the one that turned Eistered."

"Interesting. So she's turning angels into vam-pires, for what reason?"

"She is the only one that we have identified thus far. However, there are other reports on mysterious disappearances. There other angels missing or dead, too many to just be coincidence or her doing it. But that is not the most disturb-ing part." She paused again to let him think about it, then continued, "When I attempted to mark her, something happened. The branding beam, rebounded and scorched me instead." She held up the hand to show the mark of the energy on her palm as proof.

Metatron looked away from the angel, his eyes fixing on a spot over her right shoulder and up. Once his eyes moved again, they were darker. "Indeed. That has never happened before, correct?"

"No. She is, for some reason, being protected by somebody quite powerful. I was told not to mark her for her first infractions. And this time, the marking rebounded. Who would protect a vampire?"

"Who indeed? Have you spoken about this with Ranguel or Mikhail?"

"No, I sought them out, however, they are in a department head meeting. I will seek an audience with both of them when they adjourn"

"Ranguel will be there, however Mikhail will not be, he has left Heaven."

"Indeed? What is he doing?" Nida had never heard of Mikhail leaving heaven.

"Unknown. He has left an underling in the role of Ruler of Heaven, he did not include me in his plans."

"But you should be in charge. You are the next most powerful archangel in heaven. The job should rightfully be yours."

"Kafziel is in charge," He stated stoically, a tiny smirk teased the corner of his mouth. "The Warriors refuse to take orders from the Soul Reaper. Therefore, state of upheaval exists in Heaven that has not been seen since the War."

"Kafziel is a hot-head. He has the backing of the rest of the archangels?"

"Not really, a few of them are with him but he is an arrogant, malcontent and hasn't the strength or wisdom to be chief. Once the chaos has calmed, I will step in and take the reins."

"Do you really want that high pressure, thankless job when you have this one? You are God's voice and essentially run everything but H.H.A.D."

"I would, because this job really has nothing going on, God is gone and the rest of Heaven runs itself. At least with control of H.H.A.D., I could make the Enforcers stronger and get them working harder to rid the Earth of the vampires and the other paranormals."

"It's true, ridding the world of the vampires could be stepped up considerably with more than just me to do the marking. I also have a possible problem with my Warrior, Helmut. He seems to be reluctant to fully participate with the duty of being my enforcement with the vampires. He was reluctant to assist in the marking of the young woman who turned the angels. Rather than assisting me in doing my job, and letting me take the initiative when something obviously had to be done, he insisted that we let Ranguel make the call.

"You have explained to him that it's your job and his is to be there to hold the vampire while you do your job?"

"Of course, but he's not particularly bright and he adheres to the strict letter of the law. And will book no deviation. I may have to change warriors if he continues this behavior. I am the final arbiter of who gets marked and taken to Hell, not Ranguel."

"Careful, Nida, do not let anyone else hear you say that." Metatron said with a small laugh, "You could threaten someone's carefully guarded job."

Nida laughed, "Not likely, Mikhail is committed to that fool, Ranguel, and his program of attempting to integrate the vampires into the human society to live together in peace. To vampires, humans are a food source, nothing more."

"Speaking of food, how is the ambrosia?"

"I wouldn't know, I've avoided drinking the stuff. Mikhail wants sheep and isn't beyond making us all drink it to keep us in line. I will not drink it unless forced. There are many who will only drink it occasionally. I find that interesting, especially among Ranguel's Enforcers, who tend to be a bit freer with their conduct while their boss is much more of a follower of the laws Mikhail lays down."

"So, Ranguel's angels are rebels, which is fitting. If what you tell me is truth, it appears as if he's lost some to this vampire. I wonder if the goal isn't to create an army of turned angels."

"An army? Why would she want an all-angel vampire army?"

"Unsure. I want to know more about this woman, who she is, what she did before she was a vampire and what is she planning now. I will get with others and see, but I want you to investigate her as well. I want to know all about her."

"I know she's Marcus Lancaster's progeny, her name is Lilly Marchantel. Hers is an odd case…"

"Besides turning angels into vampires?"

"Well, she was tuned recently, but, she was turned over a century ago. We are not sure how her signature remained undetected but it was in New Orleans."

"Well, since there is a tremendous amount of paranormal activity in that city, it isn't surprising.

"As another weird twist to things, she has a vampire cat."

"A bat?"

"No sir, a feline, a cat."

Metatron's eyebrow cocked, "How did that happen?"

"I'll find out." Nida nodded, she had wondered about that as well.

"She is of Marcus Lancaster's House Dracenfeur, they tend to be very ambitious, driven to rule both the vampires and the humans. If any group of vampires would stand out and make a play for the angels, it would be them. Find out more, three days a complete dossier. Also, let's find out what Mikhail is up to on his little sabbatical."

"Yes, sir. Is there anything else?"

"For now, leave the young vampire alone, do not go back to re-try the marking. Let them think we have been intimidated."

"But sir! That is out of the bounds of the rules, not to mention it slows down our plan to remove all vampires to Hell as soon as possible. I have been especially interested in taking down both Vlad Tepes, the Impaler, and his brother vampire, Marcus Lancaster. House Drachenfeur is the worst of the lot of the vampires, I took another member, Viktor, to Hell, I look forward to depositing the rest of the line there."

"I know, but patience Nida. You need to leave the entire situation alone, not just Lilly Marchantel, but also Lancaster and any of his line. No tuning. No marking until I find out what is going on." He gazed into the distance for a moment, then pulling the focus back, he spoke, "Anyone who is made by anyone in that line is off-limits for marking or even tuning until I figure this out. Something is brewing...disturbances, disappearances, and Mikhail's sudden departure." His brow furrowed, "If there is a vampire uprising in the works and it is serious enough to get Mikhail's attention, we can use it to our advantage. Patience, dear Nida, you may be very busy very soon"

Nida's breath was ragged, the last thing she wanted was to back off of the vampire line she believed was the most corrupt, and the one she was certain whose lineage led back to either Lillith or even Lucifer herself. "Yes sir, I will wait...for now."

"Leave me, then, I need to find out what happens to the dog." He picked up the book, muttering to himself, "You had better not ruined this for me." Metatron waved his hand in the direction of the doors in dismissal.

Nida turned, walking way, then turned back, smiling, "The dog does die."

The sound Metatron made sounded quite like a growl.

Smiling, she turned and walked out.

Chapter Twenty-Two

M IKHAIL WALKED DOWN the Atlantic City boardwalk. It was overcast and the cold wind blew off the Atlantic. This was not a popular activity for a February afternoon in New Jersey. Most of the shops were closed and shuttered for the season, however, occasionally there would be a man hurrying down the way, head bent and holding his coat tightly around him, heading to somewhere warm. It had snowed a few days before and remnants were laying in the shade, fighting to stay around one more day.

Who goes to Atlantic City for vacation in the middle of winter, anyway?

Archangels who are bored with life and just wanting to get away, that's who.

But damn, it was cold. Even though angels couldn't actually feel cold, the gray and the wind gave him the shivers.

Mikhail had walked the beach front boardwalk for what seemed like hours, watching the birds, looking at the buildings, thinking.

Wondering what was going on back in Heaven. Trying to decide what else he was going to do. His visits to Vlad to play chess had become so routine, Vlad asked him to go find somewhere else to be.

"Look, I love having you over for chess but I also like my solitude and you're encroaching on that. Go back to your job and let's get our regular schedule back."

"Can't go back yet, sorry I've been a pest. I'll go have fun elsewhere. See you next month." Mikhail remembered the discussion.

So, here he was, walking on a cold boardwalk, thinking, walking, thinking, trying to find something to do.

Walking a few more minutes, he decided that getting out of the wind might be a good idea. He saw a shabby storefront with the word "Arcade" on it. Even with no crowds, it appeared to be open.

He walked in and scanned the room. It was full of machines, beeping, whirling, flashing, binging, everything demanding attention all at once. He walked through, stopping to look at the screens, there were shooting games, things with stationary motorcycles attached, and a few older pinball games. Turning a corner, he saw a row of slot machines against a wall. He turned and walked further.

Then he saw it, a line of pink and blue machines with a long ramp and barrels sticking out of the top with 5, 10, 20, 50 in a line on the top part of the slope and a 100 in each of the top corners.

He grinned. There was his game, one he had

come to play with his boss the last time the deity came through the system.

Skee-ball.

He remembered seeing a bill changer near the slot machines. He put his hand into his pocket and felt something materialize. Pulling out a bill, hoping it would work, he fed it into the slot. Quarters came flowing out and Mikhail scooped them up. He walked back over to the ball machine and plugged a couple of the coins into it. With a series of dings, five balls rolled out of the housing and down where he could reach them.

Skee-ball. Mindless fun aiming balls up a ramp to get scores. He didn't have to think, didn't have to follow anything but the felt on the machine and the barrels. The electronic score added up as the machine spit out tickets for prizes he didn't care about. It was all about the balls, the movement, the aim, and the mindless fun of just doing something that the universe didn't care about.

Mindless diversion.

He removed his coat and threw it onto the idle machine next to him.

Mikhail rolled balls and shoved more quarters into the machine, he managed to quiet his mind, leaving the worries and concerns as the tickets began to curl up around his feet. When the machine indicated it ran out of tickets, he merely moved to the next one, slammed more quarters into the slot, and continued without hesitating.

Which is why he wasn't aware he wasn't alone.

"Skee-ball? In Atlantic City? Really?" the voice

came from behind him and to the right.

Mikhail launched the next ball and turned around. Behind him, in khaki's and a polo shirt, polished Gucci loafers stood Sethiel, leaning against the wall, ankles crossed and arms folded across his chest.

"You and the other Angelic Musketeers are not the only ones that are familiar with pop culture and I've seen Dogma too."

"You're needed back at H.H.A.D. We've been looking for…"

"No, I'm not needed. I need a break, some of those angels need a lesson in humility. I'm doing both things at once. I'm on vacation until…"

"Essex has been turned, Metatron wants to see you…"

Mikhail fought the urge to turn to face the angel, rolling a ball toward the holes with a little more force than necessary. "I'll deal with Essex's maker when I get back, Tron can just deal with whatever it is…"

Sethiel stood away from the wall, his hands curling into fists down by his sides, his eyes blazing, "From what I understand from Gudriel, Sullivan is pissed enough to start wanting to leave. Essex's maker was Lilly and Nida has made an attempt to mark her."

Mikhail stopped, the next ball in his hand, and looked at Sethiel, "What did you say? You went to talk to Fr. Gudrun?" he used the angel's disguised-as-human name, "Did you see Sullivan?"

"I went when Sullivan was down during the

day the first time. Gudriel is very concerned about the issues Sullivan is having, although Sully is working on finding and translating the scrolls you want him to. I went back again yesterday, we sat on the roof and talked. He's unhappy about not being allowed to leave to take care of Lilly.

"Then the archangels can handle what's going on with no problem, I can stay here and relax." Mikhail rolled the ball into the goal, hitting 100 again. He picked up a ball in each hand.

"Perhaps you didn't hear me the first time. Nida went to mark Lilly for turning Essex."

That got Mikhail's attention, he hadn't heard that before. Or maybe he just wasn't paying good enough attention. "Nida marked Lilly? On whose authority?"

Seth shook his head, "She tried. No one, as far as we can tell. She didn't have an assignment to see Lilly, looks like Nida decided to do it on her own. Maybe, since she hadn't been given the assignment, that's why something went wrong with the marking. Sparks flew and Nida got burned by the rebound. That has never happened before."

Mikhail closed his eyes. When he opened them again, there was no mistaking the feelings behind them. Mikhail was pissed. "Was Helmut with her? Who was the witness?"

"There was no witness. It was just the two of them. I only found out from Helmut, he is concerned about Nida and her rebellion. He wanted to quit working with her but Simkiel talked him into staying and being the eyes for you. He's not happy but he agreed. Helmut wants to make sure that he is not disciplined for Nida's failure to follow protocol."

"He won't be. Good for Simkiel. See, I'm fine on vacation."

Sethiel shook his head. "We have a Guardian who is working for Marcus Lancaster right now, she's keeping an eye on Lilly but she's assigned to her ghoul. There are rumors that there's a second angel in the building with her but no one has seen or knows anything about this one. It wasn't...isn't Essex."

"That's interesting. Still not enough to make me to come back to that sweat shop. I need my downtime; they need the life-lesson. The longer I'm gone, the better."

Sethiel frowned, "Sir, I don't understand why you left. That little squabble? You can squelch that in seconds. Wha..?"

Mikhail raised his hand, ball palmed, like a baseball pitcher, aiming to throw the ball through the machine. He could feel the hair on his neck start to raise, the heat in his body.

"*Yes,*" he thought, "*I'm pissed. That's not normal...*"

He put the ball down and turned toward his angel, "I need the archangels to step up, they need to handle this one. What's coming, I need them to act without having to ask me for every single thing. They must think on their own. Show some initiative. And I am," he looked Sethiel straight in the eye, "and this is not for public knowledge, I have your word?"

Sethiel nodded, "Ok...."

"We have at least one mole in the company. Someone's reporting all of our moves to Hell, and it's gotten back to me. I'm pretty sure I know who it is, but I need the archangels to police their ranks, find the active quisling and any other sleeper agents there may be, and then expose them. I can't be seen dealing with it due to some other things going on. The rebellion was too well-timed and that told me a bunch of things. One is who is adhering to rules and who isn't."

"How are you doing that? Who is not obeying orders and what ones are they ignoring?"

Mikhail looked around the room, which caused Sethiel to look as well. "No shadows, angelic or otherwise."

"I didn't see anyone either, what is going on," Sethiel tacked on, "Sir."

Mikhail would have laughed at the title at other times, this time was different. He was deadly serious. "I've been messing with the emotions up there for a long time, but some of you have decided to bypass the rules and that has caused problems with making things run smoothly. I've let it go on way too long, I guess, and now my problems have surfaced."

The look Sethiel gave him was nothing short of dawning alarm. "The ambrosia. You have been using the ambrosia to change our moods and emotions!" It wasn't a question, but rather an accusation.

"Yes, I have."

"Why? How did you come to the conclusion

that this is even okay to do?"

Mikhail looked away, then back, trying to still his own feelings. "Do you remember the War in Heaven? Back when Lucy took the archangels she has and went against me for the seat given to me by God?"

"You know I do, I was part of that army that supported you, fighting our own brothers and sisters." Sethiel's words were clipped.

"Well, after she was defeated and was safely on the other side of the portal, I had to make decisions. The emotions had run high, they were out of control especially during the war. I had to calm things down. To douse any 'hot spots' of emotion that still smoldered, it is my firm belief that not all malcontents went through the portal with Lucy. So, I had Rafael and the Healers make up a mood altering solution and we added it to the ambrosia." Mikhail chuckled, "Remember when the entirety of Heaven went to sleep at once and lost about two days? That was the ambrosia, it put everyone to sleep. Rafael, once he awakened, had to mess with the formula for a few days, testing it on other Healers, until it would just mellow everyone out instead of putting them to sleep."

Sethiel just stared at his boss, incredulous at what he was hearing. Mikhail waited, anticipating the explosion. But Sethiel just simmered, and then said, "And you think that was acceptable? All of us drugged into complacency?"

"At the time, yes. And you have to admit, it was what was needed. No more arguing, no more explosions of temper. Everyone worked, rested, and some of you even found a way to play." Mikhail shrugged.

"But you abused your authority, Mikhail. It was wrong to do that to us, especially without our knowledge! We should have been able to make up our own minds whether or not to take this stuff. How many know about this?"

"The lead archangels, department heads, and a few of the Healers. It was on a 'need to know' basis."

Sethiel took a step back, running his fingers through his dark hair, blue eyes flashing. "I can't believe you did this, or that the archangels went along with it."

"I felt I had no other way to handle it, I didn't need any further problems to have to deal with on top of Lucy and her rebels."

Seth blew up, "Mikhail, that's NOT the way to do it! Seriously, man, you don't know what this has done to some of us. We thought we were crazy at times." He took a breath and then his jaw dropped; he stared through the archangel, then blinked. "Oh shit. YOU are the reason Sullivan flipped out and killed. YOU did that, with your infernal tinkering."

"Don't put that on me, angel. You forget who you are talking to. I didn't do anything to cause Sullivan to kill, and that was his choice to do or not do." Mikhail yelled back.

Sethiel moved closer, invading the space of the angel, lowering his voice to the freezer level, "No? When he lost his angelic self, he was lost. We talked about it. He started feeling all the emotions on a high level. Sure, he wasn't drinking ambrosia like he should have, none of us have been. And we had been hitting the pubs on time off, so we knew emotions. But what happened when he was turned went way beyond, it was like he was stripped of all of the effects of the ambrosia..."

"Wait, what did you say?" Mikhail stopped him.

"We were drinking at the..."

"No, it was like he was stripped of all effects of the ambrosia?" Mikhail thought for a moment, "The vampire drained him of blood. Raphael said that the ambrosia worked through the blood system to the brain. If the blood was gone, then there were no effects except residual, and that has a half-life. Once that was gone..." Mikhail blanched as reality overwhelm him just as the emotions had overwhelmed Sullivan. "He had no buffer and the inability to cope..."

"He had never experienced the intensity of emotions, he never felt their raw strength, he never learned how to deal with them, to cope and control them."

The senior archangel laid the ball down and turned, almost falling to the edge of the ramp as he endeavored to sit. He missed and sat on the floor, head in hands.

"Oh my! Dear God forgive me. You are right."

Chapter Twenty-Three

T HE SUN SLIPPED down into night, Isobel stepped out of the elevator into Marcus's penthouse. She had been patient, working with Gregory to rearrange her home. They managed to get everything into the anterior room off her bedroom but she was still annoyed about how cavalier Marcus seemed to be with her things and her life. It wasn't the first time he had made a decision and let her know once she was in the middle of it. It was like the old saying, "It is easier to say I'm sorry than to ask permission." Marcus was just an inconsiderate ass.

"Marcus?" She called out as she crossed the living room. Her boss's bedroom door was closed and even the wall of monitors was dark.

She heard bumping and a giggle come from the room behind the door. It appeared that Marcus and Jesse were back on sleeping privileges again. "Just a minute, Isobel."

"Take your time, I'll wait." She didn't want to wait, she was ready to tear into him and the longer she waited, the more she simmered.

But she was spared the raise in blood pressure when her boss walked out of the room buckling his belt, shirtless. He smiled vacantly in her direction as he ran his fingers through his unruly hair.

"You're early. What's up? Anything new?" It was then that he caught a glance at her face and stopped. "What?"

"What the hell are you doing? Have you gone insane?" Both hands on her hips, her face a snarl, without makeup and dressed down in sweats, Marcus took inventory of the woman in front of him before he answered.

"Lilly's in danger of losing the baby. The doctor put her on 24/7 bed rest. I moved Nurse King in, to tend to her."

"She's in danger because you put her there!" She felt like screaming it but kept her voice hard but controlled.

"Is that what she said? You know better than that. It appears that our dear, sweet, innocent Lilly's not so innocent after all. What I thought was a simple case of employee theft turned out to be something much more complicated. She came down of her own volition and tried to intercede on the thief's behalf, tried to convince me that the baby was his. And, to top it off, he's a fucking angel! Here to steal from me and she knew it! I didn't engineer it." He snarled back at her.

Isobel just stared at him, letting what he said sink in. It wasn't too far off what Lilly said but he wasn't telling her everything, and she knew it. "You didn't engineer it? You're completely innocent?" she said skeptically. "You broke her cat's neck. Been thoroughly churlish and berated her since she told you she was pregnant. You've been fixated on getting the angels turned, and I am supposed to believe you didn't manipulate the whole scenario in that room," she paused to take a breath then raised her voice, "You locked her in with a dying man. You made her decide whether to save him or let him die. You knew she could not let him die, it's the way she is. How diabolically cruel, Marcus. How could you even conceive of such a plan? You forced her into an intolerable situation. For her, it was a no-win. She either turned her friend or let him die. For you," she emphasized, "you couldn't lose...he either died and solved your problem or he was turned. You coerced her into it so you would not be marked. It is unconscionable. You Marcus Bleddwyn Lancaster are a coward. You victimized Lilly and the angel."

"Now wait just a fucking minute..." Marcus started.

"No, you wait. This was wrong Marcus. You were wrong. And that girl is suffering the consequences of your narcissistic bullshit."

"Isobel Kincade, you are on fucking thin ice. You better dial your ass back before you find yourself out on the street without a job. You are still an employee of Lancaster Industries and you serve at my pleasure, nothing else."

"You're threatening me? You really want to go there? Be sure before you answer. I know where ALL the bodies are buried. You know it. And you know that I can sink your ass fast. The government would frown on some of your less visible business practices. The Vampire Council, who would love to hear all the things you've done. And let's not forget Nelson Mishkoph, who wants to bring you down. And that's just scratching the surface...this week! Pick your poison, Marcus. I can do it."

Marcus turned bright red, his eyes taking on a dark blue sheen. "You wouldn't dare."

She smiled, shaking her head slowly. "Marcus, we've known each other for a long time. What do you think? I am not a foolish person. You have always complimented me on my ability to cover your ass. Well, believe me I am more than capable of covering my own! Provisions have been made. If I mysteriously disappear or meet with an unfortunate accident, like so many of your inconveniences have in the past, certain entities will be receiving some very enlightening information.

Marcus' eyes flashed. "Are you threatening me?"

"Oh Heaven's No! Just keeping you informed."

Isobel stepped forward, crossing into his space, "Now, you will back the fuck off of Lilly. She's fragile, she's on forced bed rest; this is to protect her health as well as the baby's. Stress does effect pregnant women, I'm quite sure Dr. Young went over that with you in detail."

"She's fine, the doctor said so."

"No! She's NOT!" she bellowed in frustration. "You are so fucking obtuse that you only hear what you want to hear. Because of what you did, the stress YOU caused, she went into labor early...too early! If the doctor had not been able to stop the contractions, she would have lost the baby...YOUR BABY, Marcus." She took a calming breath and lowered her voice. "Marcus, you need to let her be, stop doing things to her, to Baron. Let me handle her, let Gregory handle her. Keep your business, all of your business, out of her hearing."

"She butted in first." He replied like a pathetic chastened child, then regaining his icy veneer, he snapped, "She interfered in a situation that was none of her concern. That angel was a spy and had been stealing Lancaster Industries intellectual property. I have every right to defend my company. I don't know how she found out. Nor, why she felt it necessary to intercede. But I'll leave her to you to handle, keep her out of my way. I don't want to deal with her until that baby gets here. At which time, I will take possession and raise him..."

"No, you stop right there. That baby is not your 'acquisition'...not a piece of property. He, or she, will need his mother. You will have to let her raise the baby. She needs to give the baby the nurturing, care, and love, he or she needs to flourish, something you are incapable of. You're way too busy with your company, your wars and your new battle with the angels. You have to stop your shit, check your ass, and then make nice with the woman you got pregnant and work with her to raise your baby." Isobel crossed to the couch and sat down, "You have to do this,

Marcus."

"Why do I have to be the one to step back? Why am I the one who has to give, while she's the one to take, take, take..."

Isobel stood up and stepped toward him again, "You are not in competition with her! Slow down. Sit down and listen. You are a very smart, successful, and ruthless, business man. A high roller in high society. You are suave, sophisticated, and very much a James Bond." She pushed to reach his vanity, the soft side of him. "But in this, my friend, you are way out of your depth. Yes, you are incredibly generous and have given Lilly a glamourous life. But, Marcus, you give people what you want to give, not necessarily what they need."

She took a deep breath as she let the compliments sink in, "What Lilly needs is kindness, gentleness, and above all, patience. She has an awful lot to catch up with. Give her a chance. Or you are going to lose her and the baby both. Bending is not breaking, Marcus. You must bend."

Marcus's continued stare was uncomfortably cold. "Right now, you handle her. I'm not going to bother with her. But you need to listen to me, I'm not going to allow you to dictate to me like this. You are on dangerous ground, woman, and I'm not going to take it again."

"Okay, deal." She backed up and sat down again.

"We have a deal, why are you sitting down, this is finished." Marcus said.

"There's something else we need to discuss, please sit down." Isobel pointed to Marcus's favorite chair.

Tired of arguing with her, and hoping Jesse was still in the shower and didn't hear the prior argument, he sat down.

"Where's Essex?" Isobel asked.

"He's in custody. I will handle him."

Isobel shook her head, "I need to talk with him. See him. Lilly is worried about him. She has asked me to check on him."

"No. Tell her whatever you need to but she's never seeing him again, ever."

Isobel surprised herself by laughing, "Jealous, much? Really, Marcus, I'm not asking for her to see him. She wanted me to check on him. You owe her that after what you did. Where is he?"

"One time, you can see him once. He's on 8, in special confinement. You can talk to him but no contact of any kind."

"Thank you." She stood up. "Remember, you promised to leave Lilly alone. Let her have this baby and then we'll see what we have to do from there."

"For now." Marcus turned when he heard the door open. Jesse was standing in a towel, his hair dripping from the shower. "Go on, get out. We will talk later."

Isobel turned and walked into the elevator, the doors closing behind her.

Chapter Twenty-Four

ISOBEL ENTERED THE elevator, turned, jabbing the 8 button angrily, and watched the elevator doors slide closed on her boss. How the hell could she not see how much of an ass he was before Lilly came? She had been star-struck by the multi-millionaire who was jet-setting around the globe, running an international corporation, and who was a beast in bed.

That he was a vampire, a real one, and was a total asshole some of the time hadn't slowed her pursuit of him. Or his of her. She fell for him, hard, and had, in the last 30 years, worked hand in hand with him, had also been his ghoul and sometimes lover. The fact that Marcus took her blood during sex wasn't a problem, it was fun. And the fact he was bi-sexual and in love with his other ghoul, Jesse, wasn't a problem either. None of those pesky romantic notions clouded the relationship. And for that, she was immensely grateful.

Problem was, he was also a narcissist, like she had called him, and literally everything he did and said was filtered through his need to be the center of the universe, some of the time......strike that....most of the time.

Once Lilly had the baby, she and Isobel, with Gregory, would move out of Lancaster Industries big glass tower and into a nice house somewhere. Marcus could do his own social calendar arraigning, his own interface with his workers, and his own organization of his life. Or Jorge could do it. Or Jesse, that would give him contact with Marcus without a buffer like her standing in the gap to keep them from killing each other at times.

Once Lilly had the baby, just a few weeks.

They needed to plan......

The elevator doors opened to the eighth floor. Isobel hadn't gone down to this floor in months; it was usually mostly deserted, holding offices for visitors or storage. Now she was confronted by a giant steel wall fitted with heavy metal doors and silver doorknobs.

Silver. To keep vampires out....or in?

She hit the access panel with her key card and punched in her code. The little LED light mocked her, flashing red, denying entry. She tried it again, just in case she had missed the code.

No dice. She wasn't allowed in. She snarled as she hit the intercom.

A nice, male voice came out of the speaker, "Yes?"

"Isobel Kincaid. I'm here with Marcus's agreement, I need to visit one of the...." She hesitated, what did you call a prisoner other than just that? "People you are holding inside the room."

"One moment please."

She rolled her eyes. Used to be, her name was enough to unlock any door in the building. Yes, Lancaster Industries was a multi-national American military, security company, and consulting firm with more security than anything outside of the most secure government agency, but she was the executive personal assistant to the owner and held every security clearance the company recognized.

But not enough to open a steel door on the 8th floor. Wow, had the place, and the job description, changed.

"Yes, Ms. Kincaid, you are cleared. I will buzz you through."

She replied, "Thank-you" even though she was thinking, "Damned skippy you will."

Pulling the door when the buzzer sounded, she stepped in.

The big room was empty except for what looked to be a second-hand, military issue green metal desk, a short chair, and a man she recognized as Doyle Parker, who stood when she entered.

"Hi Doyle. I guess Marcus gave you permission to let me in to see one of the people, right?"

"Yes, ma'am. You are to visit Essex. I can show you to the holding cell." He turned and walked toward a door in the wall to the left.

When he opened it, Izzy noticed that this door also had a silver knob. Isobel wondered what Marcus was going to do if he had to open one of these doors. He was going to have to depend on someone human to open the door, or find some rubber gloves, or something. She rolled her eyes.

The hallway was lined, on both sides, with doors, spaced about four feet apart. Cells, without windows. She wondered if they were occupied, and if so, by whom.

"Doyle, before I see Essex, would you give me a tour of the floor, I need to see what we're doing so I can help Mr. Lancaster with planning and development."

The guard stopped, "I was only told of access to Essex, nothing more. Orders from Mr. Castro. You would have to ask him…"

"I'm on the same administration level as Mr. Castro, I have worked for Mr. Lancaster for many years, even more than Castro has."

Doyle Parker knew the directive he was given, no one comes and no one goes without specific authorization from Castro or Mr. Lancaster himself, but he had also worked with Lancaster Industries long enough to know that Isobel Kincade was exactly who she said she was, the boss's right-hand. And if he bothered either man with a question about her getting to go anywhere, he would probably be written up for either bothering them needlessly, or worse. A sick queasy feeling clenched his stomach, it could be the burrito he had for lunch, but he didn't think so.

"Okay, let's take a quick tour." He turned and walked back to the reception room. As they walked, he showed her where the different rooms were to house their "new vampire guests." He also pointed out the small kitchen and laundry area with a large shelving unit holding what appeared to be large stacks of sweats.

As they walked back out of the vampire area, Isobel asked, "How are these doors secured?"

"Each door is numbered and has an electronic lock controlled from behind my desk. There is a lock delay on them."

Isobel looked at him expectantly, obviously waiting for a more detailed explanation of the security system. Was this a test, he wondered? After all, she was Mr. Lancaster's right hand and for him to send her to check security was a distinct possibility. He continued nervously and more factually. "When the unlocking procedure is implemented, by pushing the numbered button behind the desk, I only have a limited time to open the chosen door; otherwise it times out and relocks. I click the lock and I have a short time to get to the door and open it; the further away, the longer the delay. Also, the doors cannot be opened from the inside."

"If the electricity goes out, what sort of safe guards are in place?" She knew that there were locks in the building that would unlock with the absence of electricity.

"They stay locked. In that case, I have a key that is a master for all doors.

"Oh?" Isobel looked at the ring of keys on his belt and he noticed her.

"Not on me." He jingled the ring, "For safety reasons, the master key is kept in the top left drawer of the desk."

Isobel knew that might come in handy if she

needed to get Essex out without Marcus's permission. She figured the security would know if a door was unlocked with the buttons.

They came to one big double door, Isobel could feel the temperature drop and there was a steady hum from behind the door.

"What's in there?"

"I don't know. We're not allowed to go in there. I don't even patrol back here."

Izzy reached out to the knob.

"No ma'am, we're not allowed to…"

She pulled the door open in the middle of his protest. The first thing she noticed was the suction trying to pull the door closed, then a blast of very cold air hit her. She stepped forward, shivering. What she saw made her stop her progress into the room.

Bodies. Men and women, stacked on silver metal shelves. There were no coverings, nothing to give them dignity in … death. Every one of them was gray with the duskiness of death. And each had multiple fang marks on the neck, arms, and some had thigh wounds.

Isobel stifled a gasp.

The room had a strong antiseptic smell, but with the cold, there was not much decomposition. Every shelf that held a body had to be sub-zero in temperature. Isobel looked at each body, each face. Some had eyes closed, most were open, staring into her face vacantly. Walking from one to another, she could see that each used to be beautiful and young. Some had contorted faces that could indicate poisoning; others seemed to sleep-soon to awaken.

In a corner lay a pile of what looked like leaves, gray, red, blue, green.

Blue?

Isobel walked closer.

They weren't leaves, they were feathers.

On further examination, they had connecting tissue and Isobel took a step back.

They were wings.

The people on those shelves were dead...angels.

She looked around quickly, trying to find the guard who brought her to the room. He was standing rock still in the hallway at the door, his eyes wide as saucers, shock registering.

"Did you know what....?" She asked as she walked quickly out of the room, pushing him out of the way and shutting the door behind her.

He didn't answer; he kept looking at the door, not moving.

"Doyle? Did you know what was in this room?" She shook his arm.

Slowly he shook his head, his breathing shallow, the blood draining from his face.

"Doyle, sit down before you fall down." She pulled his hand down as she knelt. He followed, allowing her to pull him down, putting his back against the wall of the hall. He sat, staring at the door, breathing shallowly.

Then he turned away from her, coming up on his knees, and proceeded to vomit.

It was all she could do to keep from tossing her stomach as well. She patted him on the back as he retched, then helped him move away, pulling his shirt out of his uniform pants and handing him the hem so he could wipe his mouth. She pulled him up to his feet and guided him back to the lobby of the floor, shutting the hallway door as they passed.

"Sit down here and try to get a grip, Doyle. I'll grab you some water." She helped him to the chair behind the desk and then went to the small room where the refrigerator was, found a couple of bottles of water, and returned, pulling the cap off the bottle and handing it to him.

He drained the bottle in one gulp and began to shake. "What the hell?" He looked into her eyes, searching for answers.

"They are trying to turn angels into vampires. My guess is that those were the ones who failed to turn, or ..." She hated to even think of the possibility of angels committing suicide.

"I must check Mr. Essex. Doyle, can you sit here without me for a few minutes? Are you going to be okay?"

He nodded. "I will be. Do you need me to...?" He stopped, then looked around for the trash can, finding it just in time to lose the water he just drank.

Isobel walked away, not wanting to watch that again. She went down the hallway she had been down first and finally found the room the guard had indicated was Essex's and opened it.

She wasn't ready for this sight either.

The room was totally bare, gray. There were eye-bolts in the floor, on the walls. It was cold but not like the morgue room.

There was a man, naked, spread eagle on the floor, face down. Chains ran from his wrists and ankles to the eye bolts. Under the chains that bound him, the skin was broken, bloody and oozing.

Silver.

In front of him, just out of reach, was a silver bowl filled with what appeared to be congealed blood.

He was being tortured. Hungry, bound with silver that burned, stretched out on a cold floor, naked.

Why?

He looked up, anger blazing in his brown eyes. He bared his fangs, growling at the newcomer.

"Essex?" She hesitated. "Are you Essex?"

"Go away, bitch. Tell that bastard you work for to let me go and face me like a man."

"I'm Isobel. I'm a friend of Lilly's…"

"I know who and what you are, and you work for that fucking bastard, Lancaster. Get out if you're not going to take him my message. I don't need your pity, or Lilly's."

"She sent me, she's worried." Isobel didn't want to stay; she was sickened by what she saw before her.

"Well, tell her I'm fine, I expect the dancing girls and the booze to be delivered anytime now. And then tell her "fuck you" She did this. This is her fault. She should have let me die…like I wanted."

Isobel turned to leave.

"Wait." His anger and bravo spent, he collapsed into the defeated plea. This may be his only chance, his only choice.

She turned back.

"Please, I know you work for Lancaster, but you said you are Lilly's friend. If you are her friend, you have to help me. Please. Lilly must get a message to Sullivan. Have him tell Mikhail what is going on here. What Marcus Lancaster is doing is evil. Please, that's my dying wish. I won't be here, if I get half a chance, I'll be dead..."

"What? Why?"

"I will not live as a vampire. I used to punish them; I took them to Hell. All vampires end up going to Hell eventually, so why waste time? I'll just go on and get settled in. My eternal damnation awaits." He laid his forehead on the floor.

Isobel's heart broke for him. He seemed so forlorn about the prospects of being a vampire. She found herself walking back toward him, the need to comfort him almost overwhelming.

As she got close, she frowned at the bowl of blood. She kicked it across the room in anger, the silver making considerable racket as it clattered across the floor, the coagulated blood spilling. She was surprised at the anger she felt.

Essex pulled his head up, having to turn his head sideway to look up at her due to her proximity. "That was supposed to be my dinner...."

"You're hungry?"

He laid his head down, away from her. "No, not really. Just leave. I want to die in peace."

She stepped over his arm and sat down beside him, to his right. Her warmth was radiating against his skin as she laid over him enough to place her right arm, palm up, next to his head.

"Go on, take from me. You need to feed."

Essex could hear her heartbeat from her proximity. He could smell her, a mixture of coppery blood and a perfume and he wondered what perfume she liked. He felt his fangs drop and he knew there was no way he was winning this battle with her.

He struck, listening to her breathing as he drank the warm, sweet blood she offered.

Isobel ran her left hand through the dark curls on his head, "That's it, go ahead and feed. Once you're done, we'll talk and hopefully you will see that you are more than just a monster. You are Sullivan's friend, you are Lilly's friend. Neither of them strike me as someone who would make good friends with evil. And I know more vampires than most anyone does and most of them are decent people who just have to have blood occasionally. They live, they dream, they laugh, just like the humans they used to be. You may have been an angel but before that, you were human. You're still the same as you were before. It's okay."

Essex pulled back and licked the wounds closed. "You're wrong. I was never human. I was created as an angel when the universe was born. Yes, I dress like a human, Sullivan and Seth and I used to pub crawl all over the British Isles between assignments. We used to wish we could have been human. Now heaven is lost to me and eventually Earth will be as well. Thanks to Marcus Lancaster and Lilly, I'm going to be going to Hell, no matter what else I ever do."

"Why were you here in the first place? Marcus said something about you stealing from him."

"I am, I was on assignment, to find out what Lancaster is up to. I'm not sure what they were looking for, but the assignment was to come in, find out his business dealings, and anything else he might be up to. Thing is, I got caught taking out his business information. That's why he wanted to kill me. Lilly identified me as an angel and that made Marcus decide to turn me instead of outright kill me. But he made Lilly do it, the chicken-shit."

"She's very worried about you. She didn't want to turn you. Angels showed up to mark her but it didn't work...?" Her words trailed off.

"Yeah, Nida and Helmut came to do my tuning and to mark Lilly. But the marking didn't work for some reason." He thought back over the visit, "They didn't bring another Enforcer to do it. Helmut wasn't acting right either, come to think of it."

"So what happened was not normal?"

"No, it was very far from normal, and I wonder why. I need to get out of here and I need to get to Sethiel to tell him what happened."

"I can't get you out yet, but I can work on it. I will do what I can. But if you convince Marcus that you have come over to his side, we will be able to get you out sooner. Hold on and don't do anything fatal."

"I'm not sure I can make that promise. I don't want to be a vampire."

"Then you may not be able to blow the whistle about what's going on and maybe another angel could be in danger. You need to hang on and help stop Marcus from harming more angels. You do have a purpose here."

"I'll take it under advisement. No promises."

"Just think about it, okay?"

She had been rubbing his back, and it felt good. She got up "I'll be back later to check on you and feed you again. Try to rest and I'll talk to Marcus."

She walked out the door and quietly closed it behind her.

He noted that he already missed her hands on his skin. Maybe she was right. He might be able to do what Sullivan was doing and make a life. Even though he wasn't one of them anymore, he still had to help the angels.

But he would have to kill Marcus Lancaster to do it.

Chapter Twenty-Five

H E WALKED THROUGH the park in his pajamas, the whole area just a bit off color. He could see his old house on the hill, the one he left the night he found his wife dead, never to return.

But the house wasn't anywhere near this park.

Confused.

He turned back and faced the pond, the one that, during the day, was full of little toy boats driven by old men and their grandsons. Right now, there were no boats, no people.

A balloon, red as blood, floated just a few feet above the water, then touched down in the middle and began to grow.

As it stretched, larger and larger, he saw a shape inside, at first dark, then growing more and more light.

A woman.

In the balloon.

Which burst, leaving the woman standing on the top of the water, clothed in a blood red silk dress, slit from the bottom at her stiletto heels to the hip. She had sleek, waist-length black hair, with blood red highlights, green eyes that shone in the moonlight and luscious pouty lips, the color matched her gown. He could make out the curves of her breasts in the low, cut bodice, her nipples hard.

Slowly, seductively, her hips swayed as she walked on the water.

Toward him.

His mouth began to salivate as his cock sprung to life, tenting his pajama bottoms.

Oh God, he was standing in old blue pajamas in a park, barefoot, his toupee still back in his new home on the wig stand, his bottom denture plate in a glass beside the bed soaking.

And he had a fucking erection.

With the most drop-dead gorgeous woman he had ever seen, her hips swayed seductively as she glided over the water toward him.

He wished he was dressed, but that wasn't going to happen.

"So, Nelson, you're happy to see me, I see."

She knew his name.

And she noticed the erection.

He blushed.

She smiled, her tongue teasing her bottom lip. "We can discuss pleasure later, right now we need to talk business."

Why? He didn't want to talk, he wanted to grab her, push that dress up over her hips and bury his face in the sweet spot where her legs met.

"Not yet. You wanted to talk about revenge for Lauren. I'm here to make that bargain."

She purred, like a big cat, contently as she traced her hand along the top of his shoulder and trailed her incredibly long red-tipped nails down his arm. The movement caused shivers all the way down to his bare feet and caused his erection to strain even harder against his pajamas.

Keep that up and the happy ending was going to go off in his pants and not in her.

"You realize, you get revenge and that kills your chances to go to heaven to be with her when you die, right?"

Lauren was in heaven? With all the lies and schemes she pulled on him for over the past 20 years?

There was no justice.

"Now, now, she's not there...yet. There's some negotiations going on, I'm involved with those. What you decide tonight will make the decision."

He tried to find his voice. His throat was full of cotton, like he got when he was asleep and snoring. Lauren hated his snoring, that had been her excuse to move into the separate bedroom many years ago.

That's when the sex stopped. She still wanted all the jewelry, the fine things, but she was no longer putting out for it."

"And you want revenge for that woman after the way she treated you? You're a sucker, you know that, right? No self-esteem at all if you are pining for her after that." She made a clucking sound with her tongue.

The tongue that should be running around his balls and up his cock.

He moaned, feeling the balls get tighter.

The woman reached out for the tent in his pants. He felt her fingertips tickle across his penis then her hand slid down to cradle his balls.

His moan of ecstasy turned into a scream of anguish.

She grabbed, squeezing his family jewels. All he could do was scream.

Mr. Happy turned back into a limp noodle and sought refuge in the center of his abdomen, far away from the evil bitch.

She laughed and dropped her hand.

"There! That's so much better. Now you can pay fucking attention to what I'm saying. I was saying that you need to get revenge. I need something done. We're going to work together. If we cannot reach an equitable agreement, you will be spending a lot of quality time with dear Lauren in the afterlife." She chuckled throatily. "You just thought life with her was Hell on Earth...you have no idea." She laughed again, then she got serious, "However, if we can work together, I will guarantee you a very happy hereafter with no Lauren, and just for shits and giggles, no in-laws either. Indeed, a very..." she paused for effect, "Happy eternal life, or, well, death, but you know what I mean."

She smiled, and his skin crawled.

She continued, "What you are going to do is attack the guy who killed Lauren. Well, he didn't actually do the dirty deed himself, he wouldn't get his hands dirty with such menial tasks, but he did order it done. I want him dead, and I want him dead sooner than later."

He nodded. He knew exactly who she was talking about. His balls still throbbed but he was attentive to every word.

Marcus. "Marcus Lancaster" he managed to wheeze out. Without his denture, it came out as Marcuth Lancathter but that was close enough.

"Yes, Marcus Lancaster. I have issues with the fucking bastard and since you do too. Our alliance will be quite beneficial for us both. He is a formidable adversary and thus far you have been quite lacking in your ability to perform successfully..." She paused, looking down to see if she still had his undivided attention. "...in your attempts to best him, defeat him, or provoke him to some reckless action."

Nelson nodded in resentful agreement. His hatred of that arrogant bastard was growing even more.

"So, I will provide you with information that will enable you to utterly humiliate and completely destroy him, obliterate him and all he holds dear.

Nelson smiled blissfully at the thought. "That would be marvelous. But I would make one request."

"Oh?" She purred.

"I want it to be a very public humiliation followed by a long, lingering, and very painful end." He paused, "And, I would love to watch every exquisite moment of his degradation and anguish."

Lillith chuckled, "I do like the way you think.

Now, do you need this written down or can you remember it when you wake up?"

He thought for a moment, "I can do it."

"Good. Here's what you are going to do. You've been watching his building in Houston. You will need five 50-gallon barrels, metal is preferable, but plastic will do. Fill each barrel with a slurry of fertilizer and fuel oil. Load them into a box truck, 18-feet should suffice. Use a forklift because a mere mortal will not be able to lift them."

She ran her finger over his bald head as she said the 'mere mortal' part, like she was showing him his weakness.

"Once the barrels are all loaded and secure, rig fuses and blasting caps to them. One of those cute little phones that you carry around will make an excellent detonator; they call them "burner phones?"

Nelson nodded.

"How very apropos!" Now, I know you don't like to get your hands dirty and this is a smelly job. So get your most loyal people to put it together. And, in this case, more is not better so five barrels, no more. We don't want to take out the whole city block."

"But why are you wanting to…" He struggled to say, his mouth still dry as a desert.

"My reasons are my own. Your reason is Lauren, the love of your life. That's what you have told everyone since the night Lancaster slaughtered her and your guards. Everyone knows how grief stricken you are. They have no idea that your lawyer was holding onto the divorce papers you were going to file two weeks ago."

He stared at her, how the hell did she know about that?

She burst into a grand roar of laughter. "Oh Nelson! You are so funny!" Pausing to look directly into his eyes...into his soul, "Hell? I am from Hell. You probably didn't recognize me, since you're not a vampire. My apologies for being so remiss in not properly introducing myself. I'm not just a fantasy that your lascivious little brain cooked up. I am real and I am Lillith, ruler of the vampire side of Hell."

"Vampires? Hell. Yeah, now I know I'm dreaming. Go away, you're a result of the Duck ala Orange I had tonight." He turned and closed his eyes, hoping that when he opened them again, he would be back in his bed.

A powerful hand came down hard on his shoulder and spun him back around.

"I decide when we're finished, or you get to stay in a very small room in Hell for eternity with that lovely bitch who put you through your paces while she banged every guy in your company."

His eyes widened. He figured she was fucking Carlos and Ricky, but not anyone else.

"Oh, she was a big slut. They are skimming from your company too. That missing money wasn't from bad deals or accounting errors, there's a very nice little nest egg in an off-shore bank with the name Lauren Davis on it."

He saw red. And it wasn't the dress.

"So, you see, you have reasons to do what I need. The biggest reason, other than your escape from her in the afterlife? She was fucking Marcus Lancaster when he would come to Florida. Every...Single...Time. He would come by, they would end up in bed, he would screw her, drink her blood, and then he would put her to sleep. There were many times when you came home, crawled into bed with her and took sloppy seconds, he had gone out the back when you came in the front and you never, ever knew it. He was laughing at you the entire time. He fucked you in business and he fucked your wife. What's next? Are you going to bend over and let him fuck you in the ass?"

If he wasn't convinced to kill the bastard and all he loved before, hearing that set his gums on his teeth, and it gave him the hard-on to do the deed.

"Ah, good, you finally understand. You'll kill him for that."

"But what are you getting out of it if I do thith?" He finally managed to ask a complete question without sounding like a complete idiot.

"I get to rule earth instead of sit in Lucifer's place in Hell. Lucifer wants to rule Heaven and would keep me in Hell."

"Lancather's death would let her do that?" He didn't understand. Was she talking figuratively or was she really the Lillith from Hell.

"Do I feel figurative?" She took his hand and put it down on her breast. He gave it a couple of squeezes before she slapped his hand and he moved it.

"When you blow up Lancaster's building, you

need to set up a car to blow up the parking garage as well. A car bomb parked the next level below his collection will do quite nicely. I want those toys of Lancaster's destroyed as well. Nothing left of any of it. Understand?" She sniggered, "A little boy with his little toys."

He nodded his head. Of course he could do it. Easily.

"Oh, and it has to be done Friday night, he's not there this Saturday, he has a human charity thing to do. You want to catch him in the building. Make sure the garage goes up first, so that the people will think that's the attack and the big one catches them moving. Think you have all this?"

"I have a quethtion. How do you know where he is going to be thith week?"

She laughed. "You don't think that I have my ways? Specifically, you have no idea how many people sell their soul to Hell to do things they want to do. I have people everywhere, and I do mean *every where*. And we know when his little soirée is. Trust me."

He nodded again, giving her a little, closed lip smile. "You will know when it-ith done?"

She patted his cheek, "Yes, and I'll keep my end of the bargain once you kick the bucket and end up with us."

"Do you call Lancathter a vampire because he thucks the life out of hith competition?"

She giggled. "You keep on thinking that, but the reality is, and you won't remember that when you awake, he is a real, fang-banging, blood sucking, undead vampire. The bastard really does suck." She took two steps back into the lake. "Wake up and remember to blow the garage first. Do it on Friday night."

She disappeared with a splash, covering him and his blue pajamas with wetness.

He jerked and rolled, landing with a thud on the hard wooden floor of his bedroom, soaking wet from sweat. Who scared him so much he didn't remember her face or name.

But he now had an idea what to do about Lancaster, he had to get busy getting things purchased and assembled in Houston. He looked at his watch. It was 4:45 a.m. on Monday morning. He needed to have it ready to go by Friday night, when Lancaster would be at his building.

Getting up from the floor, he reached down to adjust his pajama pants. His balls were sore. The dream, she grabbed his...balls.

Did he dream that? What did he do to himself in the dream? Was she real?

He got that creepy feeling and felt the hair stand on his arms. A shiver crawled up his back.

He shook himself and rubbed his arms. He wasn't going to be spooked, it was just a dream. He must have gotten his balls caught in his pants and twisted wrong in his sleep.

He slipped in his bottom denture, tapped his phone and listened to the ring. A very tired voice picked up.

"Yeah, what the hell do you want at this hour?"

"Freddy, I want you to wake the hell up, grab a pen and paper and take down some information. I have a job for you. If it gets done Friday night, I'll get you that condo in Cabo."

The moan on the other end was followed by a curt "Yes sir, Mr. Mishkoph" and the two men got down to planning.

The boom was going to be glorious.

Chapter Twenty-Six

"I 'M TELLING YOU, Lucy, I'm tired of dealing with the humans." Bitched the weaselly little man as he paced back and forth. His clothes were dark, which only accented his pale skin that was the sickly color of sour milk. His three day growth of stubble, grown to make him look suave only served to make him look like an unwashed aging lounge lizard. "Always whining about being here, trying to push me into doing something, anything, to let them go to heaven instead. I'm constantly having to turn down sex with them, both men and women, because there's always the string of 'I'll have sex with you if you will make sure I leave here and go to Heaven.' I'm telling you, it's depressing. The ones who want to stay aren't the type of people I would hang with, you have to watch your stuff, your life, every fucking minute because they will take you any way they can. And there's this new one, name's Lauren. She seems to think she owns not only the entire wing but me as well. I've wanted to find a nice corner some-where and lock her into it. She's driving me crazy. So, I'm going to go cruise Lillith's vampires for a while, hopefully they're a little better class of human..."

"No, Satan, you can't take the vampires. Besides, you really don't want most of them. Sit down, damn it, you're wearing a trail in my rug."

"They can't be as bad as the humans, or Lauren." He shuddered, "And don't call me Satan," he plopped into a wing-backed chair and casually slung his leg over the arm. "I'm going by Stan now, that other name seems to have a lot of baggage with the people down here and I'm over all of the comments."

"Stan?" Lucifer rolled her eyes, "Why not Satanael, which was your name before? Stan sounds like a bad piano player in a dive bar."

"I like it, it fits me." Stan waved his hand around, "I would love to be a piano player in a dive bar, it worked for Billy Joel." He laughed, took another drink of his martini, and sang "Sing us a song; you're a piano man..."

Lillith strode into the room, "I thought I heard you screeching, Satan."

"It's Stan" He sang into the tune.

"Whatever. Lucy, you summoned me?" She took a glass from the side bar and made herself a double of Jamisons.

"Over an hour ago, the last of the six times I tried, you're late." Lucy glared at her. "Drinking for two?"

"Shut up, I've been dealing with the latest vampire problem, the Enforcers dropped a vampire named Hadraniel on my doorstep and he wasn't thrilled."

"Hadraniel? Wasn't that one of Barachiel's Guardians?" Lucy asked.

"Used to be. Evidently the vampires are stepping up their attacks on the angels and he was taken, drained, and then they tried to turn him. But he managed to get fangs in an artery and keep from turning. Why do they keep dumping these 'almost turned' angels on my doorstep? They're not vampires. If anything, they are 'fallen angels' and therefore your responsibility. Hadraniel is none too happy to be with us and was tearing up the reception area. That also seems to be a hallmark of the 'Almost Turned', as well," She made the air quotes with one hand, "They love busting up my reception room. The repairs are going to take a while."

"Sounds like fun. Are you aware that you were supposed to be here for a meeting over four hours ago? It was on the calendar to discuss the need to expand your area, something I believe you have a vital interest in, and you weren't here. What were you doing that prevented you from attending?"

"I was doing my nails. I am going to say this again, for about the four thousandth time, I am not at your beck and call, I do my job, I run my area, and whatever else I do is none of your concern."

"I'm still the head of this entire dimension, Lillith. I have the right to know what you're doing because it affects me." Lucy could feel the anger building, she had put Lillith in charge of the vampire department and Satan, Stan, she corrected herself, in charge of the humans. But she retained the head of Hell and all the fallen angels and, as such, she was Queen of the Damned.

"So you had your meeting without me, I needed to finish what I was doing. If you didn't wait for me, it couldn't have been that important." Lillith turned to go.

"I have some things to discuss that..." Lucy stopped, noticing the demon wiping the furniture with a cloth. Dust? There was no dust in Hell. She raised her right arm, fiddling with her bracelet. An alarm sounded somewhere outside of the room.

Two guards came through the door. Lucy pointed at the demon, who was seized by the guards and dragged out of the room, the doors shutting behind them.

"What the fuck was that?" Stan said, staring after the trio.

"Spy, probably working for my brother."

"How can you tell?" Lillith asked.

"The energy signature was off. We were all stripped of the angelic energy once we came through the portal. That one still had one. I don't know how he got here, but I will after the torturers get through with him. Mikhail is getting bolder, trying to figure out what I'm doing and I don't have to help him with that quest. I'm also watching Mikhail and his business, he knows it, but he doesn't know who my operative is...yet."

"You've got spies in Heaven?" Stan asked.

"Of course she does, you know that. You don't have to feign stupidity, you come by it naturally."

Lillith stared at Stan, who shrugged.

"I got a visit last night. The gormless toady thinks he's helping me take down Mikhail, but he has no clue what else I've got going on. I swear, I am so glad I left the stupid ones in Heaven. That one really is revoltingly obtuse. He's giving me all sorts of information about the..." she mimicked air quotes, "...mysterious goings on with the vampires."

"You're working with them? I thought you had decided to leave that one to the vampires." Stan sounded surprised.

"Marcus Lancaster is a loose cannon and who do you think pointed that loose cannon in the proper direction? He a rogue who is going to try to take on Heaven and Mikhail's own warriors in a bid to make the Enforcers let go of them..."

"Pth, Mikhail and his warriors are weak bastards." Lillith snorted.

"True, but Lancaster has his hands full with these angels evidently. What the little spy didn't know was that more of the angels are committing suicide rather than happily accepting being turned into a vampire. That's keeping Mikhail busy as well, trying to figure out what's going on" She smiled impishly, "Which is, so far, a highly successful diversionary tactic orchestrated by yours truly," she boasted, "Because I want to get the fallen out of Hell. Imagine my brother's surprise when we bust open the door to Heaven and kick his ass out."

"You really think you're going to get out of here, then banish Mikhail to Hell with the rest of his angels? What have you been drinking?" Lillith walked over and draped herself in the throne, picking up Lucy's wine glass and draining it.

"It may take an eon or two but he has to go. I will be ruling Heaven." Lucy plucked the glass out of Lillith's hand.

"Like most of the vampires, Marcus is not nearly as smart as he likes to think he is. He's a pompous-prig. He can be manipulated so easily, it isn't even a challenge." Stan said. "You know, once you've won Heaven, you can make him a pet. Might be fun."

"That's a possibility." Lucy smiled, "Or, I could give him to you as a plaything." Stan nodded in agreement. "But there's a bit of a problem, according to my spy, Mikhail has left Heaven and just disappeared. Left a junior angel in charge, Azrael's assistant."

"How accommodating of him," chirped Lillith. "I would think you would be able to implement your plan even easier without Mikhail there."

"If we were ready, yeah, it would. But I can't get out of here yet. The portal…" Lilly scowled.

"I thought you had someone scouring the ar-chives in the various churches, in an attempt to find where Mikhail hid the scroll that allows us to access the portal." Stan said.

"I do, but even the angels can't find it. My dear brother hid it in a nice, safe place, then the stupid idiot forgot where the nice, safe place was. We think we have narrowed it down to Europe, probably north of Belgium. But that's as close as we've gotten." Lucy explained.

"Why does he want to reopen the portal? Stan asked.

"He doesn't. He just wants to make sure I can't."

"So Mikhail's just as lost as we are right now. Great. He was always incompetent, certainly was in bed." Lillith snarked. "Kept promising me he would make me Queen of Heaven, right up until he threw me down here. Now, I wouldn't even have him as a pet."

"You keep saying that. If he gave you that chance again, you'd jump on it." Stan laughed. "Or rather, jump on him."

"That is a bet you'll lose, Satan." Lillith picked back. "I would just as soon trade places with you and take over the humans than deal with Mikhail or his angels."

"Now, there's a proposition I can get behind. Give me about an hour to pack and I'll move into the Vampire wing and you can have my rooms. You can even repaint if you want." Stan jumped on her statement.

"No, there will be no swapping jobs, Satan, ... Stan, whatever you're called." Lucy said.

"But why? I want to do it." Stan whined as Lillith snickered.

"Because the vampires are Lillith's fault and therefore her responsibility. She's the one who bit the demon, infecting it with her virus. Then he went on a rampage on Earth, biting humans and turning them into vampires. All of this to get back at Mikhail for sending her down here to begin with. What do the humans say? Oh yeah, 'she made her bed, now she has to lie in it.' Now, when I gain Heaven and take over..."

"If you gain heaven..." Lillith chimed.

"When," Lucy forcefully reiterated, "I will make you the head of Hell, but the vampires will remain your job."

"Pardon my skepticism." Lillith stood and sauntered toward the door.

"I'll take the promotion," volunteered Stan.

"What a slimy sycophant" She gave a little wave and disappeared out the door, leaving the other two rulers of Hell to plan how to get out of the Hell they created.

Chapter Twenty-Seven

ISOBEL LOOKED AT the clock for the fifteenth time that hour, the evening was dragging. She had been working all day, while Lilly and Gregory slept, trying to get caught up on work before Marcus came in.

She had unlocked her office door just as the building-wide chime signaled the official time of sundown. She hoped she wasn't going to be working when the chime signaled sunrise.

There was so much that had to be finished, schedules for air flights for various employees, requests for bids to be examined and sent to the accountants, visually verifying payments on accounts both in country and out. A half-bazillion things she had to see, un-staple, read, sign, re-staple, and send on to whomever the hell needed to deal with it further.

Thanks to Marcus, she was behind on everything.

She sat back and sagged into her chair. Her shoulders ached, a combination of overwork and stress. Had it really been six months? It had been non-stop, moving from one crisis to another and no time to reflect.

She mentally reviewed; it had all begun with the aftermath of Hurricane Katrina. If Marcus had not made it mandatory for all Lancaster Industries employees to 'volunteer' a certain number of hours of community service, she never would have met Lilly.

When volunteering, all employees had to wear Lancaster Industries t-shirts, jackets or caps. They had their night at the PBS Pledge Drives, Habitat for Humanity, The Houston Food Bank, Humane Society, and one can't forget the Annual Lancaster Industries Blood Drive. Isobel smiled at the irony of it. All the philanthropic contributions and hours of community service were, by no means, altruistic, it was kept the company name, favorably, in the public's eye and was great for the image, which benefitted the company's bottom line with lucrative contracts, giving Marcus, as the head of Lancaster Industries great political influence.

It had been Isobel's turn to fulfill her community service obligation. She really did not mind because it got her out of the office. Usually, she volunteered with the Humane Society or ASPCA but this year she chose to help out with the great influx of refugees that were arriving from hurricane devastated New Orleans. She was at the social services desk that night, helping people locate relatives or friends they could stay with.

Whoever sagely observed that there are no coincidences in life; they must have been referring to incidents such as this. Amidst all the chaos in the overly-crowded Astrodome, where she was working as a volunteer registering the refugees from New Orleans, a young woman by the name of Lilly Marchantel walked up to the table and Isobel's life was forever changed.

After that, a flurry of activity; moving Lilly in, teaching her how to live in the 21st century yet another hurricane, Rita, forced them to pick up and run to San Antonio. Jesse going missing; Jesse found, beaten and dying. Marcus's intercession and turning him.

Lilly's pregnancy. Hiring Dr. Young and Nurse Reba. Gregory becoming Lilly's ghoul and all the training that goes along with that. Building-out and equipping an in-house clinic.

So much more, it made her head ache trying to remember it all.

Not to mention having to move her own life around. Her apartment had been her retreat. A place to go where she could be totally alone with her thoughts. Soak in a luxurious bubble bath, enjoy a glass of wine and listen to Enya.

When she moved Lilly into the second bedroom as her roommate, they had become fast friends. The place was big enough for them to still have their alone time. It was really nice to have someone to talk to and laugh with. Besides, since Isobel didn't have girlfriends to pal around with, female company was new and different. And teaching Lilly how to live in the 21st century was quite an experience and fun.

And Baron, the wonderful vampire cat, irascible at best and yet caring. He could communicate telepathically, something she never knew vampires, or cats could do.

When they returned from San Antonio, things really got crazy. Gregory, even though he had his own apartment next door, spent so much time in hers that he might as well have moved in. He took being Lilly's ghoul seriously and was always close by, even crashing on the couch rather than going to his own place.

Now, with Lilly's pregnancy being in danger, yet another body got moved into the apartment. Reba was great but the apartment was now growing crowded. The walk-in closet, now turned into an office for Isobel to work in away from Marcus's office area, had no window.

Her refuge was gone. Her escape that she used when she didn't want to be down here had been overrun.

It wasn't like there weren't a thousand things clamoring for her attention over the last few months.

It was no wonder she got behind.

Not that it mattered a flying flip to Mr. Lancaster at all. He was so busy, not managing his business and not chasing the next contract for security services, instead tracking down and turning angels into vampires in the hope of...what?"

She had no idea what the end-game was of this angel-vampire turning, what was he thinking? Did he think the other angels would just look the other way and not stop him? When it was discovered, and it would be discovered, what would be the collateral damage?

Maybe she should quit? Take Lilly and Gregory and go somewhere to start new?

But no, as good as that sounded, Lilly was pregnant and ill and someone needed to be there for her. Gregory was fantastic as a ghoul, very caring. But she was not going to able to move away from the care she got from Doctor Young and the resources available through Marcus. At least not until the baby arrived, and maybe not afterward.

Marcus was very possessive, not because of any tender emotional connection or concern. She could see it clearly now, he was just a greedy bastard. Lilly was a possession and so was the baby. If history was the proof, he would never let the baby go, with or without Lilly. That would keep her with him, because she wouldn't leave him with the grumpy old vampire either.

Come to think of it, what the hell would a grumpy old vampire do with a baby, even if he was one with a gazillion dollars, a gay lover, charity appearances as a human, and a business selling mercenary services, not to mention he was a guy who was picking fights with the Vampire Council and the angels themselves? She had answered her own question. The baby was a possession, something no other vampire had and that would make him the envy of them all.

What a cluster-fuck.

Talk about your narcissistic ego monsters.

The phone rang, shaking her out of her thoughts, "Isobel here."

"Come to my office, now. We need to talk."

Talking about the narcissistic ego monster...

"Ok, give me a few moments to print out the..."

"Now." He hung up.

She chuffed, rolling her eyes. Yes, she obviously worked for a narcissistic egomaniac.

She grabbed her notebook, a pen, and locked her office behind her, walking down the hallway to the double doors that separated Marcus Lancaster's world from everyone else's. A glance told her that Sophia, his secretary, had already gone home. She was basically redundant anyway, more a gate-keeper than anything else.

With a swift rap on the wooden carved door, she listened for the "come in" and then pushed the door open. Marcus was sitting behind the desk, staring into his computer monitor, tapping on a wireless keyboard on his lap, his feet up on the desk.

Good, he was at least relaxed enough to do that.

She stood and waited for him to acknowledge her; she learned early not to break his concentration when she came in.

"You screwed up." He never looked at her as he said it.

"Excuse me? What did I screw up?" She frantically checked her memory to see what he could be referring to.

"My schedule. Thankfully I got an email from the hostess of the Pause for Paws Gala asking for my notes for my speech so she could give them to the reporter who would be covering the event. That told me the event is not on Saturday like your calendar says, it's on Friday night. That's tomorrow night. It's also not at the Marriot downtown, it's at the Houstonian. If I hadn't gotten that email, I would have shown up at the Marriot Saturday night, looking like an idiot. What the hell is wrong with you?"

She raised one eyebrow, scowling for a moment before pulling it back to neutral.

"I don't remember putting that on the schedule at all, are you sure I did it and not Sophia?"

"You do that stuff, not her. You're my assistant, I expect you to do it. And I expect it to be done right the first time. Every single time."

"I'm sorry, boss. These past six months...." she started.

"No excuse. Nothing has changed much, except you. You're wrapped up in Lilly's personal drama, you're putting your nose in things you should keep it out of, you're running around all over the state picking up furniture, and..."

"You sent me on that run, remember? Me and Gregory. He could have gone alone, but no, you sent me with him, said he needed to let me talk to his grandmother..."

"I expected you to get it done, get back here, work on the way. You're spending too much time in personal stuff, not doing your job."

"Really? You just went there? I'm doing your stuff. Isobel, call the hotel and get me good rates, Isobel, find me hotel for this trip, Isobel, have the plane ready to fly, Isobel, get furniture and goods for an apartment for Jean, Isobel, keep up with Jesse, on and on and on."

"That's your..." He stopped, staring at the screen as her tirade wound up. "You have me scheduled for four events in three days in March. What the hell? Dee's scholarship thing, Houston Symphony gala, and the fundraiser for the hospital are all there, but what's this Musicians Retirement fund thing?" I don't do that one? What the hell are you doing?"

"I know I didn't put that on your schedule. I have no idea what is going on but I need to go check through all of that. I know what I did and what I didn't, I also have a paper copy in my day runner because computers get screwed up and at least I will have a back-up. I can show you everything I've got on the schedule."

"So, you're telling me that someone else is fucking around in my schedule? Who would do that?"

"I honestly do not know but I'm going to start looking into it. Meantime, you need to pay more attention to your business and less attention to this whole vampires from angels thing."

"You don't get to dictate my actions. I am Lancaster Industries, so whatever I am interested in is the business of the business. You're a secretary..."

"Personal assistant..." she countered.

"...Act like one and Stop. Trying. To. Tell. Me. What. To. Do." He snapped, pounding the desk to punctuate every one of the last words.

"Okay, fine. Yes, master. I'll do as you..."

"What the hell is your problem, Isobel? We've never had issues like this before. What?"

Isobel debated just backing out of the room and leaving, maybe even not coming back. She was about sick of his shit. She just stood, staring at him like she hadn't seen him before.

"What?" He yelled.

"It's the angels. What you are doing is wrong, totally. There's no profit in it that I can see. You're not making money on it. Why are you doing it?"

"It's not wrong. I don't need money, I need to make them understand that what they do to vampires is wrong, marking, threats, following us around, taking us to Hell. What the angels are doing is wrong and it's going to stop. I'm working for the future security of the vampire race itself. It's going to continue. If you don't want to do that, then pack your shit and leave. Be gone in the morning if you don't want to continue in my employ, but I will not have you questioning my actions or my motives and trying to triple book me to keep me from doing what is important."

"Is that what you think? I did that booking thing on purpose to distract you? If I did that, it would not be that sloppy." She turned to walk away, "I'll think about it, you'll have my answer tomorrow night if I'm here."

"If you are still here, you will keep your opinions to yourself unless I ask for it. Now get out of here and handle the things you need to handle."

His dismissal stinging in her ears, she walked out and back to her office, slamming the door behind her.

Yeah, it was immature to do that, but right now, she was over trying. She needed to think.

Chapter Twenty-Eight

S OMETHING WOKE HIM up early. According to his clock, it was 4pm local time, the sun still up, but Sullivan lay in his bed knowing it wasn't time.

Something was wrong, he could feel it. How he knew, he didn't have a clue, but he had to get up, throw on his robes, and find out what was happening.

Late February, the sun didn't set until 5:30. He knew he had to stay in the hallways, not going into rooms, the sunlight was still coming in through the many windows in the monastery.

First he walked toward the main area, most of the monks were still busy with their daily tasks but it would be time for vespers soon. He stood in the end of the hallway and looked out to see who was around. Father Gudrun's door was open but the abbot wasn't behind his desk. He saw Brother Asmund walking out of the dining area.

"Brother Asmund, is Father Gudrun around?"

"No, he and Brother Ragnvald went into Bergen for a few days to talk to the Bishop. Is there something I can help you with?"

"I'm not sure." Sullivan ran his hand through

his hair. "I awoke with the most disquieting feeling, that something is wrong. I'm not able to explain further, just a hunch, but I can't explore the building and the grounds to try to figure out why. Would you take a look around for me?"

"Okay, I'll look for you. Are you going to be in the Scriptorium or are you going back to bed for a bit?"

"I'm awake. Might as well go to work; find me there if you find anything going on. It's weird, I'm just..." he shook his head, turning and wandering back down the hallway toward the Scriptorium.

Pushing the door open, he didn't notice anything at first, until he heard the sound of a scroll opening and then being dropped. He walked around a corner to find Brother Bjarte standing in a sea of unrolled and discarded scrolls.

"What are you doing?" Sullivan asked, walking into the room. He felt a shiver as he did but the room didn't feel cold.

"I'm looking for a scroll to find a mythology I remember reading as a kid. I want to write a story about it but I can't seem to find it."

"That's not the way you look through the scrolls, you are making not only a mess but you're breaking the scrolls and crushing them. One at a time and..." Sullivan started forward to pick up the scrolls and rewind them.

"Don't bother, I'll clean up after I'm done. Go back to bed." Bjarte dropped another scroll, stepping on it, crushing it as he reached into the cabinet for another one.

"Stop!" Sullivan reached out for the monk but

missed, trying to avoid stepping on the precious parchments. He noticed that Bjarte's hands shook and the pupils in his eyes were dilated more than normal.

"Bjarte?" Sullivan stopped moving and looked closer at the man in front of him, who was continuing to unroll, glance at, and drop the scrolls.

"No time to waste, I have to find it."

"Find what, Bjarte? What are you really trying to find in here?" Sullivan softened his voice, trying to sound gentle, and reached out but didn't move forward.

"I need a ... scroll. One that says 'fallen' in it, but I can't seem to find..." Bjarte dropped another scroll into the pile of unrolled parchments that reached almost to his knees, his words hesitant.

Something didn't feel right. While he didn't know Bjarte that well, the actions, and words the man used, his inner alarms were ringing off the walls.

He decided to take a different tact, "Bjarte, is there something I can do to help you? Something you need to tell me?"

The monk's eyes grew wilder, his hands shaking so bad that the scroll rattled.

"Bjarte, talk to me, what's going on?" Concern on his face.

A single tear fell from the monk's eye, rolling down his face. Several different emotions displayed across it, from confusion to sadness, anger to fear. He dropped the scroll without looking at it. "Sullivan....Help...me..." His voice was strangled and forced.

While he wasn't sure what was going on, he pressed further, "Bjarte, what do you need me to do."

The monk shut his mouth, opened as if he was going to speak, choked, coughed, and seemed to be fighting for air. Sully tried to step forward but he couldn't move.

"Bjarte! Tell me what you need me to do! Do it now!" He was shouting.

His lips turning a bit blue, the monk finally strangled out the words, "Find the board and destroy it, a witchboard."

"What??"

"I was trying to find out....future...not me doing this...board under my mattress....stop it..."

Sullivan's mind raced. Was he dealing with...

The man coughed, then said as if being strangled, "Kill me...stop the.....demon..." and then began to cough and seemed to be trying to pull something, or someone, off of his throat.

"Leave him be, demon." Sully shouted, "Tell me what you want here."

Bjarte dropped his hands, his chest heaving trying to pull in enough air to saturate his blood again. Then his posture and face changed, grinning broadly. "Bjarte is my vessel for the moment. You can do nothing against me without taking his life."

Sullivan felt his heart speed up. He knew he was dealing with one of the fallen, something he wasn't trained to take care of. When H.H.A.D was called into dealing with an escaped fallen, they sent the Shadows and Warriors after them. He had not been trained for this. He had been an Enforcer before he was turned into a vampire. He had dealt with the paranormals, like vampires, ghosts, and such. Demons were the problem of the Shadows and the Warriors. He had to think of how to handle with this since he had no direct contact with Heaven any longer.

"What's your name? Who are you?"

"Why should I give you power over me? I'm busy, go sit down and wait for me to finish." The demon put his hand up and leveled it toward the vampire, who resisted the remote push.

"No. You must leave, you do not belong here and ...."

"And what, fallen angel." The demon laughed, "I know you, Eistered, or should I say Sullivan? And who are you to try to tell me what to do?"

"I'm not fallen, I'm ...."

The demon laughed again, dropping the scroll he glanced through, "That's the biggest lie you could tell. You're a vampire, one of us. You know the origins of the vampires just as well as I do."

"Yes, vampires came from the bite of a fallen, a demon, but we've evolved and we are no longer like you. And we aren't..."

"Evil?" the demon cackled, "You've killed, you've raped, you've fought with angels, and you say you're not evil? You are no longer an angel, so, therefore, ergo, you are fallen. So don't try to lecture me or make me leave, you can't. I don't have to go anywhere." The demon grabbed several scrolls and began to unroll and scan them, dropping them when he was finished.

"You have no power here, you're the same as me. So leave Bjarte alone, go back to Hell. You're not going to find what you want." Sullivan switched tactics again. "What scroll do you want? Maybe I've seen it."

"Why should I tell you? You lie every time your mouth opens, you're no different than any other angel."

"As you said, I'm no longer an angel. What are you trying to find?" He took a step toward the cabinet, reaching out for a scroll.

The demon stuck out his hand again and Sully was thrown backward, landing on the cold stone floor on his ass. "I told you to sit down. I need to focus on what I'm doing."

It took a lot of energy to pull himself up from the floor but Sully managed to stand, even as he found he couldn't move further.

"Okay, you can stand there and watch. But you're not going to move or interfere."

"So, you have me stopped here, surely you could tell me what it is you are looking for."

"No."

"I bet you don't even know, you're too stupid to be able to read what is in those scrolls."

"You have no idea what I know and don't." The demon dropped yet another scroll to the pile.

"Yes I do, I know how you have forgotten what you once were when you were cast out of Heaven. You are probably looking for symbols."

"Keep it up, blood sucker. I'll end up getting annoyed with you and gift you with a nice, stout stake."

"Pthththt, you wouldn't be able to, with that weak vessel you are inhabiting, you couldn't make me do anything. And I still say you are too stupid to be able to find a scroll that has the information ...."

"Ambrosia. And how that loser, Mikhail, takes wings and restores them. I want to know what is going on with the Ambrosia and how he does things."

"You think Mikhail has just put that stuff into writing and dropped it in a monastery full of humans to hide it."

"Yes, that's it. I'm going to stand right here, find the scrolls I need, then I'll drop the body and leave. You are right, it is a rather weak and trifling vessel but, it is sufficient for my purposes at the moment."

Sullivan had to stop him. The demon was searching for part of the assignment from Gudrun and Mikhail and he was destroying scrolls in the process. "You go right ahead and work. I'm going out to get some wine. Want some?"

"You really think I'm stupid, don't you? You're not going anywhere. You are not going to alert anyone to my presence. I've locked you in this room and you will stay 'till I'm done." He dropped another scroll.

"The door's open, stupid demon."

"Just try to leave, I dare you."

Sullivan tried to walk out of the door and ran into an invisible wall.

"That wasn't there when I came in." He said,

turning back to look at the demon.

"Yes it was. You could walk in because you have angelic DNA, like I do. But I've now set it against the DNA and you're stuck.

"Hey, I need help in here!" Sully shouted toward the door to call the other residents of the monastery into the room.

"Oh, it's soundproof too." The demon smiled.

Turning back toward his unwanted visitor, Sully managed to launch himself across the room and almost into the demon before he was pushed back.

"Try that shit again and I'm going to burn this whole place down, starting with the scrolls." The demon added to the pile.

"You're not as strong as you think you are, demon. I almost got you."

"Almost. You know what they say about almost, right? It only counts in horseshoes and hand grenades. Neither are present in this situation."

"You're not strong enough to hold me, hold the room, and work at the same time. I will wear you down and...." As he was speaking, he had a flash of thought, "Wait, I do know your name. You are Raumael, you were one of the messengers under Gabriel."

"Ding, ding, ding, the vampire isn't as stupid as he looks. I used to be Raumael, but now I go by Raum. But that doesn't help you either. You can't banish me because," he laughed, "Like can't banish like. Rather interesting, that is." The demon dropped another scroll.

Sullivan pulled his energy to maximum and made a dive for the demon. The demon conjured a fireball and threw it at him, then casually dropped another into the pile of parchment. Just as Sullivan's fingertips brushed Brother Bjarte's robes, Raum dropped the disguise, the body he was wearing pitched back, hitting the floor dead. Clutched in his claw was the soul of the monk, "Later" he said, smiling, and disappeared with it.

Sullivan screamed. His robes caught fire with the thrown fireball. He reached toward where the demon had been and fell into the burning pile of parchment. He felt his hair catch fire as he tried to roll out of the flames. These were not earthly flames, it was hellfire, more intense and had the unmistakable stench of underworld evil. Sully's hands came off the floor, seared flesh staying on the hot brick. He fell into unconsciousness, his last fading vision was the hellfire leaping toward the rafters and snaking toward the scrolls.

THE HYSTERICAL SCREAMS of pain echoed throughout the monastery, bringing the monks running to the Scriptorium. The intense heat held them back. Brothers Asmund and Nicholaas ran to grab fire extinguishers from the kitchen.

Brother Havaard shot a look to Brother Lukas, ordering "Move back. Leave a path for Asmund and Nicholaas." Brother Lukas shunted everyone back toward the far end of the hallway; returning to stand in the doorway with his broad back blocking the others from seeing inside. The movements and momentary crowd control diversion allowed three monks to slip into the room unseen.

What happened next would have amazed and astounded the other monks were they able to see inside the Scriptorium. Each man removed a bulky ring from the pouch dangling from their rope belts and quickly slipped them on. They rapidly stripped off their robes, giant wings burst from near their shoulder blades. The magnificent wings were the same color as the stone in each of their rings. Thorbjorn's white moonstone of a Guardian. Josef's ruby of a Warrior angel, and Havaard's citrine marked him as an archivist. Wings unfurled, the three angels walked through the hellfire. Two shielded Sullivan with their wings as Brother Havaard softly touched Sullivan's burned cheek; a worried smile crossed his face. He motioned, Josef and Thorbjorn gently lifting Sully's burned, unconscious form, they carried him toward Brother Lukkas at the door.

Havaard surveyed the room, then rose above the flames, pulling off a panel in the corner of the shelving where the scrolls were kept. He extracted three scrolls, replaced the panel, and alighted. He nodded to the other angels, simultaneously they folded their wings, removed their rings, and redressed quickly. Just in time, Asmund and Nicholaas rushed to douse the flames. The three re-disguised monks followed Brother Lukas with Sullivan cradled in his arms back toward Sullivan's cell.

"Brother Oddmund, we need you." Havvard called out over his shoulder as he passed the crowd of brothers.

A smallish man, almost as big around as he was tall, wobbled down the hallway after them.

He covered his mouth and nose as he ran. He knew that smell, burned flesh. He said a prayer as Brother Lukkas laid him on the cot. Brother Oddmund leaned closer.

Sullivan was a mess. His hair burned off down to the scalp, no eyebrows, blistered. He was unconscious, which Oddmund knew was a blessing. If he had been conscious, the pain would have been excruciating. Asmund was carefully peeling away the remnants of the robe, taking care not to pull the skin with it.

"This is far beyond my abilities. The damage is far too extensive and severe. We must get him to the burn unit at. Haukeland University Hospital in Oslo. It has a burn unit that can hopefully save him."

"We have no way to evacuate him until Father Gudrun and Brother Ragnvald return. You will have to do what you can to make him comfortable.

"Of course, I will do what I can, but I must warn you, I am very much out of my depth here. I need sheets, clean ones. Boil water and cool it down so I can use it to keep the skin hydrated until we can move him."

"I'm on it." Thornbjorn ran from the room to the kitchen, yelling instructions to the other monks.

Havvard walked from the room, motioning Asmund to follow him. Once they crossed the hallway into another cell, he whispered, "I wish we could just take him ourselves, but without Gudrun here, we can't chance it."

"You think he will die?" Asmund asked.

"We need to pray he doesn't, or Mikhail will have all our heads."

The angelic duo said a quick prayer and then walked back to see what they could do to help.

Chapter Twenty-Nine

THE RED MASSERATI glided to a stop in front of the Houstonian's valet, who hustled around the purring auto and opened the driver's door. Marcus Lancaster stepped out, adjusting his blood-red cummerbund and matching tie. He then snapped his fingers and Lancelot jumped out, festooned in a matching blood-red bow tie around his neck.

"Put it up and don't even think of driving it. I know the mileage and I'll kill you if you do." He looked into the young man's eyes, finding exactly what he thought he would. The kid was jonesing to take the expensive car out for a joy ride. Marcus pushed a bit of glamoury to the kid's brain, "I mean it. Don't even think about it."

The kid's eyes glazed over for a moment and then he nodded, "Yes sir" and handed a valet ticket to the man who was already walking away.

Marcus entered the door opened by the doorman. He was met by the hostess, a leggy blond in a black cocktail length dress holding a Yorkie. "Marcus! I'm so glad you made it. And you brought Lancelot."

"Hello Gaylynne, I wouldn't be anywhere else. We have funds to raise for the shelter, right?" He smiled and kissed her hand.

She giggled, "Of course. You're always here for us when we call." She knelt down and rubbed the Sheltie's ear, the Yorkie growled. "Astrid, stop it, Lance is a good dog," she scolded, then leaned down so Lancelot could kiss her cheek. He obliged, liberally licking her like he was trying to take her makeup off.

Marcus watched his dog carefully and when he made a move like he was going to do more than kiss, Marcus snapped his fingers and Lance sat down, pulling back from the kiss, his tail stopping its rapid wiggling of happiness.

"Aww, you disappointed him. I don't mind doggie kisses."

"He thinks he needs to nibble, a bad habit he got from the cat that belongs to one of my...employees. I don't want him practicing those bad habits on such a beautiful woman." Marcus smiled and put his hand out to help her stand, portraying a charm that he didn't feel. He was getting weary of these endless social functions and wanted to get back to work on his project.

He walked the room with Gaylynne, chatting up the assembled Houston wealthy donors who he would be convincing to part with money to fund the no-kill shelter Pause for Paws ran. His speech, scheduled for after the drinks and deserts, would make sure that the shelter ran for another year without having to raise more funds.

LILLY WAS RESTING propped up on a pile of pillows, reclining enough to keep the baby happy as she and Gregory watched the end of his latest attempt to introduce her to all of the good animated movies in the world. Lilly had a fondness for animation and Gregory was happy to indulge her. This time the movie was The Corpse Bride by Tim Burton.

"I know Victor and Victoria fell in love at first sight," Lilly said, starting to grab a bit of the popcorn, which smelled heavenly, but then she winced and ran her hand over her growing abdomen. She was certain the baby didn't want her consuming anything but blood and reminded her by kicking her hard.

"I don't believe in love at first sight, by the way." Gregory interrupted, grabbing another handful of the golden kernels, tossing a couple in the air and catching them in his mouth.

"Really? I'm not sure I believe in it either, but this movie makes me hope that it happens for some people."

"Did you fall in love with Marcus at first sight?"

"He was a client; we weren't supposed to fall in love with them. I know I thought I loved him." Lilly glanced at the skull she had talked with for those hundred years in the crypt in New Orleans.

"You don't now?" Gregory glanced at the skull as well;, Lilly had told him about having named the thing Marcus, as if it was her maker.

"I honestly don't know." She frowned, "Not really. I thought I did but the way he's been since I got here. He broke Baron's neck out of spite. What he did to Essex is cruel beyond measure. How he treated me is not that important but I am with child, his child. I'm really not interested in continuing a relationship with him."

"What are you going to do when the baby gets here? What will you do if you don't stay here?"

"I am not sure. I know he has a right to his child, but after he killed Essex and hurt Baron, I have seen a monstrous side of him that scares me. He does not even have to be angry to do horribly cruel things. I fear he might harm the child. I may need to take us away from him to protect him, or her."

"Where will we go? Do you have a plan?" Gregory knew he would have to protect them if Marcus came after her.

"Not yet. We thought of going back to New Orleans, staying with Arianne."

"Arianne?"

"She's Marcus's maker. I stayed with her and she was the one who sent me to Houston to find Marcus in exchange for Sullivan staying with her. But he didn't stay, she must be quite angry about that. Marcus would probably bully or threaten her; I don't think she would risk making him angry. I just don't know, even though it has changed so much, and it's still in such bad shape since the hurricane, New Orleans is the only place I know. I just don't know what to do." Her eyes started welling with bloody tears."

"I can talk with my grandmother. She'd help us if he decided to go there; she has lots of friends who'd hide us." He had seen his grandmother be very fierce when protecting the young women of her community and he knew that she would help Lilly and the baby if he asked.

"I wouldn't want to impose on her, but it is nice that you can count on her like that. I don't think San Antonio is far enough away to keep Marcus from finding us."

"I'm not sure the moon would be far enough away if he decided to come after us, but we can try." Gregory wasn't going to admit to her that he was afraid of the vampire; he had seen his anger and didn't relish the thought of him turning it onto them.

Lilly smiled. "I can go alone; there is no sense in you having to deal with him and a baby."

He shook his head, "Nope, no dice. You go, I go. I'm your ghoul. I protect you, I feed you, I run your daily errands. So don't even think of going without me." He laid his hand on hers and looked into her eyes, "I meant it when I said I signed on for the long run, to take care of you and I don't give up easily."

As she rubbed her belly, she smiled at him, and he loved that smile. He wondered if he wasn't falling at least a little in love with his pretty vampiress.

JOEY MASON OPENED the door of the silver 2004 Ford Focus and climbed behind the wheel. He knew his destination already, the building he had been playing wino behind for the past couple weeks. After reporting his information to Mr. Mishkoph, he got assigned to drive the car that would be parked in the next to the top floor of the parking garage of Marcus Lancaster's building on San Felipe.

Mason wasn't nervous, he knew the cargo in the trunk, fifty pounds of C-4, wouldn't just explode if he hit a bump. There was a timer in the package, which was wrapped in pretty baby shower paper, set to go off whenever he was safely away from the property. He had a date with his best girl, Kassie, to go to a movie after he delivered the car to its destination.

Creeping through the late Friday traffic on 610 wasn't easy, that part of the Loop was always socked in bumper-to-bumper. Why did they call it 'rush hour' when you do anything but rush, it should be 'sit for an hour'. Even though the thousands of workers in the Galleria area highrises had left for their weekend, others had poured into the area to hit the various restaurants, clubs, and the shopping available. Thankfully the radio was working in this car and he could listen to hip-hop as loud as he wanted without Kassie complaining about it.

He finally reached the San Felipe exit. He traveled the few blocks past Post Oak to the big pink/gold building, taking the entry road around to the parking garage. He pushed the button on the visitor ticket machine, taking the ticket and waiting until the barrier went up so he could drive up to the area just under the spot where Marcus Lancaster kept his very expensive collection of cars and motorcycles. That was going to be one ticket that wouldn't be validated. He crumpled it and threw it on the dashboard.

NADIEL AERIALLY SHADOWED the silver car, following it across Houston toward the Galleria. She had been following this particular man driving the car for days, H.H.A.D. assigned her after getting some information that someone was in danger. Whoever the human was who was the target, that person wasn't her concern, she was strictly following the man in the car tonight. She had been told to report back, not to just anyone, but to Uriel himself, or, if he wasn't available, to Ranguel. No one else was supposed to know what she was doing.

"I'M WORRIED ABOUT Lilly," Isobel said, taking the plate from the dishwasher, placing it in the cabinet.

"She's doing well, as long as we can keep her in bed until the baby is ready." Reba wiped down the counters.

"She'll be good on that count, I think Gregory would sit on her to keep her down if he needed to."

"You got lucky when that boy came to work for you, Gregory is one of the good guys." Reba replied. She genuinely liked her charge, he was an easy person to play guardian angel to.

"We really did. Lilly likes him and what's more important, she trusts him. I'm worried about how she's going to deal with the real Marcus. She invented a kind, generous fantasy version of Marcus when she was alone for all those years. He's really not the guy she thought he was and he's made it quite clear. He's not interested in a relationship past being her maker. But he does want the baby and he may take the child and leave Lilly to fend for herself."

"Would she give the baby to him and leave? She doesn't strike me as that type of person." Reba asked.

"I think Marcus will have a big fight on his hands if he tries to take the baby away. She won't move away, maybe across town but not out of Houston until the baby is old enough to fly back and forth from wherever she decides to move. She'll stick close, no matter how much of a bastard he becomes. I know she didn't have a family growing up, she grew up in a brothel in New Orleans, given to the madam as just a kid, and she has missed having a family. We're about as much of a family as she has ever had, leaving Marcus will not be easy for her. Better the Devil you know…" Both ladies nodded."

"Then we are going to have to take care of her and make sure she's got all the support and family that she needs. You, me, and Gregory, we will be her family, and the baby's too." Reba said.

"And Baron, don't forget Baron, he was her protector long before we knew her. He may be a pain in the butt sometimes, but there's something that you can never doubt, he loves his Lilly. Besides, that cat will never let us forget him." Isobel laughed.

The cat sneezed from the door to the dining room, catching their attention. *"You're damned right, on both counts. I won't let you forget me."* Baron said to both of the women. *"Auntie Isobel and Auntie Reba, I'm off for a snack. Be back later."* With a flip of his tail, he was out the door. Reba had placed a chair by the elevator so that Baron could reach the button to come and go as he wished.

BARON WALKED BEHIND the night guard, Jackson Davies, who unlocked the door long enough to let Baron out into the cool night air. As he rounded the corner of the building, he chuffed in laughter, they were right; he would always be there for Lilly. While he missed the small crypt back in New Orleans, he knew Lilly was better off in the big building in Houston. He just wanted the man who owned the building dead for all the things he's done to Lilly, and to him.

"*Bastard needs to die, that's what. Drink him dry and leave him in the woods.*" Baron growled.

He was in a mood anyway; there was a distinct lack of female companionship in the area that they lived in, so he had to roam way into the neighborhood to find anyone to party with. But, there was good eating nearer the building; the rats he loved were all over the place because of all the restaurants nearby. For nutria, he had to go down further to the north to Buffalo Bayou, those critters liked the water.

His mouth began to water and his fangs dropped down. He was hungry more than he was horny and he would find a nice juicy rat to eat before going to find...

A horn blared as the lights blinded him and Baron bounded back to the safety of the grass near the building as a silver car drove past, splashing him with the day's runoff from watering of the grass.

"*Blow it out your ass, eunuch!*" he yowled into the night.

If he wasn't so hungry, he would follow the car to its parking spot and drink the blood of the human inside instead. That was like nice, sweet canned food, a human in an auto.

But not tonight, he had to eat fast food and go find a female to spend the time with.

It was then that he noticed water on his fur. So, a change of plans, a bath before finding dinner and entertainment. He got busy cleaning himself.

JESSE WALKED BACK into the room carrying two large coffees. Jean was sitting at the conference table on the fifteenth floor, going over the list of employees that had joined the vampires and checking them against the Human Relations roster.

"Where do we stand on changing the employees?" Jesse asked.

"Right now, we've turned 472 out of the 766 employees. Some of them don't want to do it and we've wiped their memories of the discussion. We've let go over 100 of those, layoff so they are taken care of."

"Why would you do that? We have to pay for that unemployment and the severances. We could have fired them and kept the money." Jesse said, looking over Jean's shoulder at the numbers.

"Right, and firing over a hundred people for cause wouldn't raise any suspicions at all, would it. I can see it on the news now, 'Major employer, possible mercenary company owned by prominent Houston mover and shaker, fires over 100 people in one day.' That would happen. No, we do it by severance and let things settle out. We don't need any negative publicity." Jean stared at the computer screen.

"Well, you're costing Marcus money and you're on your own in telling him how you're doing it." Jesse walked to the other end of the table and sat down, sipping the coffee.

"We're using the employees for donations of blood, with the cover story that we've needed to replenish the supply to Columbia due to an industrial accident. The employees have always been good about donations." Jean took a sip of his own coffee.

"Speaking of donations, Alton Sparks says that our blood doll, that thief, Kirsten, isn't doing so well. He's telling me that we need to go ahead and drain her and be done with it. She can be incinerated with the angels that died."

"Let's keep her alive a bit longer, I'll talk to Marcus about what exactly he wants to do with her later, tomorrow night probably. Until then, feed her a bit more, get her off the bubble and back into the lineup to feed, we're too short on good blood dolls to waste one, even one who's about worn out." Jean made a note on the paper next to him. "So, what else do I need to know?"

Jesse took a sip of the coffee, "Nothing else, but I do have a question. What do you think of Marcus's plan? I know we're turning all these vampires, and angels are being made vampires, but I don't understand how, exactly, this is going to get the angels to stop harassing us."

Jean looked up from the screen, "I think he's hoping...," he sighed, "Actually, I have no idea if this is going to work or how. I feel a bit disloyal saying that, he's my maker, like you, and I want to agree with him on changing enough angels to mount some sort of attack on the angels who are marking and taking vampires to Hell. But I'm not totally sure how this is going to work."

Jesse nodded, "He's playing it close, like he does everything else. I just am not sure about all of it."

"Neither am I, Jess, neither I." Jean sipped his coffee as he went back to checking the computer.

A TWENTY-SIX FOOT box truck drove up the semi-circle drive and stopped in front of the doors to the Lancaster Industries building. A man, dressed in dark blue cover-alls exited the cab and ran around the truck and to the building.

Demarius Lincoln was running a bit ahead of schedule. His orders from Nelson Mishkoph was to attempt to make the delivery about 11:45 pm. But he wanted to go party with his wife at the new club, Sessions, in Mid-town and he didn't want to wait until midnight to do it. So, he pulled in at 11:15 and was going to hand over the paperwork to the contents of the truck, excuse himself to go back to the truck on the premise of needing to get something out of it, and just keep walking.

The truck would take care of itself a few minutes later.

He hit the revolving door and banged into it, the damned thing was locked. Shaking his head, he went to another door, but it was locked as well. He banged on the door to get the attention of security to let him in.

Jackson Davies had to put down the copy of 'A Feast for Crows', the latest in the Song of Fire and

Ice series by George R.R. Martin that he had become addicted to. When the banging started, Qyburn had showed up to tell Cersei about the imprisonment of Daemon Sand and Jackson didn't want to miss the rest of the report. Usually night shift gave him time to read and he hated interruptions. Putting the book face down, open to the page he was on, bending the spine of the book, he looked up.

He caught the sight of a shoddily painted green box truck that was obviously a U-Haul before someone got paint happy. The driver was standing at the door, pounding on it, holding paperwork. Walking up to the glass, Jackson raised his voice and said, "Deliveries are around on the side in the loading docks. Come back between 9 a.m. and 5 p.m. on Monday."

"No man, I gotta deliver this now. My boss will have my head if it's not delivered tonight. Open the door and I'll show you the paperwork!"

Jackson shook his head, "I can't let you in, man. Sorry, nobody told me about any late delivery tonight. Show me the paperwork and I'll go call ops and see what they say."

"Dude, it's cold out here, can you let me in while you call them. I will stay right here by the door but it's cold!" Demarius wanted to be in the lobby, not out in the 49 degree cold of the Houston night.

Jackson hesitated as the driver held up the paperwork for five boxes of office supplies that were supposed to be delivered on the 24th. The delivery codes were for ammunition and gun cleaner, a common delivery at the building. Motioning to another door, Jackson unlocked it, letting the driver in. He locked it back and looked at the driver, "Stay right here, I'll call ops and we'll get this figured out."

"Thanks, man,' the driver said as Jackson crossed to lobby back to the sign-in desk.

Nodding, Jackson picked up the receiver on the desk phone and called upstairs. "Parker, Davies, is the old man up there?"

The security guard nodded and gestured and Demarius couldn't help but think that if you tied the man's arms to his side, he couldn't speak a word. He watched the animated discussion happening across the lobby and looked at his watch. If he didn't get the delivery finished, he was going to be late to the party.

Jackson hung up and walked partially across the lobby toward the driver, motioning him to come across the floor. As the driver got nearer, Jackson said, "The Operations Manager is coming down to speak with you. He's got a head of steam on that you're trying to deliver this late and you might be polite to the guy, he doesn't put up with bullshit from anyone."

"Ok, point taken. Thanks man."

Jackson walked behind the desk and picked up his book, eager to get back to Cersei.

As the Ford Focus pulled through the garage,

Nadiel noticed that a truck was pulling up to the doors of the main building. Once the car stopped on the next to the top floor on the west side of the garage, she left the garage and flew to the top of the truck. Sniffing, she couldn't tell what was in the truck but it had a weird, oily smell to it. She had no idea what it was but she needed to find out and report back to Uriel.

"ANY WORD ABOUT what Nelson Mishkoph is up to?" Jorge Castro asked Ben Senai, motioning him to follow him down to his office.

Once they were away from the ops department, Ben said, "There's a lot of communication flying between Florida, Columbia, the UAE, and Georgia, not the state, the country. Someone in Tblisi is spending a lot of time talking to someone in Pricor. I've been trying to trace down what they are saying but they are switching numbers often and it's hard to get a read on it."

"Any operatives in the Houston area?"

"Not yet. We've been monitoring bank accounts and nothing so far. No airline tickets, no train in, not even a car rental. If they have someone in city, I have no idea where or how."

"Any chatter on the internet about Marcus or our business that is unusual?" Castro took the ever-present cigar out of his mouth to swill some lukewarm coffee from the "Don't Call Me Sir, I Work for a Living" mug in the Marine Corps colors. He swallowed and looked at the cup like it had just punched his mother in the mouth.

"No, si....uh... Mr. Castro, nothing unusual." Ben caught himself before saying the word.

The telephone on the desk rang, Castro picked up, "What is it now, Davies?"

The sounds coming from the phone clued Ben in that this wasn't just a random call. Castro barked a few words and slammed the phone down, jamming the cigar back into his mouth. "Make sure that we catch that bastard doing something before he does it. I don't like surprises."

"Yes, sir." The words were out of Ben's mouth before he could stop them.

The only reply was a growl as the figure of the former Marine disappeared out of the office door.

JOEY MASON PULLED the Focus into a parking space and shut off the ignition. He was so happy to be at the place. He pushed the button on the seatbelt, releasing it. He reached over and pulled the handle to the door.

It came off in his hand. Joey's breathing picked up, his heart began to pound. He reached across the car and pulled the handle to the passenger door, which proceeded come off as well.

Beginning to panic, he turned the key to the engine and tried to roll the windows down, but the electric mechanism didn't work, the window never moved. He tried all the windows.

Nothing moved.

He was trapped.

As he banged on the window, trying to shatter it, screaming, he heard his phone chime. Picking it up, he punched the message application.

"You won't double cross me twice."

Joey began to cry. He knew what was going to happen.

Fifteen seconds later, the Focus exploded.

THE CONCUSSION OF the car bomb hit the concrete above the car, pulverizing it. The vehicles stored in the garage on that floor began to fall, some crumpled, others thrown into the walls. All of the toys, the Bentley, the Ferrari, and all the other vehicles came crashing down.

The rest of the garage shook, some of the ceilings caving in as the shock wave put pressure on the columns. Cars were pushed to the walls in some areas, others caught fire and burned. Car alarms and horns blared and echoed, a cacophony of sounds, reverberating throughout the structure. The thundering continued as the building collapsed into a twisted pile of steel and concrete.

The shock wave continued; the windows on the west and south sides of the Lancaster Industries building began shattering.

Jackson Davies and Demarius Lincoln both

ducked as the glass flew from the windows and showered them, cutting both of them with shards.

Inside the security office down the hall, Brian Kennedy, the Officer of the Day, bolted from behind the desk, running to the lobby to investigate the thunderous explosion.

Nadiel, still on the top of the box truck but invisible to the people inside the building, turned toward the garage as the shock wave hit her, the garage beginning to fall on the northwest corner.

She unfurled her brown wings in an effort to try to get airborne.

UNHEARD OVER THE rumbling and crashing of debris, a cell phone ring sound started in the back of the box truck. Five seconds later, the barrels of fertilizer exploded; the fire and concussion began to climb inside and up the 25-floor headquarters of the Lancaster Industries building.

Acknowledgements

Thanks To:

Joe Rose for the help with things that go boom so I don't end up on someone's watch list. You are awesome!

Ethan Nahté for the help figuring out the sunspots that drive the Aurora Borealis and what it would look like on the day Sullivan was watching it.

Authors J.R. Ward and Anne Rice for the inspiration to keep the vampires of Fangs & Halos going.

www.chessgames.com/perl/chessgame?gid=1233404 for the online chess database and community. Game: Paul Murphy vs Duke Karl/Count Isouard "Night at the Opera."

The incomparable and always superb Cat McNulty for the help rounding up plot bunnies, reading the story over and over, fixing the continuity and the "voice", and making sure everything carried over from book to book. I would be lost without my Cat-wrangler.

Donna Morris for the "Piddling Little Details" (PLDs) of commas and spelling.

Haven Hawley for cheering on Grandma, making sure I'm working on it.

Arthur Burnett for the help with airplanes and guns and all things mercenary.

Reba King and Kirsten Skinner—because friends make great characters (and no, Kirsten, you're STILL not dead....)

And to the best husband in the entire world, Bruce Denney, who always talks plot lines and possibilities when we go out to eat and keeps me from losing my mind when he pops up and says "Yanno, I think that this may work for ...." It's HIS fault that some of this stuff is happening. I love you.

Copyright and Trademark Acknowledgement

- *Air Force One* (movie) Director: Wolfgang Petersen, Writer: Andrew W. Marlowe, Copyright 1977 by Columbia Pictures Corporation and Beacon Pictures

- *Dogma* (movie) Director and Writer: Kevin Smith, Copyright 1999 by View Askew Productions and STK

- *A Feast for Crows* (Book) Series: A Song of Fire & Ice Book 4 by George R.R. Martin, Random House/Bantam/Spectra, Copyright October 2005, ISBN 0-553-80150-3 (US hardback)

- "Hallelujah", (Song) Written by Leonard Cohen, Copyright: Sony Music,1984. Sung by k.d.Lang and Juno Awards 2005.

- St. Vigeous (Place Name Reference)—from Buffy the Vampire Slayer, episode "School Hard", 29 September 2007. Written by Joss Whedon and David Greenwalt (this is the first appearance of Spike and Drusilla, Season 2, Episode 3—"The feast of St. Vigeous is celebrated every 100 years". Buffy The Vampire Slayer copyright 1997-2003 Mutant Enemy, Joss Whedon, creator.

- *Dark Lover* (Book) Series: Black Dagger Brotherhood Book 1, by J.R. Ward, Published by Signet Eclipse, Copyright: September 2005, ISBN 451-21695-4

- *Interview with the Vampire* (Book) Series: The Vampire Chronicles, Book 1 by Anne Rice,

Published by Knopt, Copyright: April 12, 1976. ISBN 0-294-49821-6

- "Piano Man" (Song) Written and sung by Billy Joel, Copyright 1973 by Columbia Records
- "Blaze of Glory" (Song) Written and sung by Jon Bon Jovi, Copyright 1990 Vertigo Records (written for the movie "Young Guns")
- Houston Livestock Show and Rodeo (Event), Houston Texas. Founded: 1931 (as the Houston Fat Stock Show and Livestock Exposition)
- *The Odyssey* by Homer (book) In Public Domain
- Randall's Food Markets. (Place Name Reference) Founded: 1966 by Randall Onstead, Owned by Cerberus Capital Management since March 2014, Headquarters: Westchase, Houston, Texas
- Jack Daniels Whiskey (Product Trademark) produced by Jack Daniels Distillery, 280 Lynchburg Hwy, Lynchburg, TN 37352
- Guinness, (Product Trademark) produced by Guinness Storehouse Brewery, St James's Gate, Ushers, Dublin 8, Ireland
- Dalmore Selene Scotch (Product Trademark) produced by Dalmore Distillery, Alness Ross-shire, Scotland IV17 0UT
- The Brazen Head Pub, (Place Reference) 20 Lower Bridge St, Merchants Quay, Dublin 8, D08 WC64, Ireland
- The White Hart Pub, (Place Reference) 34 Grassmarket, Edinburgh EH1 2JU, UK

Chapter One

THE ASSIGNMENT ALERT buttons of all of the H.H.A.D. stations lit up at once. Requests for Guardian angels, Healers, and Soul Reapers for the Houston Texas area spiked all at once.

Ranguel looked around the room as the chaos began before seeing his own Enforcer board light up.

That could only mean one thing: something was happening in the paranormal community that overlapped with the humans.

Ranguel looked over at Uriel, studying the Shadows board, reports coming in from the angels who observe the workings of the world. Uriel turned and looked to Ranguel, who nodded as the atmosphere suddenly shifted, angels flooding out of the apertures while a few of the Shadows fought the outflow to come in.

Pangaiel glided toward the Shadows board, landing close to Uriel and pulling him aside, spoke softly. The look on her face was grave, her eyes hard. The tips of her brown wings were singed; her hair appeared to be burned a bit as well as her dress. Smudges could be seen on her arms and it looked like she had some burns on her face as well. As Uriel laid a hand on her shoulder, she dropped her head, then turned and floated back toward the living area.

Running his fingers across his board, Uriel looked again to Ranguel and nodded his head toward the archangel's break room. Ranguel glided across to the room, following Uriel through the door, closing it behind him. Both archangels were replaced at their stations by assistants.

"What is going on in Houston?"

"It's your vampire, Marcus Lancaster. His office building just exploded. It's a mass casualty event. I hope you have enough Enforcers to handle the vampires; there are a lot of them and more than I think we knew of. Pangaiel had gone to back up Nadiel on her assignment. She is telling me that Nadiel is dead. There are also several dead bodies that aren't part of the explosion, but are the bodies of some of our missing angels."

"Any idea what happened?"

"Bomb, looks like two of them from the reports."

"I guess we couldn't have gotten lucky enough to have Marcus Lancaster as one of those casualties, could we?"

"Unknown. Pang wasn't able to find him. She didn't stay too long; she was caught in the explosion. Her hearing is affected and she's going to go rest and I've sent a healer to her.

Both men turned toward the door when a knock rang out. Uriel reached across and opened it and Faranel stood with his hand up, prepared to knock again.

"I need to talk to you."

"Yes, we know. Come in." Uriel stood back as the dark purple winged head of the Media Center came in.

"The bombing, of course, is all over the human news sites."

"Bombing, are they sure it was a bomb?" Ranguel asked.

"Certain. Evidently there are a couple of witnesses. The first explosion brought down the parking garage; that got their attention. Then they saw the delivery truck in front of the main building blow. Emergency responders are already on scene. Fire and rescue, police, ATR, FBI, Texas Rangers, bomb squad, everyone they could pull in."

"Any word on who did it?" Uriel asked.

"Not yet. They're trying to get the wounded out first, the explosion was large enough to damage the cafe next to the building and broke windows for blocks. There are casualties in some of the cars on the streets, power is out, they have to bring in lights as they dig through wreckage. They're saying they know at least 10 are dead, probably more. I've got my crews watching all the various news outlets and backing the footage up so we can watch it later.

"Thanks for the update; let us know if you

hear anything specific about Lancaster, whether he is alive or dead." Uriel opened the door to let the angel leave, but found the acting head of H.H.A.D. standing there.

Kafziel stared at the three archangels, raised an eyebrow. "Plotting? You three need to get back to work, now. We have a situation and I want you on your boards, running things. Get back to work." He turned and walked away.

Faranel left the room right behind Kafziel, headed back toward the media center. Ranguel turned to Uriel, whispering, "Get your best, send them to Sethiel, tell Seth to go and find Mikhail; let him know what's going on. We need him back here, in charge. Now!"

About the Author:
Charlayne Elizabeth Denney

Given my habit of checking people for fangs, I discovered my own vampires and Lilly, Marcus, and the rest of the gang all live in the books I write. Of course, this weirds out my grandkids and kids. As the author of the Fangs & Halos series, I like sitting in dark rooms and imagining all sorts of strange things. Daylight is okay but the darkness, that's the place for me!

When not hanging with the vampires, I am a level 90 gnome mage, Rubyrose, on the World of Warcraft Argent Dawn server where I kick butt. I found my husband, Bruce, through a want-ad in the program book for ConTroll 93, he thinks it was just the button that said "I still miss my ex but my aim is improving" that did it. I've attended, worked, and guested at conventions in Texas since 1979.

Books In the Fangs & Halos Series